PRAISE FO.

"*My Hope Next Door* is a pitch-perfect romance and beautifully crafted story of second chances in a town where rumors travel quickly and reputations seem written in stone. Although Katie is a flawed and hurting character, her grace-filled transformation will make you root for her every moment and treat you with a sigh-worthy ending."

—Connilyn Cossette, award-winning author of the Out from Egypt series

"Tammy L. Gray is a must-read author for me. Powerful storytelling and exquisite characterisation mark her stories, and *My Hope Next Door* doesn't buck the trend. I soaked up the authentic challenges that Katie and Asher experienced in their journey toward God and each other."

—Rel Mollet, writer of RelzReviewz.com and an INSPY Awards advisory board member

"*My Hope Next Door* contains all the vital elements of great storytelling—conflict, tension, romance, and a fabulous resolve. Make sure you add this one to the top of your list."

—Nicole Deese, award-winning author of the Love in Lenox series.

"This beautiful story of forgiveness and second chances will stay with you long after you turn the last page. *My Hope Next* door is Tammy L. Gray's very best yet!"

—Amy Matayo, bestselling author of *The Thirteenth Chance* and *The Wedding Game*

MY
UNEXPECTED
HOPE

ALSO BY TAMMY L. GRAY

My Hope Next Door
Sell Out
Mercy's Fight

Winsor Series

Shattered Rose
Shackled Lily
Splintered Oak

MY UNEXPECTED HOPE

TAMMY L. GRAY

Waterfall
PRESS

Published by Waterfall Press, Grand Haven, MI

www.brilliancepublishing.com

Amazon, the Amazon logo, and Waterfall Press are trademarks of Amazon.com, Inc., or its affiliates.

ISBN-13: 9781542045797
ISBN-10: 1542045797

Cover design by Jason Blackburn

Printed in the United States of America

For my beautiful sister, Angel.
You're my rock, my shining example,
and one of the best people I know.
Thank you for always believing in me.

CHAPTER 1

Moonlight leaked through the dirt-splotched windows of Joe's Bar, its silvery rays glinting off the tumbler in front of Laila Richardson's saddest customer. She'd seen his type too often to be surprised when he tapped the empty glass for a refill. Silently, she switched out his drink for a fresh one and noted the transaction on his open tab.

The man was like many others who sat alone with their heads hung low and drank until last call. Each one had a story. For most, heartbreak ruled their actions. For some, they'd lost a friend, a family member, or a piece of themselves. And for a few, self-destruction reigned with a never-ending appetite.

Laila understood their stories because hers had encompassed all three versions, only she wasn't pouring drinks down her throat to numb the pain. No, her fate was far worse. She stood on the other side, serving the very poison that had destroyed her marriage.

Perseverance was what she'd called her loyalty to the bar and to her small town of Fairfield, Georgia. But in truth, she'd built a prison with walls of familiarity and steel doors of fear. And now she remained captive in a job she no longer enjoyed, in a town that refused to see beyond her last name, in an existence as empty as her home.

Laila eyed the faces she'd known for years. Young Billie Huff with his two best friends in the corner. He asked her to marry him every time he walked into the bar, and every time, she reminded him that she used to babysit him in high school.

Cantankerous Barney Richardson, dressed in dusty jeans and work boots, surrounded by his entourage of employees. He sat front and center every Wednesday. Partly because he considered himself the axis of everyone's world, but mostly to throw daggered stares at his ex-niece-in-law, aka her. His scowl lines deepened with every frown, aging him well past his fifty-seven years.

And then there was Charity Ayola, the new waitress with Kool-Aid-red hair and an eyebrow ring. She flirted with anyone who might throw a few dollars her way, which was now a trio of men who were on their fourth round. Charity hadn't noticed Barney's calloused hand in the air or the frustrated tap of his fingers on the sticky laminate table. If she didn't get his order soon, Joe would have to talk down one of his most faithful customers—a sight Laila had witnessed way too many times.

Her shift at the bar had become as stale and routine as the people inside it.

Grabbing chilled glasses, Laila filled each one with the cheap draft beer Barney had ordered earlier—a common purchase for the factory workers who made up most of Joe's clientele. Some were great tippers. Barney, unfortunately, was not.

The phone rang from the back of the bar, and Charity looked up long enough for Laila to catch her attention and point to Barney's table. Charity shrugged and turned back to her admirers.

Swallowing her frustration, Laila jerked the cordless receiver from the wall.

"Joe's Bar, can I help you?"

Silence.

"Hello? Hello? *Hello?*"

Still nothing. She wasn't surprised; they'd been getting a string of hang-ups over the last few months.

More irritated than she'd been before, Laila slammed down the receiver and loaded a tray with Barney's drinks, resigned to finish the job Charity had been hired to do.

"Here you go," she said with a practiced smile, setting a glass of cold beer in front of each of the four men at the table.

Barney didn't bother with a thanks. His familiar green eyes—like chips of painted glass—glared at the neglectful waitress in the corner. "Joe needs to fire that girl."

"You'll have to take your complaints up with him." Laila refilled the tray with their empty glassware and slipped away before those eyes played tricks with her heart. They were the same ones her ex-husband had. The same ones all the Richardson men shared.

The tears she'd been fighting all night begged for release, but she had no intention of letting Barney, of all people, see her break.

Her divorce from Chad had been finalized on February twelfth, a year ago today. She'd filed the papers as a wake-up call, a last resort to pull him from the edge and force him back into rehab. But life never took the path she wanted. After being served, he'd called her from Atlanta and asked for more time, promising to once again get his life together. That day was the last time she'd spoken to him. The last time he'd cared enough to reach out and beg her to take him back. She'd waited a month after his phone call to see if he'd come home and contest the petition. He never did, and after forty-five days of silence, the judge granted her a default divorce.

Unfortunately, the stack of documents severing legal ties to her first and only love had done nothing to end the lingering grief. Grief so crippling that on days like today, she began to doubt whether she'd ever be truly whole again.

Sighing, Laila stared out the window, past dimly lit Main Street, to a time when life and love seemed so simple.

"Hurry. I have to get back before my dad notices I'm gone," Chad says, pulling my hand and dragging me through the trees. It's dusk, and we don't have a flashlight with us. I'm a little scared, but I don't want him to know because he already thinks I'm a sissy girl, and our best friend, Katie, is so brave that I feel stupid.

"Where are we going?" I shuffle my feet faster so I can get closer to him and feel his warmth. Chad is bigger than most thirteen-year-olds and so much bigger than me that he makes me feel protected and safe.

"It's a surprise." He glances over his shoulder and grins at me. My stomach flips a little. It's been doing that lately whenever he's around, and I'm not sure why. I told Katie, and she said I'm gross and that Chad is like our brother. But I don't feel like his sister, and when I found out Jenny Harper asked him to the dance, I wanted to punch her in her big fat face. I didn't, but Katie said she would if I wanted her to.

Chad stops at a big tree with wood slats hammered in the side. I look up and see a tree house with a door and two windows. He's so excited. I feel excited too, so I climb, even though the wood scratches my hand. The inside is so huge, I can almost stand, but Chad has to duck and bend his big body over. It's kind of cute.

"How did you find this place?" I ask when we both sit cross-legged in front of each other.

"I got lucky, I guess. I come here a lot when Dad's on a rampage." His face falls when he talks about his dad, and I take his hand. I know how he feels.

He stares at my hand and then laces his fingers with mine. "Laila, can I ask you something?"

"Of course."

He pauses, and it's the first time I've seen him nervous around me. I don't like it. He takes my other hand too. "Will you, um, be my girlfriend?"

"Your girlfriend?" I'm so surprised I don't have time to control my voice, and he flings my hands away.

"Just forget it. You like Bobby, don't you? He said you did. He said he was going to kiss you." He starts to stand, but I'm able to stop him.

"Chad. I don't want to kiss Bobby. I don't want to kiss anyone but you." I think about it and I mean it. "Not ever."

He smiles at me again, and it's one I haven't seen before. One he's never given to Katie or any other girl, and I feel so special.

"Can I kiss you now?"

I nod because I'm nervous. The only kissing I've seen is what my mom does with her boyfriends, and it's gross. But somehow I know it won't be gross with Chad.

He leans toward me, and it's definitely not gross. It's soft and gentle. He tastes like gummy bears, and I'm pretty sure the feeling in my stomach is never going to go away. In fact, I'm pretty sure I'm going to love him for the rest of my life.

Laila pushed the memories from her head and trekked back to the bar, each step heavier and harder than the last. Chad had been the holder of her dreams, her hopes, her future. And he'd also been the greatest pain she'd ever known in her life.

"You're overthinking again, aren't you?" Joe's soothing tone came with a shoulder squeeze.

Laila's heart squeezed as well. She'd been wrong. Perseverance wasn't why she'd worked as a bartender for almost a decade. Joe was. He was more than just her boss—he was the father she never had.

"Reflecting is more like it." It had become their unspoken agreement—to not mention her ex. But she didn't have to say Chad's name for Joe to know the significance of today's date on the calendar. Her ex-husband would always be an echo in this town.

Rubbing his white beard, Joe leaned a hip against the counter. "How's that going for you?"

She would have laughed except for the lone tear that escaped down her cheek. With a flick of her fingers, it was gone. Starting would mean she'd never stop, and Laila had already shed too many tears over a man who couldn't love her more than his addiction.

Joe's hand covered hers, and he gave her the same sad, pitying look the entire town seemed to have memorized. She hated that look. It was why she'd begun shopping ten miles away in Burchwood, why she'd found a church there too, instead of going to Fellowship with Katie, why she hadn't mentioned to anyone that she'd met someone special, and, despite tonight's breakdown, why she was taking the first steps toward moving on with her life.

"I'm okay, Joe. Really." Today was just another dark day, but at least they had been coming less and less frequently. Something had healed inside her when Katie came back to Fairfield after being gone for so long. Maybe it was finally hearing the truth behind why she'd left in the first place, or maybe it was seeing the transformation her best friend had made in the process.

"You sure?" Joe asked, giving her hand another squeeze before letting go. "You can go home if you need to."

Going home was the exact opposite of what she needed. She'd just sit on the couch she'd picked out with Chad or lay on the bed they'd shared as husband and wife. "I'm fine. Besides, who would play interference? Charity isn't making your regulars too happy."

Joe watched as his newest hire continued to ignore the rest of the floor in favor of one table. "Yeah. I may have overestimated her potential."

"Well, they can't all be me: bartender extraordinaire." She smiled a real smile that time because, as sad as it was, her job was the only thing Laila felt totally confident in. It was the one thing she'd never failed at.

"And humble too."

She twisted a towel and snapped it at his leg. "Watch it, old man."

"Fifty-three is not old, little girl. I can still take down half the men in this bar."

And he could, even at a meager five foot eight. No one messed with Joe. That was why they'd never hired a bouncer. Joe commanded a respect most men spent their entire life trying to obtain.

He picked up a rack of dirty glasses and balanced it on the edge of the counter. "Hey, before I forget, I got a strange call today from a Mrs. Harrington about a lease in Burchwood? She wanted to confirm your employment."

Laila casually wiped the already-clean Formica with a bar towel. She'd known it was possible that the homeowner would call but had been hoping the lady would wait a little longer. At least until she'd found the courage to tell Joe herself. "My lease has been up for a while now, and I was thinking it might be time to let the house go."

He flinched with surprise, the rack slipping a little in his hand. He pushed it back securely onto the counter. "You're leaving Fairfield?"

"No . . . I mean, yes. But Burchwood is only fifteen minutes away. I'd still work here." For a little while longer, at least. But she'd deal with dropping that bomb when she had to.

"But then you'd have a commute down back roads in the middle of the night. That isn't safe."

"I know, but this new house . . ." She sighed, the memory so vivid, she could feel the shiplap beneath her fingertips. "It's like a picturesque cottage, with bright yellow shutters and three small gardens."

She wouldn't mention the other reason she wanted to move, especially since that reason was a guy Joe knew nothing about. She'd met Ben at the church in Burchwood the first time she'd gone. He was also divorced and had a six-year-old son, who stayed with him every other week. And while her relationship with Ben was only a few months old, it was . . . nice. Ben was reliable and steady. Qualities she'd forgotten existed.

Joe's brows pressed together. "You really don't think Chad is ever coming home, do you?"

Laila closed her eyes briefly, hating that hearing his name still made her breath hitch. "It's not about him. It's about me, for once." Her voice turned pleading, only because Joe's opinion mattered more than anyone's. "I've loved him my whole life, Joe. Is it wrong for me to want more?" She'd been a faithful wife. She'd supported him through his mother's sudden death, through his overdose, through three stints in rehab after Katie left town. Even after he ran off to Atlanta, she'd waited months before filing for divorce. At some point, she had to let go of a childhood dream.

"No, of course not. It's just you've never even hinted at wanting to leave Fairfield. Why now?"

He didn't understand. She didn't *want* to leave Fairfield. She *had* to leave. Every corner held a memory, and even the good ones hurt.

"I know seeing Katie get married was hard."

"This isn't about Katie either." Although, in some ways, it was, but not in the way Joe was thinking. She wasn't jealous of her childhood friend. She was blown away by her. Too much, in fact, because Katie's journey over the past year had softened Laila's heart in all the wrong places. Places reserved only for her ex-husband.

Determined, she made herself look him in the eye, made herself smile. "This is what I want, and I need you to support me."

Joe scratched his head as if warring with himself. "Chad called me on New Year's." The words stung as much as any bullet. "I wasn't going to tell you, but—"

"Stop. It doesn't matter. I don't want to know." Cold sweat coated her neck as she pushed past him, her only goal the swinging door that led to the kitchen and back office.

He followed her, his words like sandpaper on an almost-healed wound. "He sounded good this time. Strong. He didn't even ask for money. He just wanted to make sure you were okay."

She tried to block out his words as he kept pace with her past the kitchen and into the small, dusty office. She focused on her breathing. In through her nose, out through her mouth. Again and again.

But Joe persisted. "Just have a little more patience. I know he's been gone a long time, but look at Katie. She was gone four years and healed while she was away. Maybe Chad is doing the same. Maybe his time in Atlanta has been good for him."

Pain splintered through her hands; she'd curled them so tight her nails had punctured the skin in two places. This was the curse of Katie coming back to Fairfield. Everyone expected Chad to follow. It was what he'd always done, follow Katie's lead, until doing so had left him unconscious and half-dead.

Warm, fatherly hands encircled Laila's clammy arms. She'd stopped somewhere between the desk and the back wall, paralyzed by the shameful truth.

She too had begun to hope that Chad would come home.

And that hope led to a slippery slope of misery she had to continually resist.

"Come here, honey." Joe turned her trembling body around and wrapped her up in a hug tight enough to make the last of her restraint collapse. She sobbed, deep and ugly, for too long to count.

9

She shouldn't still hurt this much. Not now, not when she'd taken the first steps in moving on. Not when she had a future just waiting for her in Burchwood.

Straightening, Laila wiped away the rest of her tears. "I'm done crying over him, Joe. That's all I've done for years. No more mourning. No more waiting. No more second chances."

Stepping back, Joe must have read the determination on her face, because finally, the look he gave her wasn't pity. It was sadness, maybe even a little regret.

She squeezed his hand. "I know you loved him. I did too. But Chad is gone, and it's time all of us finally accept it."

CHAPTER 2

C had shot up in bed, the nightmare so vivid he wanted to squeeze his head until the memory was erased. He scanned the small bedroom, shuddering. Real—this was real. A truth scarier than the nightmare itself.

A night breeze flowed through the open window, drying the sweat on his back. The tiny opening to the outside world was the only gift in his eight-by-eight living space. Twin bed, white walls, stained beige carpet. It all reflected the stale place he'd tumbled into. But living in a halfway house with three other men was a lot better than a jail cell, and truthfully, it was a miracle he hadn't ended up in one.

Chad picked up the purple sobriety chip on his nightstand and rubbed his finger over the eight, then the words, *unity*, *service*, and *recovery*. For some, eight months might seem small, unimportant, but for him, it was the longest he'd ever gone without a drink.

Laila would be proud of him, if he had the courage to tell her.

That was the problem with sobriety sometimes. There was no more lying to yourself. No more excuses.

He'd ruined the only truly beautiful thing in his life.

Easing off the bed, Chad stretched his aching back and checked the time. 5:12 a.m. Trying to go back to sleep would be pointless; his shift at the hardware store started at seven.

The job he'd held for a full five months wasn't glamorous, but he took pride in every haul. Cutting and stacking lumber had put weight back on his frame and color back in his face. Gone were the hollow cheeks, the sickly thinness, and the deep black circles under his eyes. In the mirror, Chad almost looked like the man he used to be.

The man he swore he'd be again when he entered rehab eight months ago after learning Katie had returned to Fairfield. It was his fourth attempt and the only time he really believed it would work. If Katie could get clean, then somehow he'd find the strength to do it as well.

Setting the chip back on the counter, Chad shook away the lingering nightmare. He had to focus on the future. On Laila and staying clean. She was still waiting for him. Joe had practically promised as much when they'd talked on New Year's. And when Chad finally went home, he'd make sure her wait was not in vain.

A blue haze of the coming sunrise filtered through the living room blinds as he quietly stepped over shoes and discarded laundry to get to the kitchen. Mark had called a house meeting for tonight, and Chad had a pretty good idea that household maintenance was on the list of topics. None of them were especially tidy, himself included.

Two Post-it notes appeared when he flicked on the kitchen light, one on the fridge scolding them for drinking the rest of the milk, and the other on the stack of unwashed dishes that said, "Wash me or I will kill you." Chad shook his head, but welcomed the unexpected smile. Mark was a softy—soft enough to take in three recovering alcoholics and mentor all of them—so his threats fell short of their target.

Chad had met Mark in rehab during one of the group sessions. He was their success story, a man who'd walked along the cliff with one foot dangling over the abyss, yet found a way not to tumble to his death.

Mark was a nineteen-year alcoholic, four of those sober. He understood loss, understood temptation, and understood Chad's journey through years of alcoholism and drug use. He understood that though the drugs had been Chad's final undoing in Fairfield, it was the alcohol that obliterated him time and time again.

Chad had spent most of his adult life blaming his father for the affliction. But Mark had shown him that he was the only one responsible for his actions. He'd chosen to hide inside a bottle, and years later, he was living out the consequences of that choice.

Pushing away the lump in his throat, Chad rolled up the note, tossed it into the nearly full trashcan, and spent the next fifteen minutes quietly unloading and reloading the dishwasher. It was a job he knew well, one of the few Laila had trained him to do after they'd moved in together.

His hand froze on its way to grab another dish, the memory as vivid as the nightmare had been.

> *"You're doing it all wrong," Laila says, hopping off the counter.*
>
> *I pretend to be offended but I'm not. There's not much she could ever do to offend me. "Didn't anyone ever tell you that if you discourage a man from doing dishes, he'll never help again?"*
>
> *"What good is your help if none of the dishes come clean?" She's in tiny shorts and a tank top that shows the edge of her bra. I thank the universe again that she's mine, that she somehow said "I do" just a few weeks ago. "Here, give me the bowl."*
>
> *I do because it means she's going to lean over and, let's face it, my wife has the best behind in Georgia. I watch both her and the dish placement because it makes her happy. Then I grab her around the waist and lift her back on the counter.*
>
> *"Let's finish them later," I say finding that spot below her earlobe.*

*She giggles and runs her fingers through my hair.
"Mr. Richardson, you are not behaving."
"Mrs. Richardson, you knew that before you married me."*

Pain seized his heart. Eyes pressed closed, he gripped the sink and fought against the all-too-familiar ache. He was fighting for her. For them. Laila had always chosen him. And now he needed to prove himself worthy of that choice.

"I knew it was nasty in that sink, but not enough to make you hurl." Mark came around to his right and pulled the coffee pot from the corner. He was twenty-two years older than Chad, a good forty pounds heavier, and had only about half the amount of hair. But in a lot of ways, they were the same. Mark's family gave up on him ten years ago and still hadn't fully allowed him back into their lives, even after four hard-fought years of sobriety. His ex-wife was remarried, his two sons still bitter, and his daughter's only contact was a Christmas card once a year.

Chad straightened and pulled back the sting in his eyes. "Yeah. Fez needs to learn to rinse out his cereal bowl." He sprayed the almost-empty stainless steel sink, pushing the last of the soiled food down the disposal. "You're up early."

"I never went to sleep." Mark didn't elaborate on why, but a quick fear tore through Chad's limbs.

"Everything okay? I mean, are you . . ."

"Drinking?"

So matter of fact. So absent of the monumental impact if the answer was yes. Chad held his breath as he waited for him to continue.

"No, I'm not drinking. Michael let me go to his daughter's preschool performance last night." Michael was Mark's oldest son, and the only one who'd begun to forgive him. "They let me treat her to an ice cream cone, and he even hugged me when we left the restaurant." Tears swam in his aging brown eyes—happiness, regret, hope. "Sleep was a little impossible after that."

"Mark, that's, wow, man. That's huge." Chad backed away. He didn't want his lingering anxiety over Laila to overshadow his sponsor's breakthrough.

Mark scooped two heaping piles of coffee grounds into the filter. "Yeah, it really was. But seeing them is kind of like a shot of whiskey. All I want is more." With quick fingers, he dropped the lid and pressed start on the pot. His voice fell along with his shoulders. "How was I such an idiot that I didn't see the beauty of what I had?"

The million-dollar question that every recovering addict wonders.

"I don't know." Chad fell into a dining chair. "I ask myself that question at least ten times a day."

With an expression he'd been on the receiving end of many times before, Mark pulled out the chair opposite from him and sat, leaning in close with his elbows on his knees. "Yesterday was hard for you. I'm sorry I wasn't here."

Yesterday was the equivalent of an arrow through the eye, but that wasn't Mark's fault. "Don't apologize. You were with your family, as you should have been. Besides, I wasn't in the mood to discuss the death of my marriage."

Most of the year, Chad could believe the divorce wasn't real, that his not signing the papers meant Laila was still his, but yesterday, even his disillusions couldn't compete with the truth.

A default divorce.

If he'd known she could end things without his consent, he would have fought harder. Of course, a year ago, he was a train wreck. Penniless, hopping from one friend's place to another. She had every right to leave him.

"How did you cope? Honestly." Mark maintained eye contact, likely to discern if Chad was sprinkling lies among the truth. The curse of mentorship, he'd once said, was watching when a friend stumbled.

"I didn't drink if that's what you're asking, but . . . I did walk into a liquor store." Chad rubbed his hands over his face. "I admit, it's the closest I've come to failing since I left rehab." He recognized the pattern from his other face-plants off the wagon. It'd start with just driving by the store, then he'd walk through the door only to rush back out, and finally, when the temptation became too strong, he'd succumb to the darkness and buy the bottle that would inevitably ruin all his progress.

This time, though, he'd only stood there while the rows of bourbon, whiskey, and vodka called out to him in hushed whispers, using the same words his father had.

You're worthless. You're a failure. You're not good enough for her.

Lost in the haze of his shortcomings, Chad had even gone so far as to touch a few of the bottles. But in the end, he'd called Joe's Bar. Laila had picked up, her raspy voice so unique and familiar that he'd walked right out of the building, listening as she repeatedly said hello. It was the sixth time he'd called in the last two months, and every time, that small piece of contact gave him strength.

"What pulled you out?" Mark did this a lot, made Chad walk through the steps he took when fighting alcohol's plea.

"I called her." He kneaded his eyes. "Selfish, I know, but I just needed to hear her voice."

Mark's tone remained soft. "Maybe next time, you need to let her hear your voice too. Let her hear that you're sober and have kept a job consecutively for months. Heck, you've almost paid off all your debt. Do you know how few addicts ever get to that point?"

Chad's stomach sank like he was falling down a well. Not quite all the debt, which was why he had no right barging back into her life. "I'm not ready. I told myself a year. I want to be sober for a year before I go back." Because she deserved no less.

"A year may be too late." Mark held his hands in his lap and bent his head as if lost in prayer. Usually, he pushed the one-day-at-a-time mantra, refused to accept when Chad or the other guys retreated into self-pity. But today wasn't a usual day. Mark had seen, in high definition, what all his addiction had cost him.

Chad stood and placed a hand on his friend's shoulder. Mark's remorse was contagious, and Chad felt it roll up his arm and down to his already-hurting soul. "Last night was just the beginning. You'll see."

Mark simply hung his head lower. "I'm going to hit a meeting tonight. You should probably come too."

"Okay. I'll head there after work." He went to remove his hand, but Mark's own stopped his retreat. Slowly, his eyes raised until they shone into Chad's with laser-like intensity.

"Don't let her go without a fight," he said with more conviction than Chad had ever witnessed from his almost-annoyingly-steady landlord.

"Oh, believe me. I don't plan to."

CHAPTER 3

Laila hurried toward the painted Burchwood Elementary School awning, anticipation and nervousness building in her chest. For months now, Ben had been asking her to volunteer with him at the church-sponsored after-school program. She'd completed the background check, picked up the T-shirt, even pored over the curriculum, yet today was the first time she'd found the courage to show up.

It still felt impractical, her teaching children about the Bible when she'd only just begun to read it herself.

Heart pounding, she pulled open the heavy glass doors and entered, moving into a reception area to her right. Two small kids sat in chairs lining the wall, their little legs dangling as they kicked them back and forth. One held on to her pink heart-shaped backpack. The other watched the ceiling, boredom etched on his chubby face.

"Can I help you?" The woman behind the counter was young and dark haired, and wore a green Burchwood Elementary School spirit shirt.

"Yes, I'm here for the Kids' Bible Club program. Do I need to sign in?"

The young woman eyed Laila's blue volunteer shirt and name tag. "Yep. Right here." She slid a clipboard across the counter. "I also need to see your driver's license."

Laila quickly withdrew her wallet and handed her license to the receptionist, who copied it using a small scanner, then placed it back on the counter. The whole process took much less time than Laila had expected, and her nerves ratcheted up again. "I was told they meet in the cafeteria, but I don't know where it's located."

"Follow the purple line down the hall, and you'll run right into it." The young woman smiled, her eyes warm and appreciative, as if she could sense Laila's unease.

Tension uncoiled from her shoulders because for once that smile held no pity or judgment. In Burchwood, Laila wasn't the local bartender or the ex-wife of an addict. She wasn't the infamous Katie Stone's best friend or Loretta Parker's neglected daughter. She was just Laila.

"Thank you," she said, knowing the receptionist had no idea how much deeper that thanks went.

The sounds of voices and tables moving accelerated her steps to the cafeteria, the echoes of each reverberating off the waxed vinyl floor. The air smelled like markers and glue with a mild hint of bleach. White cinderblock walls were covered in various kid art projects, some as simple as handprints, others so elaborate Laila was sure the parents had offered more than oversight. Not that parental support was a surprise. The schools in Burchwood were consistently rated higher than Fairfield's. Of course, everything in this town was just a touch nicer, newer, and more expensive. It always had been.

She entered the room from the far end to see a group of blue-shirted bodies talking and laughing while they each prepared for the coming kids. Out of the seven volunteers, only two were men, so Ben was easy to spot unloading sound equipment by the stage.

"Hey, you made it," he said when they made eye contact. "I was starting to think you changed your mind."

He was dressed in khaki work slacks, and she could see his white collar sticking up through the Kids' Bible Club T-shirt he'd thrown over it. Ben was nearly six foot, wore round wire glasses, and had an adorable Clark Kent persona working for him. He was uncomplicated and kind—a small-town guy with a big heart. Not to mention, beneath the glasses and the starched shirts, Ben was a really attractive guy.

She continued toward the man who had become so significant in her life. "I'm sorry I'm late. I went by the cottage to sign the last of the paperwork and totally lost track of time."

"You're fine. We still have twenty minutes before school's over." He met her just feet from the door and took her hand, his thumb caressing a small circle in her palm. Such a minute gesture from a man who was as routine as the sunset, yet there seemed to be deep importance behind that simple touch.

She searched his face, but as always, she couldn't read his expression. Ben was a man of few words, and those he spoke were important. In the months they'd been dating, she'd yet to see him angry or even frustrated. His perpetual contentment had become a solace for her, and their time together something she looked forward to more and more.

"So, when's the big day? I plan to take the entire morning off work to help you move." He didn't let go of her hand as they walked closer to the stage. She didn't quite know what to make of his public display, something that was extremely rare for both of them.

But then again, she'd been different lately too. Happier. More ready for change. Putting the deposit down on the cottage had been a step forward, one Ben seemed to notice and appreciate.

"Well, don't mark your calendar just yet."

His hand stilled in hers. "Why? Did you change your mind?"

"No. Not at all. But you remember that leak we saw in the bathroom?"

"Yeah."

"Well, turns out it wasn't just behind the sink, but also the shower." She groaned, finding it hard to keep her usual optimism. Ms. Harrington's promised "quick" repair had now turned into a complete renovation. "They had to rip out the tile to get to the pipes. And they found mold."

She sighed. Despite her decision to let go and move on, an external force seemed to be keeping her trapped in Fairfield. "Trust me. I want this move more than anything."

He turned, facing her. "You and me both. It'll be nice to see you without having to make an appointment." His hazel eyes crinkled while his lips turned teasing, but it still made her feel bad.

"I'm not *that* busy." He was right, though; they didn't see each other much.

"You work practically every night."

"And you work every day."

"So you see my conundrum." His head dipped along with his voice. "I'm starting to miss you."

Laila's stomach tumbled at the intimacy of his words and the way his breath lightly floated past her ear. She liked him, liked spending time with him. But she also liked the fact that they could spend days apart and thoughts of him didn't consume her mind. She and Ben were the exact opposite of the overwhelming force that had been her first love. She'd had no desire to recreate that whirlwind.

Ben played with the tips of her finger, rubbing his thumb across her short and broken nails. "Caden will be here today, you know."

She had known. "You don't have to tell him who I am." They'd agreed to keep their relationship hidden from his young son for a while—a decision she respected. Ben didn't want to invite anyone new into Caden's life until he was certain the relationship was solid.

"Actually, I already did." He lifted her hand to his lips. Placed a soft kiss on her knuckle. "And I was hoping maybe we could have dinner tonight, the three of us. And if things go well, maybe we can all take a weekend trip to the beach. My parents have a house there."

Laila had to swallow the sudden need to cough. They'd had "the talk" a couple weeks ago, and Ben mentioned that he was ready for her to meet his son . . . if she was. At the time, it seemed like the logical next step.

But now, hearing those words from his lips, recognizing the significance of them, well, it suddenly made the relationship feel very, very real.

"I work tonight." Her unavailability was almost a relief. Meeting Caden, being included in their little family, was a huge responsibility, and there was still so much about her life she hadn't shared with Ben.

He knew the outlined version, that she'd been divorced for a year and her ex-husband was an addict who'd basically abandoned her. He even knew that she was a bartender at Joe's Bar, though he'd been plenty eager to help her get a resume together for a different line of work. But the intricacies of those relationships, the depth of pain she still struggled with, well, she'd been careful to keep those feelings close to her chest.

"What about tomorrow night? I'll still have Caden and . . . wait." He paused, his groan regretful. "His spring musical is tomorrow night. I'd invite you, but his mom will be there, and I don't want things to be uncomfortable."

"Of course." She squeezed his hand. Ben's wife had left him for another man several years ago, and even still, Ben tried his best to respect the times when both families combined. "You don't have to apologize for protecting your son. It's something I absolutely respect about you."

"Saturday?"

"Working again." She laughed despite herself. "I'm sorry. I swear, the universe is not on our side."

"Okay, so how about this? Caden goes back to his mom's on Saturday. I'll drop him off and then come hang with you at Joe's afterward."

Her breath hitched. For the past three and a half months, she'd been very careful not to let any part of her world in Burchwood infiltrate the life she lived in Fairfield. "But you don't drink." A fact she had made sure of before they'd ever gone out. "And it's a long drive in the opposite direction. Plus, you'd be exhausted for church on Sunday."

And she had at least forty other reasons why his crashing into her world was a very, very bad idea.

"I know, but if I ever want to see you, I'm going to have to make some sacrifices. Especially now that the move has been delayed." He scrutinized her face. "You're turning pale. Do you not want to spend time with me?"

"Yes, of course I do." But Ben showing up at Joe's would be equivalent to an atomic bomb. "It's just that Joe gets really upset when we have friends stop in. He says it's too distracting, especially on a Saturday." She hated lying to him, but there was no way she could explain the blind loyalty her town had to her ex-husband. "We'll just see each other on Sunday, okay?" In Burchwood, where it was safe and fresh and completely without her ghosts.

A glimmer of annoyance crossed his face, the first she'd ever seen. "How will we ever develop anything meaningful if we only see each other once a week?"

"Exactly, which is why I'm here now." She pressed in and playfully pinched his side. The casual touch seemed to surprise him almost as much as it surprised her. When it came to physicality, they were still very cautious with each other.

"Okay, okay," he said, his tone lifting. "I'll try to stay patient."

She smiled up at him, and to her relief, Ben smiled back.

Two of the volunteers approached, and though Ben inched away, he slid his hand back into hers. Both women were old enough to be her grandmother, and both had contagious smiles that made Laila want to brew hot tea and beg them for tales of their youths.

She'd never known her mother's parents; they'd cut off her mom when she'd gotten pregnant with Laila at sixteen. But when she was young, Laila dreamed up stories of her father's parents. How one day her mom would finally tell her grandparents about their long-lost granddaughter, and they would come rescue her from the filthy house and revolving door of her mother's cruel boyfriends.

Alas, they never came.

Ben released her hand only to wrap an arm around her. "Eleanor, Francis. This is Laila, my girlfriend. She's considering being a volunteer." He winked at her.

"It's nice to meet you both," Laila said, despite the sudden flush to her cheeks.

"Oh, you just wait." Eleanor clasped her hands together. "These kids are so sweet; you will be mesmerized the minute they come filing in. Did Ben assign you to a group?"

"Laila's just going to hang back and observe today." Ben gave her a final squeeze before releasing her. "We don't want to scare her off."

Francis patted her arm. "Well, hon, I hope you enjoy it. For me, those smiling faces are the highlight of my week."

"Thank you. I'm sure I will."

Ben found her hand again and pulled her toward the equipment he had abandoned. He kept turning to stare at her, then finally chuckled. "You still look terrified."

"I'm fine." She offered a reassuring smile, but inside she knew her unease wasn't just about the kids' program.

Ms. Harrington had promised her that the bathroom fix would take no more than six weeks, yet the move felt like a lifetime away. Ben was a patient, understanding guy, but eventually, he was going to want to know why, in all the time they'd been together, she'd never let him step foot in her hometown.

CHAPTER 4

The Kids' Bible Club was beyond Laila's expectations. Sixty kids from first grade all the way to fifth were singing praise music and dancing around, every one of them full of energy and cute giggles. Caden especially.

He was practically a duplicate of his father, the only difference being that his hair was so blond it glowed white under the fluorescent lighting. When she'd met him, he'd smiled shyly and hid behind his father's leg. Now, when he wasn't laughing at his dad pretending to be Noah building the ark, Caden would sneak peeks at her over his shoulder.

Laila sat in the back, observing from a row of chairs offered to parents, but only one other lady watched with her. She had shoulder-length brown hair cut in a bob style with streaks of gray running through the strands. The woman kept her eyes locked on a little girl in the back with identical brown braids dangling from each side of her head. The girl wasn't exactly separate from the crowd, but as the group of kids pushed closer to Ben's dramatic storytelling, she sat stoically with her head down.

Every so often, the woman would look over at Laila like she knew her. Laila simply smiled at first, but eventually the repeated stares made her wonder if she'd been recognized from Fairfield.

Ben finished his story by having all the kids make rain noises. Several kids stood and stomped; some did rain dances; others banged on the floor. Laila wanted to yell and make sounds too, just because they seemed to be having so much fun. She fully understood why Ben chose to do this with his limited spare time.

Finally, the eruption of noise subsided, and the leaders took over, corralling the kids back into their smaller groups. Ben had said this is where they'd have discussions or play games to further understand the lesson.

"If you think they're excited now, you should see them when they hand out the Bibles at the beginning of the year." The woman had scooted over two chairs and was now only one away from Laila. "It's amazing the school allows this program, isn't it?"

"Yes. I think it's wonderful." What a different life she might have had if only Fairfield had done the same. The first time she'd opened a Bible was when Katie gave her one last September for her birthday. At the time, she'd been put off that her friend was pushing her new faith on her, but now the words soothed her in a way nothing else had been able to.

"I'm Kim." The woman offered a hand that Laila softly shook. "I didn't mean to stare earlier. You just remind me of someone."

Butterflies assaulted her stomach, but Laila forced herself to remain calm. She didn't want people in Burchwood to know her history. This was supposed to be a fresh beginning. "Oh, okay. No problem."

"My granddaughter is over there. She just came to live with us a few months ago."

Once again, Laila's gaze directed to the little girl in braids. She sat unmoving in the group, neither participating nor talking. The group seemed to continue without her as if the behavior were normal or expected. Even Kim didn't seem surprised, just sad.

Compassion overruled her desire to remain unnoticed. Laila had been a bartender long enough to know when people needed to talk. "She seems to be a little nervous."

"Not nervous. Just checked out." Kim pulled a tissue from her purse and dabbed her eye. "She's been like this since they placed her with us."

"I'm sorry." It was all she could say.

"She doesn't speak. Not even to me." Kim brushed away another tear and clutched her tissue. "You probably think I'm insane for sharing this with a perfect stranger. But you look so much like my daughter that I feel like I know you."

"Your daughter?"

"Brianna, Sierra's mom. She wore her hair like yours all the time. That long, over-the-shoulder braid down to her waist. It wasn't quite as blonde, and you're a little thinner, but still, if I didn't know better, you two could be related." She sighed. "Sierra makes me braid her hair every day. I think because it helps her feel closer to her mother."

"What happened to her?"

The tears came again, and Laila immediately regretted the question.

"She's made some bad choices. Got into drugs at a young age and never really recovered. They removed Sierra at Christmas after my daughter left her alone for three days."

Laila felt her own eyes fill as she watched the girl. Another victim of drugs. Another child who would grow up damaged. "Where is Brianna now?"

"She's doing time for possession and child endangerment. Part of me is relieved, because it's the first time she's been removed from the drugs. I keep thinking maybe, if she gets the right help, she'll find her way back to the person she used to be."

Laila didn't have the heart to tell the crying woman her hope was in vain. Instead, she stared at the timid little girl and tried, without success, to stop the memory flooding her mind.

I slide through my bedroom window an hour after curfew.
Not because I'm rebellious or anything. It's just because

I've never had a curfew before, and the only reason I do tonight is because Mom's new boyfriend decided it was wrong to let a fifteen-year-old stay out all night. Katie said if I went home on time, he'd just do more and more to control me, so I stayed away out of principle.

"Laila. Come in here please." His deep voice rumbles down the hall and through the door of my room. Our trailer is small, and I should have known they'd hear me sneak in.

I square my shoulders the way my best friend would and walk into the living room. Mom's there, and she's high on her pain meds again, so despite the anger simmering off her boyfriend, she has a smile on her face.

Mr. Mortenson stands. He's not like the others. He doesn't try to be my friend, or worse, something sicker. No, he made it very clear when he moved in that I was under him, and he was to be addressed with respect.

"Are you aware of what time it is?"

"Yes, sir." My bravado falters, and I wish I'd let Katie come with me like she'd offered. She wouldn't be scared of him. She isn't scared of anyone.

"Good." He takes a step toward me, and before I can blink, pain slashes across my cheek. The force makes me stumble into the wall, and my third-grade picture—the last one my mom bothered to frame—goes crashing to the ground.

Tears swarm my eyes, and I don't know if I'm more in shock from the slap or from the fact that my mom still sits on the couch, that lost smile branded on her face.

"You're grounded. No TV. No phone." He sits back down, and my mom doesn't move except to make room for him. "Is that clear?"

"Yes, sir." I stumble back to the bedroom in a daze and reach for the phone I'm now forbidden to use.

"Hey, babe," Chad says in that lazy, tucked-in-bed voice of his. I see his house from my window and wish his arms were around me.

"Mr. Mortenson . . . he . . ." Sobs clog my throat, drowning out all I planned to say.

"Laila?"

I hear him move, hear a door slam through the phone.

"Get your stuff. I'm coming to get you right now."

I don't respond, but hang up and pack the bag in a daze. Despite all the men in and out of our house, Mr. Mortenson is the first one to hit me. I guess, in a way, I'm lucky.

I don't even get two shirts in my duffel before I hear the front door slam against the wall and shouts in the living room. Within seconds, I'm rushing toward the voice of the person who always rescues me.

The moment Chad sees my face, he freezes, his limbs going as hard as a statue. His eyes trail over my skin and land on the spot near my swelling eye.

Chad moves faster than I've ever seen him move. He grabs my mom's boyfriend by his shirt, slams him up against the wall, and punches him repeatedly until my mother is screaming, and that stupid smile is finally gone from her face.

Mr. Mortenson is on the ground bleeding. I shouldn't enjoy it, but the bruise on my face still burns, and it makes me glad he feels the same pain.

Chad crouches down and holds a knife I didn't even know he had. "Touch her again, and I'll kill you. I know what juvie is like. My cousin did two years there, so don't think I'm bluffing."

We rush away and hide in the tree house before Mr. Mortenson can retaliate. Katie meets us there. It's the night the three of us carve our names into the wood and vow to be each other's family. A unit of solidarity against a cruel world.

In the morning, I see Mr. Mortenson's destruction. My mom's cheek is the same purple color as mine, and the TV is smashed.

"He left me and it's your fault!" she hollers at me. "It's always your fault."

Laila couldn't help herself. She reached over and clutched Kim's hand. She'd wished the same thing most of her life—that her mom would wake up one day and find a way to be healthy—but time had a way of dissolving hope. Years later, her mom was still addicted to pills, floating from one guy to the next. People that far gone didn't change. Not really.

The praise music began again, chasing away the memories. Laila let go of Kim's hand, and they stood, now focused on the little girl who had suffered so much.

Sierra untangled her legs, but instead of joining the rest of the kids, she seemed to search for someone. Kim waved, and Sierra began walking in her direction. She wore the same Burchwood uniform as the other girls there—a khaki skirt and green polo shirt. Her white socks were pulled up high on her shins, and her tennis shoes were pink with green laces.

"I make her stay until small group is over," Kim whispered. "I keep hoping she'll start to like it, but not yet." Kim's concern morphed into a big, happy smile when Sierra came close. "Hey, honey. You did so good today." She hugged Sierra, but the young girl didn't return the embrace, nor did she smile. "This is my friend . . ." Kim stopped and seemed embarrassed that she hadn't asked Laila her name.

"Laila." She crouched down so that she was eye level with the girl. "You must be Sierra. It's very nice to meet you."

That same curiosity that Laila had seen in Kim now colored her granddaughter's expression. Sierra tilted her head and reached for the braid over Laila's shoulder. The touch was hesitant and only lasted a fraction of a second, but it was enough to make Kim's breath catch.

The noise seemed to startle Sierra, and soon that glazed, disconnected look returned to her eyes. Laila stood, and Kim ushered her granddaughter to a chair to wait for her.

She walked back to Laila and spoke only loud enough for the two of them to hear. "That's the first time she's initiated contact since coming." The hope in her eyes was so familiar and so heartbreaking. Kim glanced back at her granddaughter, who stared absently at her hands. "The counselors say she will come out of her shell when she's ready. I'm just trying to be patient."

"Sometimes that's all you can be."

Kim suddenly pulled Laila in for a hug, squeezed her tight, then released her just as quickly. "I'm sorry. I just needed to do that." A beat later, she retrieved her purse, took Sierra's hand, and led her out before the final song was over.

Laila watched them disappear, still thrown by how quickly they'd invited her into their pain and by how much she now wanted to help in any way she could.

"So, what did you think?" Ben's voice came from behind and startled her enough that she let out a small squeak.

"Sorry." He squeezed her shoulder and kept his hand there.

"It was really wonderful. I can see why you are all so dedicated to doing this."

Ben let his hand fall and tucked it into his pocket. "It means a lot to me that you came today. For a while, I worried . . ." He trailed off, then shook his head as if reprimanding himself. She found herself wanting to know what he was about to say but, after their earlier conversation, figured it was better to let it go unsaid.

"So, Caden wanted you to know that he thinks you are very pretty and very cool, since you both have the same hair color."

She chuckled. "He's as charming as his father."

"Charming enough that you'll be back next week?"

Laila remembered Sierra's ghost of a touch. "Yeah. I'll definitely be back."

CHAPTER 5

The warehouse was hot and stuffy, making Chad feel as if a fog of dust had settled and clung to every pore on his face. He'd been warned of the springtime shipment of mulch and topsoil and yards of flagstone. Then again, he couldn't complain. Last week he'd logged ten hours of overtime, and this week he might log even more.

He was almost there. Just a few thousand dollars shy of his goal and only three months left to earn it.

Then he'd go home.

The thought of her spurred him on, gave him that extra strength he needed to lift the fifteen-pound bag of soil and walk it over to the display.

"Nice job, Richardson. You keep this up, and you'll get the employee award every month." His manager chuckled and grabbed his own bag. Chad liked that about him. Scott didn't have to do the manual labor stuff, but he had no problem getting his hands dirty.

"As long as it leads to extra hours, I'll do whatever you want." Chad dropped the load and stretched his back. He was getting stronger than he'd ever been, even before the drugs. His shoulders had broadened, and his arms were now cut with a definition that made his sleeves tighter than he wanted.

He imagined Laila's hands running over them, the softness of her fingertips as they explored the new body he'd formed. He shook his head, trying to force the images out, but the closer he got to returning home, the stronger they became.

Following two of his coworkers back to the pile, Chad flexed his aching fingers and prepared to lift another bag.

"Hey, Chad, I've got a question for you." The voice belonged to the new guy whose name he kept forgetting.

"Yeah. What is it?" Chad squatted to protect his back and picked up a bag.

"Well, my girlfriend and I are heading out to Club Metro tonight, and she has a friend who, well, I'll be blunt, likes the way you look in your jeans. The girl's pretty friendly, if you know what I mean."

Chad knew exactly what he meant, and the thought sickened him. "I'm married." He wiggled the fingers of his left hand, letting the gold band catch the light. No stack of papers was going to change that either. "And I don't drink."

"Okay. Your loss."

Chad quickened his steps as he carried the bag away, not wanting to be anywhere near that idiot. But the new guy's invitation brought on a wave of memories Chad now had no hope of suppressing.

The club is packed tonight, despite it being a holiday weekend. We've just finally scored some seats at the bar, and both Katie and Laila are on the dance floor, grooving to whatever the heck this music is.

Katie shimmies over to her new boyfriend. "Baby, come dance with me, I'm lonely," she begs like an ignored southern belle. She's pretending, and Cooper knows it. There's not a weak or desperate thing about her.

"In a minute, Firecracker. We just sat down."

She dances as she walks backward, shaking her head. "Your loss. I'll just find someone else who will."

The "someone else" is my wife, who looks hot enough to make me want to leave this place and make our own sweet music in our own sweet bed. But she's laughing and swaying those hips, so I'm content to watch, for now.

Cooper shifts over so we can talk above the music. This is only the second time we've gone out as a group, and I only agreed because Katie threw a hissy fit. Laila doesn't like Cooper much—she says he brings out the worst side of Katie—and I don't like to see my girl uncomfortable.

"So you've all known each other since you were kids?" He's watching Katie dance with a goofy grin on his face. The poor sap is in love, and I don't have the heart to break it to him that she's just not wired that way.

"Yeah, since kindergarten. Laila put out a lemonade stand, and I went to get a drink. One look at her, and I knew I was going to marry her one day." She was the most beautiful thing I'd ever seen. An angel, right there in front of me with two pigtails and pink ribbons. "Katie challenged me to an arm-wrestling match right in front of her, so I couldn't say no."

"She win?"

The question makes me like Cooper a little more. "Yeah. She won, sort of. Laila came over and sat with me after, so in the end, I kind of did."

My gorgeous wife throws her head back on the dance floor, and it's all the invitation I need. I set down my drink and join her, our bodies swaying to the music with promises of more. My lips graze hers, and my heart flutters.

Call me a sap, a sucker, whatever you like.

I'll love this girl forever.

"Richardson!"

Chad pulled himself out of his head just in time to see the forklift coming down the aisle. He hurried to the side and ignored the scowl on his boss's face. Three long months, and he'd hold his wife again.

"I'm at two hundred forty-five days with no injuries in this warehouse. You pull that again, and you can forget the overtime."

"Sorry. My mind wandered, but I'm good now." Only he wasn't. His mind was stuck seven years back in time. Right before everything went to hell.

CHAPTER 6

Joe's was slammed, even for a Saturday. The sports crowd had mingled with the weekend crowd, and despite the extra help from their busboy, Eric, Laila was still barely keeping up with the orders.

She filled two more draft glasses, offering the guy across the counter a smile she didn't feel. The roar of the crowded room had become a throb in her ears. Her feet ached, and all she wanted was a hot bath and a good night's sleep. Unfortunately, she still had five more hours before either would be possible.

"I told you adding those two sixty-inch flat screens would pay off," Joe said as he passed her with a fresh rack of clean glasses.

"Yeah, you also promised you'd hire on more waitresses. Danielle barely takes shifts anymore, and Eric can't work the bar solo." Laila reached around him and grabbed a tequila bottle along with two shot glasses.

"I did hire more."

She practically groaned. "Charity doesn't count. I meant good waitresses."

Joe simply laughed. "I can think of a time when I thought the same about you."

She could argue with him, but honestly, he was right. At eighteen, she could barely walk across the room without spilling something. Now, she could serve multiple customers without breaking a sweat or messing up an order. The problem was, she hated herself for doing so. Hated how many people left needing cab rides or sturdy friends to lean on. It made her feel like a hypocrite. For years, she'd begged Chad to stop doing the very thing she made a living enabling others to do.

With quick fingers, she slid a twenty into the register, took out the five-dollar bill the customer had said to keep, then stuffed it into the tip jar.

More people crowded in front of her.

"What can I get you, Frank?" she asked the balding man who'd somehow shoved between two giggling girls.

"Three house beers, and Cooper said you'd know what to make him."

Laila's gaze swept across the mass of bodies. Somehow, she'd missed Cooper's arrival, and he was now making his rounds across the floor, shaking hands with coworkers from the factory.

Cooper had been one of Chad's closer friends and Katie's boyfriend for two years. And even though Laila had never really approved of his explosive relationship with her friend, they had bonded after Chad split town, mostly because Cooper was the only one who missed him as much as she did.

Laila took Frank's credit card and promised to bring the drinks to his table in a minute. Once again, she was doing Charity's job, but that had become so routine, she'd stopped expecting otherwise.

"I need to run to table four," she told Joe after loading the drinks on a tray.

"Okay, I've got the bar," he murmured from his crouched position in front of the leaking ice machine. "Try not to kill her on your way there."

"Don't hold your breath." A joke, but in some ways, not so much. People rarely got under her skin, but Charity was exactly like Laila's mother. She floated from guy to guy, falling in and out of love at least twice a week. They'd use her until either she found someone better or they tired of her. The pattern was as sickening now as it had been when Laila was young.

The crowd kindly split as she pressed through with her full tray balanced carefully in her right hand. A few steps later, she reached Frank's table, and he stood to help her with the load.

"Thanks, Laila. I tried to wait for Charity, but you know how she is."

"It's no problem. I started a tab for you, so just wave at me when you're ready for refills."

"See, this is why the whole town loves you." Cooper came over and draped a heavy arm around her shoulder. She pushed it off, immediately smelling evidence that he'd been indulging long before showing up at the bar.

Great. Now she'd have to babysit him too.

Frank shifted away, obviously sensing the tension between them. Cooper wasn't especially tall, but he was big and burly, and the air of intimidation that clung to him wasn't fabricated. When he drank, he got angry, and when he got angry, he looked for people to take it out on. She'd seen him fight, and every time, it was vicious and dirty, like a darker side took over the second that first punch was thrown.

"It's crazy in here." Cooper scanned the room like he was looking for someone. It used to be Katie, then Chad. Now, he just seemed to do it out of habit.

Her irritation softened a little. "Yeah, it is, but the game's almost over, so it will clear out soon." She handed over his drink and noted to make it weaker next time around. "So, where's Piper tonight?" Laila didn't exactly like Cooper's on-again-off-again girlfriend, but since Katie's return, their new normal was awkward small talk. The last several months had been tough on their friendship. Cooper still resented Laila for forgiving Katie, and Laila was still angry that Cooper had lied about Chad's overdose.

"Don't know. Don't care. I ditched her ages ago." Cooper turned to shake another hand while Laila subtly eyed the men across the table. Frank mouthed "Katie" and shook his head.

Yep. Cooper was definitely chasing away some demons tonight.

When his attention returned to her, she laid an empathetic hand on his arm. Despite their recent distance, Cooper had been her shoulder to cry on more than once. "Do you want to talk about it?"

"Nope." He lifted his drink, swallowing half of it in two big gulps. She eyed his white knuckles as he concentrated on the opposite end of the bar. He'd come a long way, but Cooper still hadn't fully accepted that the Katie he'd loved and waited for was truly gone and married to someone else.

It was the curse of Fairfield: desperately clinging to the past, no matter how ugly and broken.

He finished off his drink and placed the empty glass on her tray along with his credit card. "Keep these coming all night."

"Coop—"

He lifted a finger. "All night."

Frustrated, she slipped his card into her apron pocket and spun around. This wouldn't help him any more than it ever did Chad. In the morning, Katie would still be married to Asher, and Cooper would still be alone.

Edging through the crowd, she forced herself to calm down. Why things were getting to her tonight, she didn't know. She could usually push them aside, get lost in busyness, and forget that she was playing a part she no longer wanted.

A hand encircled her arm, and she tugged it away right as she jerked her head to see who had dared to grab her.

A blink. Two blinks. Then the haunting realization that her two worlds had just irreversibly collided.

She glanced at him head to toe twice before she could utter a word. "Ben?"

He stood out like a beacon in darkness. Not only was he dressed for a big city business convention, but everything about him was clean cut and scholarly, from his wire-rimmed glasses to the tight trim of his hair. Even his slacks had perfectly ironed creases down the front.

When someone bumped her from behind, she was pushed closer. "What are you doing here?"

"I know you said not to come, but I wanted to see you." He had to yell over the crowd, and she prayed no one around them was listening. Even worse, he took her hand and brought it up to his lips. "I'll just stay for a few minutes, I promise."

Laila fought the urge to stiffen, all while feeling a treacherous heat flood up her neck and across her cheeks. Subtly, she angled her head to check how many people were paying attention. But only one pair of eyes met hers. Cooper's. He'd been watching them. Watching her with a guy who wasn't Chad.

This was exactly why she hadn't wanted Ben here. Why she'd worked so hard to keep him a secret.

Doing her best to hide her panic, she pulled him toward the far end of the bar and away from the worst of the crowd. The alcove by the restrooms created a blind spot to the TVs, so only two or three people lingered near the wall.

As soon as they stopped moving, it took all of Laila's self-control not to start yelling. "I don't understand," she finally said.

He ran a hand over his short hair, his eyebrows furrowing behind the glasses. "I know. And I'm sorry. I had no idea this is how busy it got." His gaze swept the crowded room. "I just needed to see you tonight. Courtney and I got into another fight about Caden."

She fought the rising guilt. "No, it's okay. It just surprised me is all."

"Laila." Joe pounded the bar like a bongo drum, sending a bolt of panic through her. She hadn't seen him approach. "I need some backup here."

"Coming." She called over her shoulder, all while trying to figure out how to politely ask Ben to leave.

He didn't give her the opportunity. "You must be Joe," Ben said, holding his hand out to her boss. "Sorry to show up like this. I know she's busy."

"Yeah, no problem." Joe carefully returned Ben's handshake, but his eyebrows rose in a not so hidden question. "And you're . . ."

"Ben."

"Ben," Joe repeated as if testing the word in his mouth. "How do you know Laila?"

Now it was Ben's turn to bristle. He glanced from her to her employer. "We're dating."

Laila cringed, while Joe practically fell over the bar. "You're dating?"

She could hear his thoughts. *He's nothing like Chad.* And he wasn't. Ben didn't command a room when he entered or lift a crooked smile that promised danger and seduction. But he also didn't stumble into the bathroom after closing and puke his guts out every night either.

Someone shouted Joe's name across the bar.

"Just a minute," he hollered back, his eyes still fixed on hers. They were angry and disappointed and a gamut of other emotions she'd never seen directed her way. "Is he why you suddenly want to move to Burchwood?"

Not daring to look at Ben, she pleaded, "Can we talk about this later?"

Joe grumbled something under his breath that she was fairly certain she didn't want to hear and pushed away from the counter.

Ben remained a step away, utterly silent. And unsmiling. She put a hand on his arm, needing to touch him just to make sure he was still there.

"You were right. I shouldn't have come," he said in heartbreaking stillness.

"Ben—"

He brushed past her, his long legs carrying him to the door quicker than she could follow. The crowd had now noticed him, and her following him. They moved aside, but the murmuring had only just begun. It suddenly didn't matter, though. She just wanted to make things right.

He slammed through the door, and she got to it just as it was about to click shut. The weight knocked her back, but she trudged forward, the night air a cool relief from the sticky heat inside.

"Ben. Please stop. My legs are much too short to chase you."

He slowed until finally she caught up. "Don't make jokes," he said, lacking any of his usual good-natured humor. Finally, he stopped moving altogether. "You lied to me. Joe didn't say you couldn't have friends come by, did he?"

Ben wasn't stupid. She didn't have to spell it out for him to realize she'd kept him a secret. "No." She hung her head. "I didn't know how to explain why I didn't want you here."

"Do your best now, or you won't ever need to." Such a simple ultimatum, yet so complicated. She knew Ben's standards. After being lied to and cheated on by his ex-wife, he'd made it clear on their first date that honesty was number one with him.

She sucked in a deep breath, knowing her words could very well end whatever it was they had started. "I fell in love with Chad when I was thirteen. He's the only guy I've ever dated. The only guy I've ever even looked at. This town is where we grew up. Those people are *his* people, and they expect—in some cases even demand—that I spend the rest of my life waiting for him to come back. No matter how great you are." She pointed her index finger back and forth between them. "They will *never* accept the two of us." Her hand dropped listlessly to her side. "Maybe I'm a coward, but I just wanted to live in our bubble as long as I could."

A breeze whispered across her neck, sending goose bumps down her arms and legs. Ben inched closer and ran his hands up and down her chilled skin.

"I guess your reasoning makes sense, even if hearing it stings a little." He didn't exactly smile, but his mouth showed less of a scowl than it had before.

She tilted her head up to look at him. "In Fairfield, Chad will always be a ghost between us. It doesn't matter that he's been gone for so long or that we're divorced. To them, I will forever be his wife."

He flinched. "Please don't call yourself that."

"I'm sorry. I'm not explaining this well." She shifted on her feet, half expecting him to walk away.

But instead, his hand cupped her cheek, his palm a warm print on her skin. "So I'm the only other guy you've ever looked at?"

She chuckled. "It's the glasses. They sucked me right in."

Ben smiled too, but it wasn't one she recognized. She'd hurt him, and that wasn't fair. "I really am sorry I misled you. This is all very different for me, and I don't know how to navigate this new world."

"Well, let's start with something easy." His hand fell to her shoulder, his thumb brushing the bare skin of her neck. "I don't want you to keep me a secret anymore. Your friends may not like it, but eventually, they're going to have to get used to the fact that you're seeing someone else."

"I know."

Ben leaned down slowly. "Thank you for telling me the truth, even though some of it was hard to hear." His lips were gentle, like his spirit, like his patience.

It wasn't their first kiss or even their second. But this one felt alarmingly significant. Maybe it was being in Fairfield or her proximity to Joe's, but as he kissed her, she felt her throat close and her eyes burn with unwanted moisture.

She tried to blame it on her guilt for having kept things from Ben when she knew what it felt like to be lied to. But deep down, the feeling was more like grief. The loss of something she'd never find again.

CHAPTER 7

Laila watched Ben's car until its taillights disappeared. She knew she needed to go back inside the bar. Joe was probably drowning in orders without her, yet she couldn't seem to make her feet move.

Ben wasn't the only one affected by her calling herself Chad's wife. Ever since the cursed words had left her mouth, her mind wouldn't stop replaying that day.

> "Ugh. I do not want to go to class," Katie moans from her spot under the tree. "Why even have it? We're graduating in two months." She's lying on her back, and her black hair is spread out around her like a halo. There are four rips in her jeans, which is against the school dress code, but they stopped sending her home when the principal realized she was doing it on purpose for just that result.
>
> "Two months," Chad murmurs from behind me. I'm tucked between his legs, and his arms are wrapped tightly around my waist. He leans down to kiss my favorite spot behind my ear and lingers for a second. "Laila Richardson." He says it with eager anticipation. We're getting married soon—the Saturday after graduation—and every day he reminds me we'll soon have the same

last name. "I wish we could just go do it today." His hand gradually trails down my arm to the gold engagement ring on my finger. It's thin, with only three small diamonds in a row, but it's by far the most beautiful thing I've ever worn.

"Why don't we do it today?" Katie sits up, her face full of renewed energy. "You're both eighteen. Let's go."

"We have class, and we need a marriage license." As usual, I'm the practical one. The one who barely manages to keep these two from chasing rainbows and leprechauns.

"Mr. Tolver owes me a favor. Ten bucks says I can get you a license in an hour." She's on her feet.

"How does he owe you a favor?" Chad's skeptical, but I can see he's starting to catch her vigor. That's how they always are. One idea, then another, until they're both doing something crazy.

"Let's just say, I was in the right place at the right time, and the woman he was kissing was definitely not his wife." She grabs my hand and tugs me up. "We'll meet you at the courthouse at four."

Chad jumps to his feet, and I can see his smile grow. He pulls me away from Katie and cups my face. "I love you. I've wanted to marry you since the day we met."

My stomach flips when I see that look in his eyes. "I love you too."

"Then let's get married. Today."

It's March 28, but somehow that day seems perfect now. We have no house, no car, no stuff, but I don't care.

"Okay. Today."

Katie squeals, and we're running to her car. I think she's just as excited as I am.

Laila glanced toward the streetlight a few feet away, then across the road at the dimly lit realty office and coffee shop. The courthouse where they'd said their vows was just around the corner.

Her right foot scooted back and forth across the gravel until a line of dirt appeared. The breeze once again caused her skin to tingle.

They were just babies. She should have waited, should have listened to the warnings. But her love was blind back then, just like it had been for years afterward.

With a final sigh, she shoved her hands into the pockets of her jeans and turned back toward the entryway to the bar.

A silhouette leaned by the door, his foot propped up on the wall behind him. Her steps slowed until she could see Cooper's hardened expression, despite the shadows around him. He pushed off the wall when she approached.

"How long have you been standing there?" she asked.

"Long enough to see you kiss the wrong person."

She tried to edge past him, but he used his big body to block hers.

"Don't do this to him, Laila. It'll ruin him. All the progress he's made will be for nothing."

She wanted to slap him for making her the bad guy. "What progress? When's the last time you've even spoken to him?"

"Joe just told me he called on New Year's, and he was sober."

"So?"

"So? He was *sober*, Laila . . . on New Year's."

"Stop it. I'm done wishing. Done reading between the lines of every little scrap of hope just to convince myself that this time things will be different."

He gripped her shoulders, forced her to look into his now-blurry eyes. It stopped her cold, the heartbreak in them. In the seven years she'd known Cooper, she'd never once seen him this broken. Not even when Katie had left town. "I'm begging you, Laila. *Begging* you . . .

to try one more time. Call him. Just see if he's good now. Joe has his number."

"And what happened to the number you had? The one you used when you called to tell him Katie was back in town?" Cooper had begged her then too. Swore up and down that Chad would come home if he knew about Katie. "If I recall, you insisted he was getting his life together then too."

Cooper glanced at the ground. "I should have known better. I should have known any news of Katie would send him spiraling."

"Chad's addiction is not Katie's fault," she practically yelled. "It's not my fault or your fault. It's Chad's choice. One he's made over and over."

Three people stumbled out the door, forcing Cooper to release her. She wiped away the wetness on her cheeks. When would it be enough? When would she have cried enough to be over that man?

"Go home, Cooper. Sleep off whatever is twisting you up inside tonight and let this go." She squared her shoulders, worked to stand almost as tall as him. "Ben is my boyfriend, and like it or not, that isn't going to change."

This time, when she went to open the door, he didn't get in her way.

"What if Chad had come home?"

Her feet stilled and her body stiffened. "It wouldn't have changed anything." She swallowed and pulled open the door.

"You're lying. To me and to yourself."

She didn't bother arguing, just shut the door behind her.

The crowd had thinned slightly, and to Laila's surprise, Charity moved from customer to customer like a bee during pollen season. The reason was easy to see, even through the crowd.

Joe's normal cheer had been replaced by curt order taking. He filled drinks, passed them along, and then moved on to the next order. A complete departure from his usual *everyone's family* mantra.

Laila slipped behind the bar and took the next order. Side by side, they worked in silence, a silence so heavy it suffocated the room. Most of the bar's patrons closed out their tabs and bolted to the doors.

When the room was down to ten customers, Joe snapped his fingers. "Charity, come take the bar. Eric, you've got the floor." Without a word to Laila, Joe pushed through the swinging door and disappeared.

She'd worked with the man for almost ten years. She knew when she was expected to follow.

Trudging forward, she entered the back room and sat, feeling a lot like she'd been summoned to the principal's office. Joe stood by the window, his back to her, his hands on his hips.

"You're going to quit on me, aren't you?" he asked without turning around.

She'd been avoiding this conversation, mostly because she knew the truth would upset him. The house was just the beginning. Eventually, Laila would sever all her ties to Fairfield. "I have my resume at a few places, but I won't leave until I know you have a proper replacement."

He spun around. "What if I made you a partner? You'd still get your salary and tips, but I'd add profit percentage, and let you take over the waitstaff."

She'd never before seen him beg. It made something within her strain. "I can't."

He sat in the chair opposite her and leaned in close. "Why not?"

"Because."

"Because why?" he demanded. "You know every corner of this place. You could serve in your sleep. Tell me what you want and I'll make it happen."

"Okay, fire Charity."

"Done." He shot to his feet, and Laila had to grab his hand and tug to keep him from bolting to the door.

"Sit down, Joe. I'm kidding. You don't need to fire her."

He returned to his chair, looking far older than his fifty-three years. She took his hand in hers and squeezed. "This job was never meant to be my lifelong profession."

"I know, kid. But we're your family, and this feels a lot like you're running away."

Maybe she was. But after all this time, it was definitely her turn.

CHAPTER 8

The buzz in his head started slowly, then continued to grow louder and louder until his consciousness could finally decipher reality from dream. Chad pried his eyes open, flipped onto his side, and grabbed the vibrating cell phone off his nightstand.

Darkness leaked into his room, confirming what his groggy mind was telling him—it was the middle of the night. He pressed the round button on the bottom of his phone and flinched when his screen flashed bright. He'd missed four calls from the same number.

Awareness came slower than usual, so it took him a few seconds to register that the three-digit area code wasn't from Atlanta or the surrounding area. It was from Fairfield.

Chad swung his legs off the bed, and his bare feet hit the thinning carpet. Still gripping the phone in one hand, he rubbed the sore muscles in his chest with the other, hoping to wake the rest of himself up. His body was tired. His mind was tired. Neither of which were good when facing his past.

He studied the number closer and vaguely remembered dialing it many times when he could barely stand upright. Cooper.

Chad gripped the phone and pressed his eyes closed. There was a reason he hadn't called his old friend since entering rehab. They were too much alike. Shared too many of the same triggers. They also shared the same propensity to let anger rule their emotions when alcohol was involved.

Yet all the same, Chad felt his finger slide to the "Call Back" button. If Joe had given out his number, then it had to be important.

Cooper answered after the first ring. "Hey." He said it like he hadn't been the one to call four times in the middle of the night. "I was hoping you'd be awake."

"I wasn't, actually."

"Oh. Okay." He'd been drinking, heavily. Chad could hear the slur in his voice, the effort to sound lucid, the catch in his throat that often came with his drunken anger. "So, you're still in Atlanta, I guess."

"Yeah. I'm still here. Is there a reason you called?"

"A reason?" Cooper's voice turned sour. "You really have the audacity to ask me that?"

Chad tightened his fingers around the phone. He didn't need this kind of drama right now. "How did you get my number?"

"Great question. Maybe Joe thought I should know you're still alive. It's been months, Chad. Where the hell have you been?"

He took a ragged breath, his anger edged out by guilt. "Rehab. I checked in a week after you told me Katie was home. Been sober nine months now."

The line went silent for just enough time to make Chad wonder if the call had less to do with him and more to do with his old friend. Awake now, Chad tried to think of how Mark would deal with the situation. "What's going on in your head, Coop?"

"Nothing," he said, but his voice begged to differ. He sounded exhausted, and not the kind that came from sleepiness, but the kind that Chad often felt when he'd reach for the bottle. "Joe said you were doing better. I wanted to hear it for myself."

"At one in the morning?"

"It's a Saturday night. I figured you were out."

"If I were out, I wouldn't be doing better, now, would I?"

"No, I guess not."

Heavy silence fell between them again. In such a state, it wouldn't surprise Chad if Cooper passed out talking. "Coop, you still with me?"

"Yeah. I'm here. Just trying to understand why you aren't."

"I have my reasons." Reasons that still haunted him when he slept. Reasons that had him working every hour he could at the hardware store just to earn the money he needed to get out of the mess he'd made. "How's everyone doing?"

They both knew he was asking about Laila.

"You sure you want to know? Nine months sober, and you don't call her?"

"I told you, I have my reasons." If Chad could reach through the phone and strangle his friend, he would. "Just tell me how she's doing."

"Why?" Cooper's voice turned hard and sarcastic. "Your life is so freaking fantastic now. That's all that's ever mattered anyway, right? You and Katie. The two suns in our little universe."

Chad responded with equal aggression. "Is this really why you called? To make me feel guilty for getting clean?"

"What do you want me to say, man? You're asleep on a Saturday night. You're sober. Bravo. Good for you. Be sure to send us a postcard when you go get married to some preacher's kid."

Chad shot to his feet. "What are you talking about?"

"You, Katie. You're the same selfish person. Maybe Laila was right to move on and forget about you. You've obviously forgotten about us."

Chad pushed down the rising nausea. "What do you mean, that Laila's moving on?"

As if Cooper could sense the shift, he too lowered his voice. "A guy came to the bar tonight."

Suddenly, Chad couldn't breathe. He pressed on his sternum and rubbed. "To see Laila?"

"Yeah, to see her. She kissed him right outside Joe's, for the whole town to see."

"She kissed him?" He gulped, but his mouth was so dry he had nothing to swallow. Cooper was wrong. She wouldn't betray him. She loved him. She'd always loved him. "Are you sure?"

"I saw it with my own two eyes."

Chad couldn't speak. He stumbled through his bedroom door, counting each step to the bathroom. He pressed his palm to the wall, using its sturdiness to support his weakened legs.

"And then I defended you." Resentment laced each word. "I begged her to give you another chance. But she knew. Somehow she knew you wouldn't care. I guess I'm once again the fool."

Chad couldn't hear anymore, not through the blood roaring in his ears. He pressed "End," let the phone drop from his trembling fingers, and fell to his knees. Hands gripping the toilet bowl, he shut his eyes, willing the churning in his stomach to stop. But the words pushed through.

She kissed him. She's moved on.

With one last cramp, Chad vomited for the first time since detox, trying his best to contain the sounds of his heart breaking. But the walls were too thin, his retching too monumental.

"Why is Nathan texting you?" I'm ticked, and I have no right to be. It's not Laila's fault that he can't take a hint. The guy's a douche with an ego. He's the star quarterback, and he's had his eye on my girl ever since she got runner-up for homecoming queen.

She's ticked too, but for completely different reasons. "That's not the point. The point is you lied to me."

"I was going to tell you."

"When?"

"Don't change the subject. I don't want him texting you. He's trying to cause trouble between us."

"There is trouble between us, Chad. You did Ecstasy."
She whispers the last word like it's a curse. "You promised
me nothing stronger than weed."

"I know. I'm sorry." I reach for her arm, but she
pulls away. From over her shoulder I can see Nathan at
his lunch table across the grass. He's smirking. Smirking
because he comes from a wealthy family with connections,
and he's used to getting what he wants. Not this time.

I'm walking before I have time to process the two
linemen flanking him.

"Where are you going? Chad, stop." She's chasing
after me, and I hate the plea in her voice, so I stop, but
I don't want to. I want to punch someone, namely him,
because the worst truth is that he would be better for her
than me. Anyone would be.

She pulls me to the parking lot, knowing I'm about
to lose it, and the school already said that if I get another
suspension, I'll have to repeat a year.

We stop behind Katie's car.

"Do you want him?" I have to ask because right now
I can't figure out why this amazing girl is mine. I'm a
mess, and I'm dragging her right down with me.

"No, I don't want him. I love you."

I feel the tears the same time Laila sees them, and
she hugs me. I grip her tight, so afraid that if I let go,
she'll be gone forever, and what would that leave me?
Nothing. 'Cause I'm nothing without her. "I'm so sorry. I
don't know why I do these things. I don't want to."

Lights flooded the hallway, illuminating the dark bathroom.

Panting, Chad braced himself over the bowl. "Go back to bed. I'm
fine."

He didn't know who was in the doorway, but it didn't matter. There was no one he wanted to see him like this.

"Is it a stomach bug?"

Oh, how he wished it were.

"No." Chad finally felt the end of his torment, grabbed a handful of toilet paper off the roll, and wiped his mouth. He stood slowly, shut the lid, and flushed the toilet, still too embarrassed to look Mark in the eye. "Sorry I woke you. Really, I'm fine." He turned on the faucet, cupped the icy water in his palms, and splashed his face. In the mirror, he saw Mark watching him, the doubt starting to play on his features.

Mark had a two-strikes-you're-out policy, and based on his expression, he was definitely thinking Chad had earned his first one.

"I'm sober."

"Probably, but I'm gonna need to make sure."

Chad gripped a towel, spun around, and let Mark get close enough check his breath for alcohol.

"Satisfied?" he demanded when Mark bristled.

"No. You smell like rotten cabbage. But I am glad you haven't been drinking."

"Good. Now go back to bed." Chad pushed past him, his mind set on one task alone. He had to get home. Tonight.

Spurred on by an uncontrollable desperation, he didn't bother to acknowledge that Mark had followed him into his room. His duffel was under the bed. He grabbed it in one fierce tug and unzipped the worn fabric.

Mark continued to watch, wordlessly.

"If you're trying to figure out what to say to stop me, don't bother." He thrust open his drawer, grabbed a stack of T-shirts, and shoved them into the bag. "Laila met someone." He choked on the words, felt the lingering acid in his stomach. "I'm going home before it's too late."

"If you have to run out of here in the middle of the night, don't you think you're already too late?"

Chad fisted another stack of shirts, his anger the only thing keeping him from completely breaking down. "Weren't you the one who said I needed to fight for her? What do you think I'm doing?"

Mark crossed his arms, his stare as pointed and steady as a boxer's in the ring. "I think you're putting yourself in a situation where you're going to relapse."

"I told you, I'm fine."

"You're not fine. You're shaking. Your lips are colorless; your eyes look crazed. You're panicking."

Again, his gut twisted, but he dismissed the ache, along with Mark's words. Two more trips to his dresser and he had his duffel almost full.

"So what happens next? You just walk out on your job? Don't even give your boss notice? You hop a bus, show up at her house? Let her see you're exactly the same as you were when you left?"

Chad froze. "I am not the same."

"Right now, you are. This behavior, it's erratic. It's these kinds of moments that make you fall right back into the pit you've crawled out of. What you need to do is calm down. You need to take five minutes and think rationally, instead of reacting." He inched closer. "I've been here, Chad. I've blazed a fire trail to my ex-wife's house. I've beaten down the door; I've demanded a second chance. It doesn't work. It's not what they want to see."

Closing his eyes against the pounding in his head, Chad collapsed onto the bed. "I can't lose her," he whispered. Yeah, they'd been separated, but she had always been there, in his head, in his blood. They were connected. It was why he'd never taken off his ring, why he'd never touched another woman, no matter how far gone.

"Take a few days. Talk to your boss. Calm yourself down. Then go to her, rationally. Let her see the man you've become. Not the one you used to be."

The panic was still there. The grief, loss, fear, and even anger still lingered through each of his veins. Yet, with a voice he barely recognized, he told Mark he'd wait and honor his obligations.

Mark knelt by his bed, took one of his shaky hands in his, and did something no man had ever done in Chad's life—he prayed for him. For strength, endurance, and reconciliation.

And for that span of a few minutes, Chad clung to the hope that this God Mark believed in might actually be listening.

CHAPTER 9

The twenty-minute drive to her mother's current double-wide seemed longer and ten times more daunting this time. Usually, Laila enjoyed this part of the winding highway, the one reprieve in her otherwise miserable monthly obligation. But today, the road seemed never ending, and every inch of her felt edgy and electric.

She'd joined Sierra's group during Kids' Bible Club that afternoon. Watched as the little girl stared, then studied her own hands, then stared some more. She hadn't participated in the life-sized tic-tac-toe game or worship time, but she did stay. Even after the program was over, she remained by Laila's side until they walked over to Kim together.

With teary eyes, Kim had asked if Laila would be willing to help, noting that her granddaughter's budding interest in Laila was likely because of her resemblance to the girl's mother. Kim admitted she was willing to use any inroads to draw Sierra out of the fog she'd been living in.

"Of course," Laila had said, but something about seeing that spark of hope made her viciously angry.

Why children felt that desperate need to love unspeakably selfish parents, she'd never understand, especially since she too seemed to fall into that category. Or at least, she had for the last twenty-seven years. Maybe she always would.

A buzzing from the passenger seat pulled Laila from her tumble into bitterness. She grabbed her Bluetooth earpiece, relieved by Katie's distraction.

"Hey," she said, adjusting the speaker in her ear. "Sorry, I meant to call you back earlier."

"It's fine. I just wanted to follow up and see if you were planning to come to our barbeque this weekend?"

Laila felt a sting of jealousy roll through her. Katie's new husband, Asher, loved to host parties; he had invited at least thirty other guests to the last one Laila had attended, most of them couples with little kids. Asher had spent the night wrestling with the children in the yard while Katie watched with a sappy smile on her face. They were already trying for a family of their own.

The sting came again, sharper this time. Laila had wanted a family too. Wanted kids and a dog and a white picket fence. She'd even drawn her dream home once when they were kids. Chad had kept it and promised he'd build it for her one day.

Laila swallowed the emotion that came whenever she thought of how close she and Chad had come to being parents. "No, I'm sorry, I can't make it. Joe put me on the schedule after all."

Katie sighed through the receiver. "That's the third weekend in a row. Laila, you need to take some time off. Go do something fun for once. Maybe we can plan that girls' trip we've talked about. Just me and you."

Laila glanced out the window. Trees lined the road on either side of her, boxing her in and blocking the view of the water channels from the coast. They were the only beautiful thing in this area and would end the minute she turned right.

Katie felt sorry for her. Laila could hear it in the softness of her friend's voice.

"Yeah, a girl's trip sounds fun," Laila said without any enthusiasm. "I'll let you know when I'm off again."

"Okay . . . Laila, you know if you ever need to just talk, I'm here for you."

"I know. Thanks." The line went eerily silent and uncomfortable. A common occurrence these days. They'd come a long way since Katie's return but were nowhere near being the friends they'd once been. "Listen, I'm driving and the road is getting tight. Can I call you later?"

Katie hesitated. "Yeah, sure. Be safe."

Laila tossed her earpiece back into the console, wishing she'd never picked it up in the first place.

The smell from the nearby wastewater treatment plant filtered through her vents. She pressed recycled air and fought the urge to turn around. If she couldn't even have a phone call with Katie, how in the world was she supposed to deal with her mother?

The same way you always do, she told herself.

The smell worsened as Laila drove over the dirt in front of her mother's trailer and parked along the weeds. The blue plastic skirting had two new holes, out of which a litter of stray kittens maneuvered to see if she'd brought them anything. She had, because she was a sucker that way.

After tossing each cat a treat, Laila readjusted the grocery sacks in her arms and stepped onto the cinder-block stairs leading to the trailer's front door. The ripped screen door gave a familiar hiss as she pulled it open and pushed through to the sagging plywood door.

The smell of old cigarettes and beer was the first to assault her, then the chatter of the Home Shopping Network, though no one was currently watching. Arms starting to ache from the load, Laila slid between the recliner and the couch and dropped the bags on the counter.

"Mom?" she hollered down the hallway. "I have your stuff." She didn't dare walk back there, not after the time Victor greeted her with only a towel wrapped around his oversized, wrinkled body.

Loretta appeared a beat later wearing a tight Def Leppard tank top and even tighter jeans. Gold hoops dangled from her ears, and her blonde-streaked hair fell just shorter than midback. Black script encircled both her thin biceps, and a pack of cigarettes was tucked securely in her exposed bra.

"My life would have been a whole lot easier if you'd just picked up my prescription while you were there." She didn't bother with the niceties, though Laila hadn't expected her to.

"You know I won't do that." The sigh in her voice could be felt all the way to her toes. Loretta's first love would always be a little round pill.

Her mom had been addicted to pain meds since her motorcycle accident nineteen years ago. She'd suffered a broken femur, a broken wrist, two collapsed vertebrae, and a third-degree burn on her right calf that left her with a three-inch-long scar, but more debilitating was the decades-long addiction the ten weeks of recovery had caused.

The rustling of bags and slamming of cabinets pulled Laila back to her mother's complaints. "I only have enough medicine for the rest of the week. Now I have to figure out a way to get into town."

"Or you could find a way to live without it." Laila had stopped enabling her mother the first time Chad had gone into rehab. Not that it helped. Her mom always found a way to get more. She'd find a new pain clinic or some doctor in another town, one who'd believe her sad, tear-filled plea. Or she'd buy it illegally, paying money she didn't have for the escape she needed.

"I could if the pain would ever stop." The bite in her voice came with a quick grab of her prescription bottle. Funny how even the slightest hint at stopping sent her straight back to the source.

Laila glanced away when her mother opened the bottle and threw back two pills, then busied herself with unpacking the groceries. "When will your car be fixed?"

"Don't know. Victor's trying to find the parts. He's checking the salvage yard in Brunswick this weekend." Loretta leaned against the counter, closed her eyes, and smiled. It was enough to make Laila want to grab the bottle right out of her bony fingers. She didn't, because her mother was unpredictable and erratic. Not to mention, she'd already tried that tactic once, and it hadn't gone well.

"Okay. I'm going to go, then."

Her mom's eyes popped open. "Wait. Sit and talk to me. You're always rushing out of here."

"I have to work. This trip was already out of my way."

"Your shift isn't until seven. I called Joe myself to make sure."

She must not have told him who she was because Joe would never disclose Laila's schedule to the woman he called a *self-absorbed junkie.*

"Well, I still need to shower, and it might be nice to eat a dinner that isn't from a fast food joint." Laila inched toward the door while her mom closed in. The tears would come soon. The drama about her poor life, her pain, how bad Victor treated her, the fact she was trapped in the house without a car. All of it her own doing, yet she was always the victim.

Loretta's face crumbled. "You don't love me. My only child, and you're just like your deadbeat father."

Laila had heard this country song before. When she was young, she'd begged to know who her father was. Now, she didn't even bother asking. "I do love you, Mom. I just need to get back."

Her mom stumbled to the couch, the pills taking the effect she needed. "Back to your boyfriend, I suppose.

Laila felt her face heat, hating her small town and the gossips who seemed obsessed with her love life.

"I heard he's the stuffy type. Not much of a looker either. Not like our Chad." Her mother's face remained cold and calm, her words having the exact effect Laila knew she wanted them to. "When am I gonna meet this guy?"

"He's no one you need to worry about. It's not serious," Laila said, still trying to calm her sudden surge of adrenaline. She wasn't letting her mother anywhere near her relationship with Ben.

"That's not what I heard. I heard he had his hands all over you. I also heard that Joe was so mad that he threatened to fire you right on the spot. Seems like your new reputation might just match mine. You must be dying inside." Her mother leaned back, satisfied. She'd always resented Laila's choices. Resented that Laila didn't drink or smoke or sleep around. Resented that the man she fell in love with loved her back. "Heaven forbid the world doesn't think you're perfect."

Laila fought against the sting in her throat. Her mother's accusation wasn't the only backlash she'd experienced. Sally at the deli counter ignored her for five whole minutes before taking her order. Monday night's tips were abysmal, and on Wednesday, not only did Billie not ask her to marry him, he didn't speak to her at all.

"Do you need anything else before I go?" Laila had learned long ago that engaging with her mother when she was high was as pointless as it was counterproductive.

Loretta closed her eyes and waved her hand, likely having already forgotten the callousness of her words.

Laila slipped though the screen door and trekked back to her car. The tears came faster than usual this time. She furiously wiped them away, resenting every one, and grabbed her cell phone.

Ben answered immediately. "Hey, this is a surprise."

She forced a smile into her voice. "A good one?"

"Always. What's up?"

"I wanted to tell you yes; I'll go to the beach with you."

"You sure? I thought you said it was too soon."

He'd mentioned his parents' beach house more than once. Separate rooms, no expectations, but a chance for them to spend more than a few hours together. Up until now, she'd always declined, finding some reason to avoid that level of closeness.

"I'm sure."

"Okay, then. I'll take care of the details." He paused for a second. "Laila?"

"Yeah?"

"Will you surprise me again tomorrow?"

She smiled through her tears. "Sure."

Laila ended the call and pushed against the weight in her chest. The ratty trailer stood in front of her, paint chipping, siding loose and drooping. The woman inside should have no bearing on her life. So how was it possible that, after all the neglect and abuse, Laila still wanted her mother to love her, just once, more than she loved herself?

But alas, that was another fantasy that would never, ever come true.

Safely tucked inside her old car, Laila hit reverse, turned around, and drove back the way she had come. Back to the town that had suddenly forsaken her, like all the people in her life. Well, they could all keep their opinions. She didn't need them or their judgment. She was moving to Burchwood, anyway.

Finally steady, Laila turned on the radio and went through the self-soothing exercises she'd learned as a kid. Deep breath in, deep breath out. A mental pep talk about boundaries. Then another deep breath in.

The pattern continued until she passed the Fairfield sign.

POPULATION: 9,468.

Soon it would be 9,467, and her life could finally begin again.

She turned the wheel, slowing to navigate the huge pothole that had formed at the beginning of her driveway. Her little white house came into view through the trees, but that wasn't what made her slam on the brakes ten feet from her front door.

The silhouette stood. Broad, muscled shoulders, a powerful frame that stood exactly four and one-third inches taller than hers. He shoved his hands into his jeans. A large black duffel sat inches from his scuffed black army boots.

She couldn't move, so she just stared through the windshield, her throat so raw it felt like she'd swallowed broken glass.

He took only one step down out of the shade, one step closer to her, but it allowed the sun to frame his beautiful face. Not just handsome, no. *Beautiful.* His chiseled features were a work of art. His skin tan against black, unruly hair, his green eyes a dramatic almond shape and that mouth, all sensual lines and softness that burned into her memory. That face was just as much a weapon as his ability to make her believe in him time and time again.

Finally, her trembling hands found the gear, and she parked, still stopped in the middle of the driveway. She inched open the door, her body cold despite the rising temperature outside.

He stepped down one more time, and they were level with each other. His black T-shirt hung to his hips; a thick chain encircled his neck and fell just past the collar. And there was more, so much more, that her memories and her reality began colliding and fighting for dominance.

It was a dream and a nightmare all rolled into one.

Chad Richardson had finally come home.

CHAPTER 10

When Laila's car halted in the driveway, Chad stood and shoved his hands into his pockets. She was only a slight outline though the windshield, but just that was nearly enough to take him to his knees. Panic seized him. He didn't have a game plan. He'd thought he would just wing it, that the right words would find their way, but words felt impossible right now.

He took a single step down. She hadn't moved, and he didn't know if that was good or bad. The sun's reflection shielded her face through the glass, but he could feel her all around him, like a current across his skin. He wondered if she felt him the same way.

Her driver-side door finally opened, and he took the last step down to the ground. Golden hair came first, then her beautiful eyes, wide enough to show her shock. She slammed the car door, and it was all he could do not to run, wrap her up in his arms, and kiss that perfect mouth, still hanging slightly open.

She walked with hesitation, her eyes never leaving his, past the edge of the asphalt and into the front yard, shaded by the tree they'd planted together on their second anniversary.

"Why are you here?"

They were still too far apart. At least six feet. The hair around her face blew slightly in the breeze while the rest stayed locked in a tight braid. He wanted to tug out the hair band, loosen the pieces, strand by strand, and pull her to him, like he had in every dream for the past two years.

"For you." Why else would he have come home? Without her, Fairfield was empty.

She closed her eyes, took a deep breath. "But why are you *here*?" She stressed the word like it was bigger than just their house, like it encompassed the town, maybe even the state.

"You told me to come back when I had my life in order."

Her lip trembled, and it was all the invitation he needed. Three long strides and he was within arm's length. His hands itched to touch her skin, to kiss the spot on her neck that would make her purr. To have her run her fingers down his back.

"Laila, I've missed you so—" He reached for her, unable to do anything else, but she slipped away before he made contact.

"I can't . . . No . . . I won't do this." As if she were shaken out of a fog, she steadied her gaze. "You need to go."

That's not going to happen.

He stepped closer and she stepped back, almost colliding with the tree behind her. She set her hand on the bark and moved until the low hanging leaves were practically a guard in front of her.

"I just want to talk to you."

"I don't want to talk to you. I don't want you here." Her voice was hoarse, as if she'd been yelling for hours.

"You don't mean that." He stepped toward her again, wishing they were enclosed so he could keep her from running. He could see she wanted to, and he didn't blame her, but the guy who had hurt her was gone. That horrible, destructive guy no longer existed. "I've changed."

"You always say that. It's your favorite line." Her words came sharper this time, less strangled. "But honestly, it doesn't matter, because I don't care anymore."

For one horrifying second, he believed her, but then moisture filled her eyes, and he knew she cared just as much as she always had. Too much, she used to say, but that was what made Laila so special. Those who had the privilege to be loved by her were forever changed.

He swallowed and glanced up at the live oak they'd envisioned their kids climbing on one day. It'd grown close to ten feet since he left. "She's gotten tall. You were right about it holding a tree house. It's perfect." A dead branch blocked his vision of her, so he snapped it off.

"Are you really talking about our tree?"

Frustration rippled through him. "Only because you keep saying things you don't mean." It was torture. Absolute torture standing there, this close, her perfume weaving its way into his senses. He'd picked out the scent himself. Had kissed every inch of the skin it lingered on, and now he couldn't even touch her.

"I'm sober now." He said the words like he used to say *I love you.* Maybe that would break through the fortress around her.

But it only made her eyes go cold. "You don't get to show up here after a year of no contact and say that to me."

"You kicked me out and changed the locks. You told me not to come back until I had my life together. Well, I'm here and my life is together."

"Stop saying that." Laila's voice caught in her throat. She could barely breathe.

Those words. Those beautiful, gut-wrenching, manipulative words.

Chad moved toward her, but she put up her hand. She didn't want him closer. It was already too hard to look at him and not get sucked back in time. He'd changed so much from the last time she'd seen him, yet the way he looked at her was exactly the same.

She exhaled, reminded herself to be strong. This was what he did. He reeled her in, then ripped her heart out.

"Things have changed. I'm happy now, and you're not a part of my new life."

Sheer pain washed over his face, and she immediately felt guilty. Then angry because she shouldn't feel guilty. He was the one who had done this to them.

"I just want an hour. After all we've been through, please tell me you can give me that." The hurt was evident in his voice. She couldn't let it get to her. She had to be strong.

"I have to work. I'm already going to be late," she bit out.

"Tomorrow, then."

"I don't know." She shook her head, gnawing the inside of her cheek. She knew why he'd come home, and she hated Cooper for it. Everything had been moving forward, and now it wasn't.

"Tell me what I have to do. I'll do anything."

She didn't have time to react before he was next to her, his scent overwhelming. It made her heart beat faster. Made her cheeks flush with a heat no one else could evoke from her. Fingertips lightly grazed her cheeks. The feel of him was worse than anything else, a deep stab of memory forcing her back in time so that all she could remember was the smell and taste of him.

Chad must have felt her weakness, because he shifted closer. "Please tell me it's not too late."

She wanted to both slap him and crawl inside him with equal passion. "Don't" was all she could say; anything else would expose her longing.

The minuscule gap that had existed between them was now a memory as his chest grazed hers, his mouth so close she could feel every breath, every heartbeat hammering in both their bodies.

"Please stop," she all but begged. Her instinct was to touch him. To kiss those lips, to wipe the tears from his eyes. To love him.

His whole body deflated. Eyes and arms dropped. "Sorry," he said, brushing a lock of black hair off his forehead.

"I know you are. You always are." Her voice sounded as lost and empty as she suddenly felt. She walked toward the house, and the echo of crunching grass followed her. Seeing his bag on their porch, the audacity of it, brought a new wave of anger. "You can't stay here." She attempted to lift the bag and throw it at his feet—dramatic effect and all that—but it only moved an inch.

"I know. I didn't expect to." He easily picked up the duffel and tossed it away from the porch. Her eyes lingered on his arms. They were strong, healthy. A man's arms. Arms that had held her, protected her.

She grabbed the tip of her braid. "Just tell me why. After all this time. Why now?" She knew the answer, so maybe it was a test to see if he'd still lie to her.

"I know you're seeing someone."

She huffed out a dry laugh. "So, what? You came to break us up?"

His wince was noticeable, and again she felt a wave of guilt. They'd been together since they were kids. Neither had ever dated anyone else.

Chad's eyes pleaded with hers. "I came because if I waited any longer I might lose you."

Laila fought to keep the tears away. She'd been the dutiful wife. She'd given him chance after chance.

"We're divorced, Chad. You have lost me."

"I never signed those papers."

"That doesn't matter. It's still legal. It still happened, whether you wanted it to or not."

He lifted his hand, the gold band gleaming in the sun. Seeing it on his finger was like a dagger in her gut. The ring contoured to him like it'd been etched there, the white skin underneath a sharp contrast to his now-tan fingers. "'Til death do us part. I said those words and I meant them." His voice was angry, and it rumbled through her.

Very rarely did Chad get jealous. She never gave him reason to. When they were together, no one else existed. But they weren't together anymore, and his spouting out wedding vows when he'd dishonored them time and time again with his addiction was unacceptable.

"I really can't do this with you right now."

"Okay." He took a beat and seemed to pull himself back under control with an ease that unnerved her. Anger was a natural emotion for him, after growing up with his father, and it usually took brooding time and a stiff drink to make it go away. "My showing up is a shock. I can see that. Let's just try this tomorrow."

"I have nothing left to say to you." She turned away so she didn't have to see him or this new steadiness he seemed to possess. She was moving in a few weeks. She had a life. A boyfriend. She was finally on track.

"You expect me to walk away? Now that I'm clean. Now that I have my crap together. You honestly think I'm walking away from you?"

A tear slipped down her cheek, and she quickly wiped at it. She'd waited so long to hear those words. So long to see him this way. Strong. Determined.

She heard him take a step. She should flee, slam the door, and never look back, but her feet remained planted.

Hot breath blew over the top of her head, and the warmth of his body pressed against her back; he wasn't close enough to technically touch her, but close enough that every nerve in her body came alive. "I love you, Laila. I never stopped loving you, and I never will stop loving you."

She closed her eyes and swallowed the words that had become so automatic for her. It was too easy to remember what it was like to be loved by Chad when he was himself and not the nightmare he became when the alcohol and drugs took over. But she couldn't forget. Couldn't let herself forget how bad it had become.

I watch as Chad stumbles in the door, tripping over his untied shoelaces. I can tell he's trying to be quiet. He probably assumes I'm asleep, and I should be. It's after three in the morning.

"Where have you been?" I rise from the couch, where I've been waiting since coming home from work two hours ago. Chad promised he wouldn't use tonight, but I can see it in the brightness of his cheeks, the way his eyes stay permanently dilated. "You told me you were only going to a movie. And why didn't you answer your phone?"

"The battery died." Chad stands there. He won't look me in the eye, and right now I don't really want him to. His behavior is getting worse, his excuses more frequent.

"I told you I couldn't live with an addict. You know what my mom is like." I'm crying now, and I can see the way it hurts him. Chad promised me he would never be like his father, yet ever since his mom passed away, he hasn't been able to stay sober.

"I just needed to blow off some steam, and Katie had a little pick-me-up." He comes closer, wraps me in his arms, and kisses the side of my head. "I love you. You know I'd do anything for you."

"I love you too, but it's been five months now. You have to start dealing with the grief. Your mom wouldn't want this for you."

His kisses get heavier, and I let it continue, because I do love him, and for two hours I honestly feared he wouldn't come home. "I won't do it again," he whispers, his fingers undoing the clip in my hair. "I promise you. It's the last time."

Chad's sudden feather-soft touch pulled her back to the present.

"Laila, please." He said the words with so much longing, she wanted to melt and crawl into his arms, but that was the naïve Laila. The older, wiser Laila knew she had to put some distance between them.

She stepped away, pulled open the screen door, and shoved her key into the lock. A second later, she was inside, the barrier she needed between them.

He stared at her through the mesh, chest fallen. "I was wrong to just show up without warning. I realize that now." Chad moved closer, and for a brief second she thought he might pull open the screen and force his way in, but he only placed a hand on the door frame. "When I left, it wasn't because I didn't love you. It was the opposite. I left because every day I saw the pain I caused. I left to save you, and believe me, it broke my heart." His free hand gently touched the screen, his fingers tracing an imaginary line down her cheek. "You don't have to forgive me, but please, at least give me the chance to tell you why I hope you will."

It wasn't fair that she still loved the man in front of her. That she wanted to reach out and press her palm against his. That she still wanted to trust him.

"If I agree to talk to you tomorrow, will you leave?"

"Yes."

"Fine. I'll meet you at the Sandwich Hut at one o'clock." It was out of town. Away from prying eyes and from the memories he'd use to convince her to take him back.

His green eyes shined like sea glass. "Thank you."

Laila shut the door and pressed her back against the wood.

Chad was home. He was sober.

She closed her eyes, and suddenly all she could feel was an empty, hollow echo of the life they once had.

CHAPTER 11

The trek to Cooper's place was two miles long, lined with thick pine trees, and one Chad had walked many times. His shoulder ached from his duffel, now hanging diagonally across his chest, but worse was the lingering pain inflicted when Laila had slammed her front door.

He'd hated seeing the tears, but the emptiness was worse. He couldn't read her. Not like before, when he'd had every facial expression memorized. Too much time had passed, and she'd changed. There was now anger and bitterness where there had once been only love and softness.

Chad kicked a rock in front of him and cursed. He'd spent the last five days dreaming of this moment, sure that the minute she saw him, Laila would run into his arms. He'd been careful, responsible. Had done everything Mark had recommended before rushing home.

Home.

What a fool he had been. Nothing was the same.

The house was smaller than he remembered. The trees were overgrown, the stairs weathered and cracked. The pothole at the front of the driveway could eat a Kia or two.

It was his fault. He'd done this to her. He'd left her alone without any help.

The trees broke at Cooper's rusted mailbox, and he turned the corner, boots crunching the gravel beneath him. Chad didn't know how his old friend would receive him. Chances were, he'd kick him to the curb as quickly as Laila had.

The screen door opened, and Cooper stood there, still in his work uniform.

"I guess my phone call worked."

"You knew it would." Chad unhooked his bag, let it drop to the ground. "I don't suppose you have any room in this place, do you?"

Cooper stepped forward and hugged Chad without any of the lingering animosity he'd released on the phone. For a moment, they were brothers united by history and heartbreak. Who would have thought that when all the dust settled, Cooper would be the one standing by his side?

His friend smacked his back twice and let go. "You stay here as long as you need to."

"Thanks, man." His duffel felt lighter when he picked it up and stepped inside. The familiarity took him back in time, even though the place resembled a partial demolition zone. The bookshelves were empty. There were no pillows on the couch, and every strip of wallpaper had been torn and tugged without regard for appearance. Even the curtains had been ripped from the windows, leaving gaping holes in the drywall.

"Excuse the mess. I'm doing some redecorating."

"I see that. How come?"

"Because I needed to." Cooper pulled the fridge open like he wanted to assault the thing and stopped his hand before reaching for what Chad assumed was a beer. Instead he took a breath, closed the door, and leaned his shoulder against it.

"You can take the spare room. Not much in there but a mattress and a dresser, but it will work. Sheets are in the top drawer." He stuffed his hands into his back pockets. "You know where the bathroom is.

We'll have to share, but don't go using my towels. There are some old blue ones in the cabinet."

Chad smirked. For a guy, Cooper was particular about the oddest things. It used to drive Katie crazy to the point where she'd mess with his stuff just to tick him off.

His smile suddenly faded, and heat raced through every limb.

He had a lot to say to Katie. About leaving. About the drugs. About breaking Laila's heart. She'd avoided him for five years, and he wasn't about to let her get off without a confrontation. But that was an issue he'd deal with later.

"How's the factory?" Chad continued through the dining room, his eyes immediately drawn to the tall liquor cabinet in the corner. He refused to let them linger and quickened his steps to the hallway.

"Good. Steady. I'm a crew leader now, and Hank says there's already been some talk about management."

"Hank, huh? How is Katie's dad?"

"Okay, I guess. Maureen's been pretty sick, but they finally found some medication that's working." Cooper shook his head. "Hank's a great man. Not sure I would've made it through the past few years without him."

"And Katie?" He shouldn't have asked, but it just slipped out.

"You sure you're ready for that conversation?"

Chad ran a finger along Cooper's old dining table, his heart beating a bit faster. Katie leaving had been another horrific turning point when his life had gone from bad to far worse than he'd ever expected. The years between her disappearance and Laila changing the locks held some of the darkest moments in his life. Katie was supposed to be his best friend, yet she'd abandoned him when he needed her the most.

"No. I guess I'm not."

"Yeah. Me either." Cooper moved from the kitchen into the living room. "Feel free to grab the shower first. I've got some things I need to take care of."

TTammyammy L L.. Gray Gray

"Okay. Thanks."

The spare bedroom wasn't big, but it was nicer than his room at Mark's. At least there was a double mattress, and the dresser had a fancy mirror attached to it. Of course, looking at himself in the mirror right now wasn't his favorite pastime. Atlanta had been lonely, but it'd also been safe. Mark kept the house clear of temptations. His roommates made sure to keep him accountable with meetings, and he could convince himself that even though she was three hundred miles away, Laila still loved him.

My girl is perched on a towel at the beach in the tiniest bikini I've ever seen. I want to cover her up because every guy who passes has a rubber neck, and, well, I'm old-fashioned, I guess, 'cause I don't like them looking.

I toss her my T-shirt. "You should put this on before you get a sunburn." I'm full of it, and she knows it, but because she always puts me first, Laila slides the shirt over her head.

"Better?"

"Almost." I roll from my towel to hers, cover her up more with the weight of my body. My fingertips slide down her face, her skin beneath them like the finest, rarest silk. And that's what she is: rare. She gives every part of herself without hesitation or expectation, and for some blessed reason, she's mine.

"I love you." It's the first time I've told her. I know we're only sixteen, and people think we don't know what it means to be in love, but I do; I lived in a house that didn't have any of it.

Love is special, and it's not something you take for granted.

*"I love you too." She says it so easily that it makes
me want to toss my man card and do a dance right there
on the sand.*

"Promise me something?" I ask.

"Anything."

*"When I say I love you, will you always say it back?"
I slide my hand down her arm, lace my fingers with hers.
"I know I'm a screw up, and I'm sure I won't always
deserve to hear it, but will you say it anyway?" I hate my
insecurity. I hate that I need her so much, but I do, and
there's no point in denying it.*

*She kisses my neck so softly; it feels like an angel's
whisper. "I promise."*

Chad continued to stare at himself in the mirror, no longer able to deny
the truth that had followed him all the way down that dusty road.

For the first time in eleven years, she hadn't said *I love you* back.

Unable to stop the emotion this time, he dropped to the bed, put
his head in his hands, and wept.

⋊⋉

The shower seemed to wash away his depression, and for the first time
since stepping off the bus, Chad didn't feel a pressing weight on his
shoulders.

Cooper had been busy. The liquor cabinet was empty, and the case
of Miller Chad had seen on the counter was now gone as well. He
wished he could tell his friend not to worry about it, that having alcohol around was no biggie, but it would be a lie. And the smarter part
of himself, the one that had fought the battle for nine straight months,
felt a new surge of respect for the guy he had assumed would only be

around for a season. Seven years later, Cooper had certainly shown he was the type to stick.

Chad made his way to the couch, flipped on the TV, and watched the news until Cooper emerged, towel drying his hair in shorts and a T-shirt. The guy had bulked up quite a bit since Chad saw him last, which seemed unnecessary since Cooper's size had already intimidated everyone. Well, not everyone, which had been a big part of the problem for Cooper and Katie.

He tossed the towel on the dining chair. "That room work okay for you?"

"Yeah. It's fine."

"I can make a pizza." He opened the freezer, shifted things around. "I have some chicken too, but it has to thaw. Just tell me what you need, and I'll—"

"Coop."

He glanced over his shoulder, and Chad leaned forward, set his elbows on his knees.

"What I need is for you to stop being so ridiculously polite and sit down. I'm not a charity case, but you're sure making me feel like one."

Cooper shut the freezer door and ran a hand through his hair. "I'm sorry. It's just . . . different. You being here, sober. I don't think you've ever been here when we weren't partying or . . . you know."

"Yeah, I know." He didn't say her name again, but Katie was the connection between them. He'd used Cooper a lot after she left. A place to crash. A friend who wouldn't tell his wife how bad his addiction was getting. His ride to rehab, twice. "I've never said thank you."

"No need. I should have done more." For a moment Cooper looked embarrassed, which was uncomfortable for both of them. "I know I was a jerk on the phone the other night, and I didn't mean for it to come out that way. I am proud of you, and I know Laila is gonna be too."

"Yeah. Not so much." Chad leaned back on the couch and muted the TV. "I could barely get her to look at me."

"She'll come around." Cooper pulled two Dr Peppers from the fridge and tossed one his way. "So, what's the plan?"

To get her back. To keep his word this time. To clean up the mess he'd made two years ago.

"I need to lay low for a few days, and then I need a job."

"I can help you on the job end. Just tell me when you're ready." He lowered himself into the recliner and popped open the can. "Joe know you're back?"

"No, and I'd like to keep it that way. In fact, apart from you and Laila, I don't want anyone knowing I'm in town." He was still short the money he needed, and the person he owed didn't play around. Not when it came to loyalty and definitely not when it came to cash.

"They won't hear it from me, but won't Laila say something?"

Chad had considered that, but her choice of meeting place implied she wasn't any more ready for Chad to go public than he was. "No, I don't think so."

"Okay. Just remember this town has eyes and ears everywhere. Our little Firecracker didn't make it one mile past the water tower before the gossip started."

A wave of heat rolled through his stomach and up his neck. "Well, I'm sure they had a lot to say to her. I know I certainly have a list with Katie Stone written right at the top."

"Powell," Cooper corrected, his voice as tight as his expression.

"What?"

"Laila didn't tell you?" Cooper rolled his shoulders. "She got married. Blew into town, acted like none of us ever existed, and convinced the preacher's kid and half of Fairfield that she's changed."

Chad couldn't speak. He stared at his friend, more shocked than if he'd just been told the sun turned purple. "Katie married Asher Powell?" The guy was gangly, with glasses. She used to kick his chair and blow spitballs at his back.

"Yep. Right after New Year's." He took a swig of his soda like it had something harder in it, and knowing Cooper, he probably wished it did. "It's like she never abandoned us. Like she gets a free pass to come back and start all over. But whatever. She's not my problem anymore." Cooper's voice was way too angry and hurt for a man who no longer cared.

Chad should have warned him. He knew Katie would break his heart. It was what she always did. But to get married? That didn't make any sense. Katie was all about freedom with no boundaries or limits.

Cooper tossed him a side-glance. "Katie's not the same. Whoever that person is, it's not my Firecracker."

Chad fell back into the cushions and pretended to watch the news anchor talk about politics. He and Katie shared the same darkness, the same ferocious need to escape. If she used, he did, and vice versa. They were connected by it, like DNA they both shared.

Katie had been his greatest ally, but also his worst enemy. She'd been a part of every bad decision he'd ever made, and the catalyst for every good one. Imagining life in Fairfield without her friendship, without her laughter and insanity being a part of the world he'd share with Laila, it felt wrong. Bleak. Empty.

All this time, he'd been preparing to come back and be with Laila, to yell at Katie for deserting him after destroying his world. But never once did he consider that life wouldn't go back to how it had always been—the three of them, united against the world. Katie had been their anchor, their glue. And now . . .

She'd moved on, forgotten him, and now Laila wanted to follow.

How in the world was he supposed to stop that?

CHAPTER 12

Laila checked the clock for the fifth time. The numbers hadn't changed. Her palms were sweaty and her mouth dry, despite the fountain drink she'd ordered several minutes ago. She'd picked the Sandwich Hut because it was one of those places most people in Fairfield avoided. The attached multipump gas station jacked up their prices, and interstate travelers constantly funneled in and out.

She'd considered changing locations at least three times last night, but the subsequent flurry of butterflies kept her grounded. Being alone with Chad was too dangerous. And while this loud, sticky restaurant wasn't ideal, it was, at least, safe.

Each time the door swung open and closed, her heart raced faster. She shouldn't be surprised that he was late. Chad was always late. She checked her phone again. Okay, so he wasn't late. He still had five minutes.

Closing her eyes, she willed her system to settle. She could do this coolly, pragmatically. This wasn't a reunion; it was a business meeting.

"You're early."

Laila didn't turn around. She'd never forget that faint drawl, not slow so much as rich, like a fine aged scotch. Whether he was telling a joke or yelling at the TV or whispering in her ear. That voice had haunted her for years.

"I always am," she choked out.

He walked around the table and slid into the chair across from her. Of course, he'd used the side door, the one that gave her no warning, no preparation for how ridiculously good he looked in his snug gray T-shirt.

His demeanor was different today. Smoother, cockier, more like the guy whose charisma repeatedly captivated the town. When her eyes finally lifted to meet his, something like a smirk appeared on his face. Her cheeks burned.

"Nice bun." His lips twitched. "You do that just for me?"

Laila ran her hands up the sides of her hair, tucking in any stray pieces she encountered. "Honestly, I wasn't thinking of you at all." Not totally true. He hated her hair tied back, and she enjoyed his poorly hidden annoyance a little too much.

"Sure you weren't." Chad leaned back in his chair, not the least bit fazed by her words. "So, how have you been?"

"Good. And you?" There, she could be just as calm, even if her hands were trembling against her plastic cup.

"Did you start taking classes at the community college like you wanted to?"

She hadn't done anything she'd wanted to. "No, but I'm already working on next year." Well, she'd picked up the application, but that was as far as it had gone.

"And Joe? He's been good to you?"

"Yes, of course he has," she said, feigning a coolness she no longer felt. "What's with the small talk?"

"I'm just catching up. But if you want to get deeper, I can do that too." He crossed his arms. They were more defined than ever, the sleeves tugging against his biceps. "Tell me about this guy you're seeing."

"I'm not having that conversation with you."

"Then what conversation would you like to have?" He swallowed, and she watched his Adam's apple move up and down, remembering all the kisses she had put there.

Stop thinking about kissing him.

"Why is this on me?" she asked. "I came because you asked me to give you an hour."

"And I still have fifty-five minutes." His eyes were devious as he stared at her. "You want something to eat?"

"No. This food sucks." *Almost as much as this conversation.* What was he doing, anyway? He was too calm. Too . . . in control. She'd come prepared for his lies. Prepared for all the same types of manipulation tactics he'd pulled on her when she'd finally gathered enough willpower to leave him.

"Okay, a refill maybe?" Again, with that stupid grin.

"I'm fine, Chad. Let's just . . . move this along, okay?"

He eyed her a little too closely, like an artist trying to sketch from memory. She bit her lip, looked off toward the frazzled cashier with a line wrapped around the corner.

His fingers grazed hers, warm and soft, and those pesky butterflies returned, the ones she hadn't felt in years. The ones that only seemed to respond to *him*.

"I've thought of you every day." He said it so softly that she felt her heart break all over again. The coolness he'd come in with was now replaced with a vulnerability she'd only seen in their most intimate moments.

Despite the ache in her chest, she allowed herself to look at him. Really look at him. His face was tan, his cheeks full and strong. He needed a haircut. Dark wisps fell over his forehead and almost into his eyes. Her fingers wanted to reach out and brush the strands away. Her heart wanted to know how he'd gotten to this point when the last time she'd seen him, he was bloody and bruised.

But instead, she slid her hand into her lap and reminded herself that this was the same man who'd broken his promises time and time again. "You said you wanted to explain. I'm listening."

Chad cleared his throat, and the world seemed to come alive around them. People scooted by their table; kids begged parents for all types of junk food.

"I'm not really sure where to start." He exhaled and settled back in his chair. "This environment isn't exactly what I pictured."

"Would you rather we do this in town? Let a thousand people weigh in on what we should say and do?"

"No. I'd rather do this alone."

"That isn't an option." She glanced at her phone. "You're at fifty minutes."

He stretched his neck to each side, something he'd always done to calm himself. His frustration was evident and almost as simmering as hers. "So Katie's home, I heard."

For a second she wished he'd stuck with the small talk. They'd been linked, the three of them. Too much, she now realized.

He leaned in, leveled those piercing green eyes at her. "Is she why you're so determined to move on? Why you didn't wait for me?" Hurt and betrayal lined every word.

"There's a lot we need to discuss about Katie and what happened the night she left, but Ben has nothing to do with any of it."

"So you just forgave her. Just like that?"

"It took some time. Especially when I learned the truth." A wave of resentment washed over her. Katie had given Chad the drugs that he overdosed on. "You should have told me."

"The two people you loved the most basically destroyed each other in one night. Can you understand why I didn't want to relive that?"

"I had a right to know that Katie was involved. But as usual, you kept secrets from me."

His gaze locked with hers. "If I'd told you, would it have made a difference?"

"I don't know." Her shoulders fell because he was right. That night had ruined all of them, and no matter how many scenarios she'd imagined, the end always looked the same.

He took a breath, one that seemed to get both of their emotions under control. "Cooper told me you were in her wedding."

"I was."

"And yet, you wouldn't even let me past the front door yesterday." His bitterness came again, coating every word.

"It's not the same."

"It is! How can you forgive her so easily and not me?"

"She wasn't my husband, Chad." The bite in her voice turned the air silent, and they both found other things to look at. He fixated on the table, while she watched a family of four argue all the way to the restrooms.

Finally, he moved, reached into his pocket, and slid a coin across the table.

No, not a coin, a sobriety chip. She picked it up, ran her fingers over the raised lettering that was more significant than any apology.

"Nine months." His hand covered hers. It was strong and calloused like he'd spent all that time using it for hard work. "I wanted to wait a year and prove to you it was going to stick. But, well, you obviously know why I couldn't wait."

She felt the tear fall before she ever knew she was crying.

Nine months.

Never. Not since he took that first drink with Katie in their tree house did he ever go nine months without some form of substance.

And just like that, he was the wounded boy all over again. The one hiding from his house to avoid his father's wrath. The one fighting in the halls at school just because it gave him some sense of control over his life. The one who loved her with every inch of his soul because no one had ever loved him back before.

His voice hitched. "I'm asking for another chance. The same chance you gave Katie when she came home. I know I screwed up. I know I don't deserve it, but this isn't lip service this time. I've had a job. A good one." He reached into his pocket again, pulled out a folded piece of paper. "Employee of the month. Twice."

Another shocking truth. Chad hadn't kept steady work since high school.

Laila wiped her eyes, feeling so many things. Pride, elation, confusion, anger. Why couldn't he have done this sooner? Why couldn't he have done it when he was here with her, when he saw their marriage falling apart? Why did he wait until it was too late to give her what she had always wanted?

She eyed their joined fingers and tried to get the fumbling thoughts and emotions in check. It wasn't fair of him to put this pressure on her. To make her wonder if her words would send him spiraling. "It's not that I'm not proud of you . . . I am. This is . . . It says a lot about how far you've come, but . . ."

He eased his hand away, shock and disappointment etched in the lines of his face. "It doesn't matter, does it?"

"No, it *does* matter. I want you to stay sober. I want you to have a great life."

"Just not with you." His voice was so chilling it slid over her skin like an ice storm.

How could she explain how much she'd grown while he was away? "There's so much history here. It's not all bad, but a lot of it is. I didn't recognize the dysfunction before because it was all I'd ever known. But now . . ."

"You have Ben."

She'd been able to brush off most of Chad's looks until this one. It made her squirm, made her body react in ways that defied every promise she'd made to herself.

"He's not the only reason." She hesitated but decided it was time to get it all out. "I'm moving to Burchwood, and I really think you should go back to Atlanta. You've obviously been doing really good there."

He didn't speak. Just stared with those devastated eyes.

"Or stay. Whatever you need to do. I haven't given notice on the house yet since my new cottage isn't ready. But if you want it when I'm gone, you can have it. Your name is on the lease." She drew lines through the condensation on her cup. "We probably need to split up our stuff too. I mean, a lot of it is yours, and I'm sure you don't want me to haul—"

"Please stop talking." The ache in his whisper was almost enough to do her in.

She felt herself weakening. That face. Those eyes. She had to go before all her progress came tumbling down around her. "I'm sorry, Chad. I just can't go through this with you again." She stood, left him there, still frozen in his chair, and did exactly what Joe had accused her of doing.

She ran away.

CHAPTER 13

C had sat under the dimming sky watching the water lap against the swampy shore. After Laila walked—no, ran—out on him, he'd trudged to Fairfield Lake to forget his faults, or maybe to remember them. Both options were equally painful.

A slight breeze blew over his sweat-dried face and rippled the water's surface. Calling this a lake was a bit of an exaggeration—a large pond was more accurate—with only the young and stupid willing to step foot into the murky water. Chad smiled when he saw the large rope swing hanging in the distance and remembered how often he'd come here with the crazy crowd from high school. Laila never jumped, but she'd cheered him on, scoring his flips off the swing and offering long kisses for the best ones. Those were their happiest days, before bills and jobs and fallen dreams seeped into their lives.

The buzz of his phone had him sliding his thumb across the screen. He'd ignored the last two calls from Cooper, and his conscience wouldn't allow him to blow off a third. Considering their long, sordid history, the guy probably thought he was drunk in a ditch somewhere.

"I'm alive and sober." Not the cheeriest way to answer the phone, but it was the best Chad could do under the circumstances.

"Where are you?"

"The lake. I needed a minute." Or six hours, to be exact.

"I guess that means things didn't go well."

Chad could only grunt a bitter laugh. "No. Things did not go well."

"You need a ride?"

A ride. If only that were all he needed right now.

"Nah, man. I'll walk home when I'm ready." Though ready felt so far away, the word made Chad's skin prickle. He'd lost her trust, her belief in him shattered to a point at which even he didn't know if it could be repaired. "Don't wait up."

When the screen went dark, Chad dropped the phone between his knees and stared at the ground. Memories were his enemy today. They weren't the good ones that drove him toward his goal, encouraging him day after day that he had a life worth fighting for. They were his chilling reality, the nightmares that woke him in a cold sweat.

"Laila!" I pound on our front door for the eighth time and shake the doorknob. She changed the locks. Forced me out of my own house. "Baby, come on, I just want to talk to you. Let me explain." My forehead presses against the door, my body sagging in a plea she refuses to hear.

She's mad because I left rehab again, but she doesn't understand. It doesn't help. They just want to get inside my head. Make me talk about my family and my emotions. I can't go there, not with a bunch of strangers, not after all I've done.

"Laila, please, let me in." I slam my hand on the door, strongly considering smashing the blasted thing in, or maybe I'll bust a window. Whatever I have to do to make her see I had no choice.

"She's not in there."

I spin around to find Cooper standing at the bottom of the porch steps. He's lying. I know she's here. Our car is in the driveway, and I heard her slam a door earlier.

"This isn't your business, Coop. Go home."

He takes a step up, and I feel the adrenaline kick in. The same adrenaline that came when Slim tried to shake me down for the money I owe him.

"You're bleeding, and you're scaring your wife."

I touch the slice in my lip. It's the first time the cut has stung. I know my face is bruised, and I'm guessing the blood on my shirt is from more than just my lip. Slim's lackey had a real good time, before his boss stepped in making some remark about messing up my pretty face. I spit blood on his shoes.

"Did you know she was going to do this?" I turn my fury onto Cooper, who's now only a few paces from me. He's trapping me on the porch like I'm feral. I'm not, the buzz has already started to wear off, and I can feel my limbs weakening.

"I'm just going to take you to my place, okay? Let you calm down, and then we'll talk."

"I'm not talking to anyone but my wife." I slam my fist into the door, again and again. "Laila! Don't do this. You promised you'd never do this!"

Before I can duck, Cooper has one arm around my neck and the other locking my hand behind me. It's the same chokehold they used at the center when I punched my roommate, and like then, I have no control as Cooper pushes me down the steps.

"Get off of me!" I try to fight back, but the trees seem to spin around us.

"You don't want her seeing you like this," he hisses in my ear, but the warning comes too late.

Laila opens the door, her face blotchy and red from the tears I've caused, once again. "It's over, Chad. I want you to leave, and I don't want you back until you have your life together."

I wrestle in Cooper's hold with no relief. I just need to touch her. It always helps. Always makes her change her mind. "You don't mean it."

"Yes, I do."

I stop fighting because the look in her eyes slices right through my heart. It's hatred and disappointment and gut-wrenching truth.

"Get him out of here, Coop. I can't look at him."

Chad fisted his hair, the sensation he constantly fought exploding inside his chest. Panic. Regret. Pain. He craved the emptiness. Craved the ability to escape and find that hour of bliss where his head was silent of all the screaming. He'd called Mark an hour ago, and the little strength he'd gained from the conversation with his sponsor was already starting to wane.

"I figured if you're going to brood, you should have some company." Cooper's voice was a light in the darkness. Chad hadn't even heard him approach, too lost in his struggle to notice.

"You didn't have to come." The strangled sound in his throat was as haunting as the reality that he desperately wanted his friend to stay.

"I needed the air anyway." Cooper lowered himself down into the weed-riddled grass beside Chad, keeping a few feet of distance between them. Silence gathered around the men, cut only by Cooper periodically tossing a pebble into the water. After his fifth throw, he dusted his hands off. "You were gone too long, Chad. You gave her too much time."

"I didn't have a choice."

"There's always a choice." He said the words regretfully. "I made mine, took the advice to stay away, and let her adjust to being home." Chad knew exactly the "her" Cooper was referring to. "I should have pushed harder. I should have been there every day, forcing her to deal with me. Instead I let her run right into his arms." Cooper swung his head to face his old friend. "Don't make my mistake."

Pain struck Chad in his chest. Laila wanted to run away too. She wanted to move to Burchwood with another man and forget their marriage ever existed. "She acts like she doesn't care. Like my being here has no effect on her at all."

"If that were true, she wouldn't have called in sick to work yesterday and today."

For a moment, he let himself hope. Laila never called in sick. Not even when she needed to. "How do you know?"

"Joe called me to see if I knew anything he didn't. He knows she hasn't been herself lately, and he's worried about her. "

Chad felt his whole body tense. "Did you tell him I'm back?"

Cooper's eyes sparked with disapproval. "No. I said I wouldn't, and I keep my word. But I don't like it. Joe isn't the kind of man you lie to."

"I know." Chad lowered his head, wondering what he would say if he were on the other end of this scenario. If he were the one watching his friend cope with consequences of his own making. He'd want the truth, that much he knew.

"Laila kicking me out wasn't the only reason I left. I owe Slim money." A bitter reality. "It's why I don't want anyone knowing I'm back."

Chad felt the weight of Cooper's gaze, but didn't look up. He couldn't stomach the judgment.

"How much?"

"Ten grand," he said, finally meeting his friend's eyes. "After I left rehab the second time, I started working for him."

Tammy L. Gray

Disgust colored Cooper's expression. "For how long?"

"I guess it was about six months, total."

"What the hell were you thinking?" The glare Cooper turned on him burned, but he'd dealt with worse. He didn't even flinch. "You grew up in Fairfield. You knew the risk."

Unlike the bigger cities that had gangs and street fights, Slim's underground network was laced together with good ole boy systems and generational secrets. In Fairfield, reputations mattered as much as family names, and Slim exploited every bit of that southern mindset. He kept their indiscretions private, and the town did the same for him. And once you were entrenched in his web, there was no getting out.

Chad's mind returned to those dark months. After his overdose, he'd spent years trying to get sober, but failed again and again. Eventually, he'd given up trying, had lost any hope of ever being happy again.

"I wasn't thinking back then. I was spiraling. Katie was gone. Laila would hardly look at me. I needed a fix and I had no income." Not an excuse, just the truth.

Slim liked him to work the yacht clubs and the beach parties. Said Chad had a respectable face that wouldn't raise suspicions. Slim would set him up in a fancy hotel and give him a weekend's worth of blow to dish out. Chad had done what he'd felt he had to at the time. He'd worn the suit. Flirted with the women. And walked away with money lining his pockets. He'd justified his actions by telling himself the partygoers were adults with too much money anyway, but every time he came home, the guilt and lies only deepened the chasm between himself and his wife. "The last time I went to sell, there was a sting operation. Slim had been giving the concierge a cut to keep silent, and thankfully, the guy called up to the room with a warning. I barely got rid of the drugs before the cops searched the place."

"Let me guess, Slim still expected payment in full," Cooper murmured, so low he barely heard him.

"He said I was responsible for the inventory, and therefore, I was also responsible for the money he lost." Slim might be a small-area dealer, but he was lethal and unforgiving. "I checked into rehab again right afterward, but as you know, I was in too dark of a place for any real recovery. I only stayed a few days, and Slim was waiting for me when I got back to Fairfield. He said he had ways for me to pay off the debt. When I told him I wouldn't sell for him anymore, he gave me a closed-fist reminder that he owned me. That was the same night Laila kicked me out, so you can see why I had to leave. I'd hit rock bottom. I basically had nothing to live for."

Silence followed his confession, a prickly kind, magnified by the singing of cicadas and croaks of nearby frogs.

"What did you expect to happen when you came back? Did you think Slim was just going to forget?" Cooper asked, speaking for the first time after many long minutes. His eyes were on the lake, but his words bit into the air.

"No, but I wasn't exactly thinking past the news that Laila was kissing another man."

Cooper hopped to his feet and chucked a fistful of rocks into the lake. He brushed his hands on his shorts and turned without a word.

"Where are you going?"

"Home. Enjoy the walk. I'm too ticked off right now to coddle you, and I'm tired of watching you feel sorry for yourself." A few steps later, his silhouette disappeared into the darkness.

The rebuke seemed to echo across the still water. Katie would have said the same thing, but she wouldn't have walked away. She would have yelled, cursed more than once, possibly even kicked his butt a few times for being so stupid. But in the end, she would have sat down next to him and come up with a plan.

An acidic burn of nostalgia clawed at his throat.

He and Katie shared a bond—a troubled one forged in kinship and addiction.

They were connected, despite the betrayal, despite the words exchanged, despite the unfathomable truth that she might not even care that he was home.

"Ah, Katie, what should I do?" he asked no one but the wind. For as much as he hated her, he missed her, and the feeling only grew every moment he stayed locked in the past.

Try as he might, he couldn't forget the shadow of who she'd once been in his life: the leader, his north star, the only one who ever truly understood.

Chad lumbered to his feet, shaking his limbs to wake them after so long on the ground. He was out of options, out of ideas. The time for confrontation had come. And Katie Stone—Powell—or whatever name she felt like wearing that day, was about to get a big heaping dose of the history she seemed so eager to forget.

CHAPTER 14

Anticipation whirled in Laila's stomach as the valet handed her a ticket in exchange for her car keys. Ben had a late meeting in Brunswick, and despite his protests about her having to drive herself out there to meet him, she had insisted that they keep their dinner reservation. They were celebrating four months together, and too many things had already derailed her momentum this week.

Plus, she had yet to tell Ben about Chad coming home, and she had no idea how he would respond. Heck, she still hadn't fully grasped her own reaction to the shocking news, choosing instead to hide away in her house and tell everyone in town she wasn't feeling well. Not completely a lie. Her stomach had been a wreck since finding Chad on her front steps.

Another attendant opened the door, decked in the same black slacks and red polo shirt as the valet, and ushered her into the lobby of the five-star restaurant. She had expected to wait, and had even assured Ben that she didn't mind if his meeting ran a little late, but there he stood, hands casually in his pockets, watching fish climb and dive in a massive crystal-clear salt water tank that separated the hostess stand from the dining room.

Laila allowed herself a second to linger. Ben was the picture of elegance and stability in a dark-blue suit with subtle pinstripes. No glasses tonight. A surprise, but one she enjoyed. Rarely was he unpredictable.

Still under her perusal, he turned his head to check the door, finally seeing her. His responding smile sent a wave of relief down her every limb. This was her life now. She had a steadfast man who wore a suit and showed up early, even when he had an excuse to be late.

She moved toward him, her black dress swaying across her hips as she walked. The fine material dipped in a V at her neckline and exposed her shoulders, a style she almost never wore. But she wanted to feel elegant and beautiful tonight.

"Wow, you look . . ." Ben paused, his eyes trailing a line down her face. "There are no words." He took a step closer and touched the same blonde strand she now had twisted around her finger. "You should wear your hair down more often. It's stunning."

Her hair was thick and long, reaching to her waist. In Georgia, that meant braids and clips and ponytails pretty much year-round.

"Thank you," she swallowed, her nerves making every word feel stretched.

Taking a rare initiative, she raised up onto the toes of her high heels and eagerly pressed her lips to his. A rush of warmth spread through her, an invigorating curl of happiness. *This* was the life she wanted.

Chad coming home didn't change anything.

When she pulled away, Ben's hand cupped the back of her head, though disbelief flickered across his face. "You're full of all kinds of surprises tonight."

She beamed at the sight of his small but genuine smile and lowered her heels back to the ground. "I'm happy to see you. And feeling a little pampered."

"It's our semianniversary. You should be pampered." His warm hand embraced hers, smooth and soft, so different from Chad's rough fingers.

"Two for Gates," he told the hostess.

The woman moved quickly and with practiced ease. Arm poised around two hardbound menus, she smiled brightly and requested they follow her. Her sharp stilettos clicked against the marble floors, but Laila was too overwhelmed with the sheer elegance of the dining area to pay much attention to the beat. Large crystal chandeliers hung every five or six feet across a checkered, molded ceiling with hand-painted inlays. The lights were dim, and on each table flickered a votive candle nestled within a red-and-cream blown-glass casing.

Her treacherous mind returned to the past. To homemade sandwiches and tall glasses of milk, and if the money wasn't supertight that week, to fried chicken from Lucy's. Nothing about Laila and Chad had ever been fancy or decadent. They'd had love and each other, which had been enough, until . . . all of a sudden, it hadn't.

The hostess stopped at a reserved table in the back, and Laila forced herself to return to the present and the wonderful man who'd so carefully picked out this restaurant for her. Tucked into an alcove, the small rectangular booth featured a wall for seating on one side and two large windows on the other. Diners were granted a view of Brunswick's historic downtown, the light of its buildings shining like bright stars.

Ben moved to the side, allowing Laila to slide across the seat, holding her dress down as she scooted over. A second later, he was next to her. They sat thigh against thigh, and ever so subtly, she pressed closer, wanting to snuggle into the crook of his arm and the safety of his touch. His hand automatically found her back, rubbing up and down, but the tilt of his head and press of his eyebrows reflected the same curiosity as earlier. He wasn't used to this kind of affection from her. But that would all change. She'd been holding back, waiting on something . . . who knows what. But now she was fully ready to give all of herself to this relationship.

The hostess picked up the extra place settings and turned their glasses over. "Would you like to see a wine list this evening?"

"No thanks," Ben answered with an ease that once again reassured her that he was the right choice. "Just water for now."

The woman left with a nod, and Ben shifted, looking at Laila with eyes that promised sonnets and roses. She'd never noticed their depth before. Light brown with a circle of green around the edge.

"And to think I almost missed you like this," he said, and she felt his fingers tunnel through her hair, caressing the pieces like fine artwork. "Remind me to always take you out of town to fancy restaurants."

"What do you mean?" She smiled, but a hint of unease crept up her spine.

"I don't know. You're different." She withdrew slightly, and he tickled the tender skin on the nape of her neck. "I'm not complaining, by any means."

"Okay. Good." She leaned back in and took his other hand in both of hers, squeezing tightly. "Because I'm so excited about our trip."

"Yeah?"

"Definitely. Does Caden like water slides? I've been doing some research the last couple of days, and there's a great waterpark not too far from the beach house. And there's also a sea turtle center and plenty of parks."

"Slow down." He lifted his hand from her grip and gently slid aside a piece of hair that had slipped in front of her eye. "This is the first time you two will spend a significant amount of time together. We should probably let you ease into that kind of exhaustion."

"But I want everything to be perfect."

"It's sand and water. To a six-year-old, that is perfect."

She closed her eyes, suddenly feeling silly. "I guess I'm nervous. This is important for us. A step forward and I'm ready to take it. I wish we were leaving tomorrow, in fact."

He shifted away slightly, his earlier curiosity turning to skepticism. "Laila, are you sure everything is okay with you tonight?"

"Yeah. I'm fine." But her tone wasn't believable, even to her own ears.

The waiter's approach gave her a minute to do some deep breathing exercises. The man held himself like a regal gentleman in dark pants and a crisp white button-up shirt. He gracefully detailed the chef's specials while offering suggestions on which cuts of meat were the restaurant's best.

"That all sounds delicious." Ben shifted his focus to her. "Do you know what you want?"

"Um, sure. The filet sounds good. The small one." She closed her menu, answered more questions on how she wanted her meat cooked and what sides she wanted.

Ben ordered the bone-in rib eye, his eyes bright and eager, and suddenly she wished she'd never have to tell him about Chad.

"Very good. I'll check back in a minute." The waiter dipped his chin and collected their menus.

"I love this place," Ben said with a satisfied smile. His fingers trailed up her arm, rubbing small circles on her bare shoulders. Goose bumps prickled where his touch had been, and she twisted the napkin in her lap, once again shoving down the conversation she knew she needed to have. His fingers stilled. "Seriously, Laila, what is going on? A minute ago, you were bouncing out of your chair. Now you look like a petrified puppy."

Her plan was to casually mention Chad's blowing into town over dessert, after she'd sufficiently proven to Ben that she was all in. One hundred and ten percent committed. Unfortunately, not only had her tactics backfired, but she could sense Ben's growing irritation.

She offered him a weak smile. "I wanted to wait until the end of the evening to mention this, but you're becoming far too adept at reading me."

"You think? I feel like I'm chasing a moving vehicle half the time." His thumb brushed her fidgeting fingers, the touch gentle and kind. "You're by far the most complicated woman I've ever known."

She lowered her head, feeling a twinge of regret. She hadn't meant to be a challenge. She so wished she'd been able to jump in like Ben had, with no doubts or reservations. And how did she explain that she was ready to now, when all evidence pointed to her feelings being corrupted by the sudden appearance of her ex-husband.

"Chad returned to Fairfield two days ago, and I know that seems like a big deal. But it's not. Or at least I don't want it to be. Not between us."

His eyes widened as he processed the information. "I thought you said he was completely out of your life?"

"He was . . . is. Unfortunately, Fairfield is a town with a very long grapevine. One that apparently reaches all the way to Atlanta." Regret immediately followed when Ben's shoulder's stiffened. Her intent was never to blame him, even if his unscheduled visit to Joe's a week ago had started this unfortunate chain reaction.

"So Joe learns you have a boyfriend, and suddenly your long-lost ex-husband strolls into town? Do you have any idea how messed up that is?"

"Joe isn't the one who called him." She shook her head when his eyes practically screamed that she was in denial. "Whatever. It doesn't matter. What does matter is that I'm here and you're here, and we have a fabulous dinner on the way."

"What is he asking of you?" Ben waited for her answer, his usual calm now strained and grim. He'd been through a bitter divorce. He knew the dynamics that came with a less-than-civil history. "He obviously came back for a reason."

For a fraction of a second, she considered withholding the truth, but that would only make her like Chad. She hadn't wanted that kind of relationship back then and certainly didn't now. "He wants to reconcile. He claims he's been sober for nine months and that all the drinking and drugs are behind him."

Ben fell back against the booth, his breath coming out in a shocked whoosh.

She tried not to let it panic her, the way he'd shifted away like any point of contact was unwelcome. "Ben . . . what are you thinking?"

"I'm thinking we should have had this conversation two days ago." He eyed her with a distrust that mirrored the night at Joe's. "Why didn't you call me?"

"I don't know. I was still processing it all."

"And tonight?" Suspicion colored every word. "The dress? The hair? Your eagerness to rush into next weekend? Are you telling me all of it has nothing to do with him?"

A wave of guilt slammed into her so fiercely, her only counterattack was anger. "How am I the one on trial here? Chad showed up on my doorstep. I didn't ask for it and I didn't want it. Maybe it's not my baggage that's the issue here. Maybe it's yours."

His shoulders drooped in a show of defeat so severe it made her curse her upbringing. She hadn't been taught decorum and restraint. She'd been taught to survive, to fight back when cornered, to hurt those who hurt her.

"I'm sorry. I shouldn't have said—" she started.

"No . . . it's true. Trust doesn't come easy for me." He squeezed her hand, but she still wanted to apologize profusely. This wasn't how the night was supposed to go. They were supposed to make plans and laugh and confirm that her decision to move was the absolute right one.

The waiter returned with their appetizer, although the earlier joy had been stripped from Ben's eyes and replaced with a palpable friction.

She tried moving closer. "What can I say to make you feel better?" There had to be a way to mend their sudden rift.

"I'm not upset with you. I know his coming home isn't want you wanted." He placed a hand on her leg as if to reassure them both. "But at the same time, I don't think us running off to the beach together is the best idea either. You need to close this chapter with him before we can move forward."

"It is closed. I promise." She pleaded with her eyes, but she could tell he had no plans to relent.

"I hope so." He kissed her, but it was sharp and quick. "Come on. Let's enjoy our meal."

"Okay." She ran a hand across the back of his jacket, hoping her touch would make all his unease go away.

It only seemed to make it worse.

CHAPTER 15

Chad's sneakers methodically pounded the pavement as he hit mile five on his morning run. He'd never been the type to work out, figured it was for those with far too much vanity and time. Now the sweat and endorphins were a necessity almost as critical as the AA meetings he'd attended in Atlanta.

The road stretched in front of him, long and winding, and he tried to ignore the hammering of his heart as he counted the landmarks leading up to his old house. Two blooming dogwoods, a battered red mailbox, and the pink crepe myrtle Laila planted for the child she'd lost just a week after the stick turned blue. They'd only been married two years and weren't trying for kids, but the miscarriage wrecked them all the same. Laila withdrew, and he found solace in the bottle, a cycle that only worsened after his mom passed away a few months later.

Cooper had been right. Laila needed to deal with him, not send him away or pretend she no longer loved him. They'd spent the last year of their marriage tiptoeing around the issues, ignoring the pain in whatever way they could. Not anymore. He wouldn't let the denial continue.

Chad's footsteps slowed as the trees thinned out, and he came to a halt near the pothole at the edge of the driveway. With a turn, his legs moved quicker, more deliberately. He wasn't naïve enough to think that Laila would happily welcome him this early on a Sunday, but her car had been gone last night when he'd come by, and she *had* said he should get his stuff. His choosing to do it without a shirt on was just a bonus.

The house appeared seconds later, a dark silhouette against the morning sun. He glanced at the small tilled garden. Laila had planted flowers like she always did in the spring. Pinks, purples, yellows, they all blended together among green bushes and ivy vines that covered the front of their porch. He'd missed it. Missed it so much that he had to stop walking just to keep his body from trembling.

Taking another calming breath, Chad continued toward the front door, but one glance to the oil stain where Laila's car should have been and his steps faltered. It was before nine on a Sunday morning. She should be here. Unless . . .

She didn't come home last night.

The runaway thought chilled his blood. As much as she'd changed, as damaged as their relationship was, he still knew a small piece of her heart. She wouldn't go there with another man. Not after their conversation and all he'd told her about his journey over the last nine months.

Unless she did it to hurt you.

His knees felt like they would buckle any second, but he refused to go down. There had to be another explanation.

Forcing himself to turn away from the emptiness, Chad took off with a speed he didn't know existed, running out every tear he refused to shed. He wouldn't accept that she'd taken that final step.

Screw the judge, the law, and everything else. She was his wife. End of story.

Cooper's red front door appeared sooner than he wanted. He hadn't run out the emotions yet. Hadn't even begun to process the sight of their empty house. But he'd already gone seven miles without water, and he didn't feel like passing out either.

The screen door slammed as he entered, the fury refusing to subside.

"Whoa, killer. You're gonna make me feel lazy," Cooper said with barely a glance in Chad's direction. He sat on the couch, his feet propped up on the farthest cushion, the TV tuned to *SportsCenter.* "How many days a week do you run?"

Chad pulled on the refrigerator handle, the force rattling the condiment bottles tucked in the door, and grabbed a sports drink. "Every day. Sometimes twice if it's an especially hard one." Today would be a double-run day for sure.

"An outlet is good. Healthy." Cooper swung his feet off the couch and stretched when he stood. "But if there is a time when you don't want to Tom and Jerry it all over town, here's something that goes a little faster." He snatched a set of keys from the coffee table and tossed them to Chad.

On instinct alone, Chad caught the set and stared down at the old Chevy symbol etched into the key. "What's this?"

Cooper grinned, an action Chad found just as unnerving as he did unusual, coming from his old friend. "Betsy. I didn't have the heart to sell her when I got Big Blue out there."

Chad welcomed his sudden chuckle. Betsy was a 2500 Silverado that had at least two hundred thousand miles on her, leaked more oil than an offshore rig, and spent more time in the shop than most mechanics. But on the outside, she was a pristine maroon beauty that Cooper had been babying since Chad first met him.

"You'd really let me drive Betsy?" He stared at the keys, then up at his new roommate. "Your truck? Your baby?"

Cooper only shrugged. "You're gonna need some wheels if you stay here, and she's just sitting out back anyway."

Chad clenched the keys in his hand, felt the rage slip away without complaint. "Thanks, man."

"It's no big deal." But it was a big deal. Everything Cooper had done over the last couple of days had been a big deal.

Chad hadn't planned to discuss Katie with him, but now his silence felt like a betrayal. He didn't have many friends left, and if time had taught him any lesson, it was to value the ones worth having. "I need to talk to you about something."

"Okay." Cooper sat back down and muted the TV. "You mind putting a shirt on before this little heart-to-heart? I like you, but not that much."

Chad downed the rest of his drink and tossed the bottle into the trash on his way to the hallway. The shirt he'd worn yesterday lay crumpled on his bedroom floor, and he threw it over his sweaty torso before walking back to the living room.

"Does this appease your delicate sensibilities?"

"What can I say? Betsy's a jealous girl." Again, the man smirked, and Chad hated that he was about to wipe the grin right off his face.

"Speaking of jealous girls . . ." He lowered himself to the chair across from his buddy. "I wanted you to know, I'm going to see Katie today."

As expected, Cooper's entire body stiffened, and his mouth turned into a tight, thin line. "Why are you telling me? She's married. I'm not her keeper anymore. Or yours, for that matter." A creature of pride, even now, with pain splashed all over his face.

"I'm telling you out of respect. I'd want to know if you were going to see Laila." And he would, but his declaration was more than just a courtesy. Chad saw how badly Katie had wrecked his friend.

"She won't be home on a Sunday." Cooper scratched his head and rolled his shoulders, but the tension didn't seem to ease any. "That's part of the new good-girl manual. Church, then lunch with the in-laws. It's all very sugary in her world now."

"Sounds like you know her schedule well." A little too well.

"There was a time when I thought she'd come back, so I made it my business to know. I imagine you would too." Their eyes met for moment, and Cooper's shoulders sagged. It was the only sign of weakness he'd probably ever let Chad see. "Anyway, you have my blessing or whatever you think you need. But don't fool yourself like I did. The girl you're looking for no longer exists."

Chad didn't doubt any of Cooper's conviction, even if it was skewed by heartbreak. The difference was that Chad didn't have romance clouding his judgment or heightening his emotion. Whatever change she'd made, it wasn't significant enough to erase a twenty-two-year friendship.

"I'll keep that in mind." He pushed to a stand and watched as his friend went back to his sprawled position on the couch. "Thanks again for the ride."

Cooper nodded dismissively, and Chad knew that was all his friend could give at that moment.

He wasn't being a stalker, although staring at the exit door of Fairfield Fellowship for the last thirty minutes had certainly made him feel like one.

The building looked different through sober lenses. More commanding, more intimidating, for some reason. Maybe it was because two more structures now crowded the campus, or maybe it was because the fiercest person he knew was behind those glass doors.

With a groan, Chad lightly hit the steering wheel. Cooper's warning had messed with his head. Made him question too many things about seeing Katie again.

Another five seconds ticked by, and he beat the seat with the back of his head. This was so stupid, his waiting here just for a glimpse. Knowing his luck, she'd see him, storm up to the truck, and they'd end five years of silence in front of an audience. With all the resentment and anticipation he was feeling, he doubted anything that came out of his mouth would be appropriate for the Sunday morning crowd.

But even that thought brought a shiver of doubt. Katie Stone attended church. Not just any church. The same church they'd vandalized at least twice in high school. He was pretty sure it had also been the victim of a drive-by egging on Katie's twenty-first birthday, but his memory of that night was a little fuzzy.

A flash of color through the glass doors had him straightening. A few couples and some families with small kids straggled out. Then the crowd thickened, and soon the exit doors were propped wide open as a stream of people in ties and dresses and fancy shoes began their rush to the parking lot.

His heart galloped every time he spotted a dark head of hair. Katie had been dying hers since junior high, and the jet-black color was as distinctive as her eyes. But none of the passing figures were the girl he'd known most of his life, and soon only a small crowd remained, talking just outside the doors. He turned the key in the ignition, feeling like an idiot. She wasn't here. Of course, she wasn't here.

Hand on the gearshift, Chad glanced over his left shoulder to check for pedestrians, and suddenly every muscle in his body locked up.

Katie had walked right by him, and he hadn't even noticed.

With hair to her shoulders in a soft brown color he barely remembered, she stood by an SUV, hand in hand with Asher Powell. The guy had filled out since high school, Chad could give him that, but still the picture of them together was . . . well, it wasn't her. Katie didn't do public displays of affection, and she certainly didn't wear . . . he squinted for a closer look . . . pantyhose? She'd morphed into one of *them*—an exact replica of the people they'd vowed to hate.

But worse than the hair and the clothes and the nauseating sweetness was her smile. She radiated joy.

Suddenly all he saw was red. A livid anger. It rushed to his fingertips, trapped just beneath his skin. He clenched the steering wheel, and in a flash the last night they'd spoken to each other came hurling toward him like a fatally placed spear.

The third bottle clanks against the other two in the trash bag, and I tie it up, knowing I'll need to drive the evidence to the dump before Laila gets home.

She already found one bottle, but I managed to convince her it was from before. If she finds out I lied to her again, she'll leave me for good. I know it, and I can't live without her. With a new wave of panic, I grab my keys and pull the door open.

Katie stands there, staring at me like I appeared out of thin air.

I drop the garbage bag and hear a bottle shatter within. "What are you doing here?" I ask with a cringe. I don't want Katie to know I'm drinking again either. But a closer inspection of my best friend makes me forget my planned diversion.

Her face is white, her hands are trembling, and her eyes? Good night, her eyes look as wild as the Mad Hatter's, the Johnny Depp version.

She's tripping, and it's on something I'm not familiar with.

"I left him. I left Cooper." She glances over her shoulder like she's being chased. "I can't do this anymore." Tears stain her face, and I'm frozen for two seconds, because in all the years I've known her, I've only seen her cry twice. At my wedding and now.

"Where's Laila?" Katie begs. "I need Laila."

"She's at Joe's."

Katie spins around, like I'm going to let her leave in this condition. She can hardly stand without swaying, let alone drive.

I grab her hand and wrestle the keys out of it. Her other one is fisted too, but I don't bother to find out why.

"What did you take?"

"Just leave me alone." She fights me, but I pull her inside. She starts pacing, talking like there's some imaginary person in the room and pulling at her hair. Its normally sleek black strands are tangled at the nape of her neck.

She's obviously been this way for a while.

"Take a deep breath." I pull her hands from her hair and force her to look at me. "Tell me what happened."

"Slim gave me something new." She rubs her hands over her face, then over her arms and legs. "I feel ants all over. They won't get off. I want them off. Get them off!" She's losing it.

I grip her shoulders and shake her until she's back from crazy town. "Calm down, now! Or I'm taking you to the hospital myself."

The shaking works a little too well, I think, because she collapses into the chair in front of me, sobbing. For the first time, I see what Laila must see when I'm strung out, and the picture disgusts me.

"You have to stop this," I say, harsher than I intend. "We can't keep doing this to her. She's stressed and tired all the time, and she can't take care of you anymore." My words are not just for Katie, but for me. Laila deserves better than both of us. I know it. Katie knows it. "Laila will be home soon, and she doesn't need to deal with you. Not like this."

"I'm sorry. I'm so, so sorry." She's bawling now, and I can't stand it. I shouldn't blame her for the mess I'm in, but I do. I've followed her over a cliff, and now we're both dangling.

"Sorry isn't enough, Katie. You're twenty-two. You have to grow up and stop relying on Laila for so much."

"I know." She's finally calm, but it's a hollow kind. The kind that can change in a finger snap.

"How much do you have left?" I ask because I need to know what I'm dealing with. If she has more at home, this madness will only happen again.

She loosens her hand and sets a half-empty vial on the table. The white powder coats the side, and I feel my nose twitch the minute I look at it.

"How could you bring this here?" I grab her arms again, pulling her out of the chair. I want to throttle her, but my eyes keep returning to the cocaine.

"I'm sorry. I just had to leave. I wasn't thinking." Her runny nose and bloodshot eyes make me shove her away. She stumbles slightly but finds the edge of the table.

I pick up the container and roll it back and forth. I messed up with the drinking, but it's been four months since I indulged in drugs. Four amazing months of clarity, yet my mouth salivates. Katie knows the drugs are always my final slide into oblivion. She knows Laila will never forgive me if I use again.

"Let me have it," Katie slurs. I see her eyes droop. They flutter shut and open again. She's coming down, and the fall is going to be catastrophic. *"I'll throw it out. I promise."*

I've heard promises from addicts. I've made those promises. I know they're worthless. *"You won't throw it out. But I will."* I look her in the eye—my best friend, my wife's anchor—and all I feel is hatred. *"The only thing you're capable of right now is finding a way to ruin my life."*

I barely make it five steps into the bedroom when I hear the front door slam.

Katie's gone, and I'm left with a vial of kryptonite in my hand.

Chad blinked, as if waking up from a bad dream. In a way he was, because the Katie he didn't recognize stared right at him, her eyes narrowing. He knew she couldn't see him through Betsy's tinted windows, but she would remember Cooper's old truck.

With a quick check of the rearview mirror, Chad backed out of his parking space and spun the wheels toward the exit, the resounding squeal of his tires as brash as the puncture wound in his heart.

CHAPTER 16

Laila twisted the screwdriver to the left, and once again, the metal refused to budge. She grunted, used her other hand for leverage, and to her total frustration, the driver only managed to slip off the screw for the third time. Changing an air filter should not be this difficult. Then again, she'd let Cooper replace it last time, which was why it felt as though it were imbedded in concrete. The man didn't know his own strength.

Why she felt so determined to change it at eight o'clock on a Sunday night, Laila still didn't know. Maybe she just wanted control over something in her life. Nothing in the last few days had gone according to plan. Her date last night had ended up feeling edgy and uncomfortable, even with Ben's attempts to shake off his frustration.

Worse, she'd told him she'd be going to the early service at church, and he hadn't come. She tried to think up excuses for why—he was tired, he picked up Caden early, he got called back into work—but none could erase the depressing truth in the back of her mind. For the first time since they met, Ben hadn't gone out of his way to spend time with her. Not that she blamed him. As far as girlfriends went, she was pretty lousy.

A knock echoed from her front door, and once again, she wanted to bang her head against the wall. Joe had threatened to send his wife over with some chicken soup for Laila's nonexistent cold. Now, she'd have to lie right to the woman's face.

A perfect end to a perfect weekend, she thought, with more than a little bitterness.

With an aggravated huff, Laila dropped the useless tool at her feet and stood, brushing off the residual vent dust that had settled on her thighs.

The knock came again, louder this time.

"Chill out. I'm coming," she mumbled as she wove around the two corners necessary to get to the entry.

Lifting on her tiptoes, Laila peeked out the tiny hole in her door and realized her weekend was about to get a whole lot worse.

With two turns, one to the dead bolt and the other to the knob, she opened the door and stared right into the eyes of the man who'd jacked up her entire past and now, it seemed, her future. Worse, he held a bag from her favorite café, and the smell of hot, rich chocolate immediately made her mouth salivate.

"What do you want?" she asked, trying to look at him and not the bag of treats. The jerk knew she'd never turn down a homemade brownie.

In his other hand, Chad lifted a cardboard tray containing two coffees, as if the answer were obvious. "You said I should come by and get my stuff." He smiled, all innocent and unassuming. "The coffee is for sustenance, and the brownies are my way of saying thank you for not burning all my clothes."

"Well, now is not a good time."

He tilted his head, letting his gaze sweep over her loose T-shirt and faded striped pajama shorts. "Why's that? Do you have company? Your boyfriend?"

She would never let Ben see her in this state. Her hair was a tangled mess piled on top of her head, and she'd taken her makeup off an hour ago. "Maybe."

"Good. I wouldn't mind meeting the guy." Without an invitation, Chad was inside the door and close enough that she had to step away or their chests would collide.

"Sure, come right on in." Her sarcasm rang through the house almost as loud as the warning signals blaring in her head.

He paused in the entry, not at all fazed by the bite in her voice, and stretched his neck to peek around the corner. "Your boyfriend appears to be missing."

"Your point?"

"No point. I just find it interesting that you're avoiding being alone with me."

"I'm not avoiding anything."

"Really? I came by this morning, but you were gone. Odd, especially since word on the street is that you're deathly ill with the flu."

"I went to early service at church," she said defensively.

He seemed to stand a little taller. "Good. It's settled then. You're here, I'm here. And I even brought boxes. They're in the back of my truck."

She peeked outside and saw Cooper's old truck gleaming in the residual porch light. Ugh. When she saw that man again, he'd better plan to run. He'd started this mess and now seemed determined to keep her ex-husband in town.

Chad wandered to the living room, and part of her was relieved to have some distance. The other part was furious that his presence in her home felt more natural than it did foreign.

"I like what you've done with the place." He didn't bother to look up, too busy setting down the brownie bag and drink tray on the coffee table.

"I haven't done anything with the place."

He smirked. "I know. That's what I like about it."

With an audible sigh, he plopped down on the couch and spread his arms out wide. "Oh, man, I forgot how comfortable this thing is."

"It should be. We spent an entire month's paycheck on it, remember?"

"Of course I do. I remember a lot about that night on this couch." He peeked over his shoulder with a wink, and for a fraction of a second, it felt like she'd been transported back in time. To days when they'd laugh over silly, mindless things that eighteen-year-old newlyweds laugh over. To when he'd tickle her until she gave up and then kiss her until they were both running toward the bedroom. Or the times when they didn't bother to leave the living room at all.

"You hungry?" Chad pulled the first brownie out of the paper bag and set it on a napkin. He held it out to her like a peace offering. Either he didn't notice how flushed her cheeks had become, or he was considerate enough not to mention it. When she continued to stare, his hand dipped a little. "Or do you want me to just get started packing?"

She scowled and took the offered dessert, annoyed at something, though she wasn't sure exactly what.

He patted the space next to him, but instead of sitting there, she leaned against the wall in childish defiance, slowly picking at the brownie in her hand.

"You're more stubborn than I remember." Chad chuckled, looking amused. "I like it. It's kinda sexy."

"I'm not trying to be sexy."

"Then sit with me. If you really don't care anymore. If my being here has absolutely no effect on you, what's the harm?"

The question stung more than she wanted it to because she did still care, and his presence absolutely did have an effect on her. So, what did that make her, then? Stupid? Naïve? A masochist?

"No harm. I just feel like standing." His grin widened, but she ignored it and went on. "So, what kind of things were you thinking you wanted?"

"I don't know. CDs, movies. I probably need to get the rest of my clothes." He was being so nonchalant. So accepting. It put her off guard.

Her Chad, or the Chad who used to live here, would have already started manipulating her in some way.

"Okay, we'll start in here, then." She tried to sound just as unaffected, but the words came out stilted.

He took a bite of his own brownie, eating half of it in one swallow. "I missed Lucy's." Eyes closed, the man practically moaned. "I swear it wasn't this good before. She's added magic cocoa or something."

Laila couldn't pull her eyes away. He was still so achingly handsome, all six feet of him. He wore a tight-fitting T-shirt and loose jeans, and she found herself staring at his newly formed muscles again. Her gaze wandered up his left arm, then across his chest, until it landed on the sharp line of his jaw.

He opened his eyes, all too aware that she'd been checking him out.

She expected him to call her out on it, or make a move toward her, but he simply smiled. "I guess it's time to get to work." Leaning over the coffee table, he brushed the crumbs into his hand, then into the bag. "Trash still under the sink?"

"Yeah." She could hardly breathe as he put the coffees on the table, grabbed the empty tray and bag, then strolled to their kitchen—*her* kitchen.

Shaking her head, Laila pulled out the decorative wicker baskets filled with years of shared music and memories and set it down on the floor. Her mind was too foggy, and she needed to keep her senses clear. Beautiful or not, that man in her kitchen was the same one who'd lied to her and broken her heart for years.

Plus, she was dating someone. Ben. A great guy who'd probably hate that Chad was over here collecting his stuff. She'd call and tell him first thing tomorrow.

No secrets.

"So, how was your weekend?" Chad asked.

She jumped when he spoke, too lost in her head to notice he'd returned to the living room.

"It was fine. Yours?"

"Odd, actually." He lowered to the floor, kneeling in front of the container.

Laila joined him, careful to keep the basket as a barricade between them. "Why's that?"

"I don't know. It's like I'm home, but everything's different." He shifted through some of the CDs, pulling out a few and setting them to the side. "We all kind of had our roles and expectations, and now I feel like I don't know exactly where I fit. Or if I fit at all."

"Is that why you haven't told anyone you're in town?"

He shrugged and his eyes found a spot on the far wall. "How do you know I haven't?"

"Because I've talked to Joe twice, and he hasn't mentioned you." Neither had Katie. And even though Laila still resented her a little, especially when it came to Chad, their friendship had slowly begun to heal. Katie would have plenty to say about both Ben and Chad, if she knew. "Plus, I'm pretty sure my phone would be ringing off the hook."

"True. Is that why *you* didn't tell anyone?"

"No. I just figured you'd be leaving soon, so there wasn't any point."

He snorted. "Wow. Thanks for the vote of confidence."

"I didn't mean it like that."

"I know." He smiled, but the motion felt sad. "Truth is, I appreciate your discretion. There are a few people I'm not ready to deal with yet, and my sponsor thinks I should take my time and adjust to all the changes first. Mark is big on slow and steady."

Fear and vulnerability rang openly in his gaze, and she had to sit on her hand not to reach out and comfort him.

"I won't say anything until you're ready."

"Thank you." He picked through another stack, chose two of her favorites, and set them down.

"Hey, you don't just get a free for all," she said pointing to his growing pile. "I like some of those."

His brows pinched. "Since when?" He grabbed his pile and began laying each out in front of her. "This one I bought before homecoming, and you said if I played it in the car, you'd dance with Bobby McMahon just to spite me. This one was Katie's, and if I recall, it took me begging on two knees for you to even let it inside the house." He continued on, a nostalgic smile forming as he reminded her of the origin of every album.

What he didn't realize was that after he'd left, she'd listened to all of them. Sometimes to remember him. Sometimes to make her angry enough to forget the pain. And sometimes just because it filled the house with a familiar sound. After a while, she listened simply because she liked the music.

"Well, my tastes have changed, and I want . . ." She grabbed two cases. "Both of these."

"Fine. But I get the next five without complaint, and I may take *Overexposed* just for spite."

She gasped. Maroon 5 was her favorite, and he knew it. "You wouldn't dare."

His face suddenly softened, the teasing smirk disappearing. "No. I wouldn't. I just like to see you riled up."

The air shifted, and she could sense that old chemistry sparking between them. Laila played with the hem of her shorts, not wanting to add to the sudden tension.

"So, I guess this is the last time we'll hang out together," he said, his voice regretful. "It's going to be weird being in Fairfield and not being around you all the time."

"We'll adjust. It just takes time and . . . space." Loads of space, acres of space.

"And you think that will do it?" He touched her knee, and the ache in his eyes did more to rattle her than the idea of coexisting in their little town. "Make me stop loving you?"

"I think we have to start somewhere." Quickly enough to make her stumble, Laila jumped to her feet. "The movies are in ou—my room. I'll go grab them."

She ran to the bathroom instead and splashed cold water on her face and neck. Of all the scenarios she'd fabricated in her mind, never once did this one play out. Chad accepting her decision. Chad walking away without an army forcing him to the truck. Chad being completely upfront and honest with her.

Grabbing the blue hand towel that shouldn't bring more memories but did, Laila forced herself to relax. It was the house. His things. Once she moved to Burchwood and out of this town, all these feelings would finally disappear.

When she went back to the living room, the scene was comical. Chad must have run out to the truck and grabbed the boxes, because they were now barely balanced in his arms, the top one teetering.

"A little help here," he groaned, taking another step toward the piles they'd made.

"They're made of cardboard. Just let them drop."

And he did, all three crashing to the ground in front of him.

She tried not to laugh when he ran his hand through his hair, leaving a trail of what looked like Styrofoam scattered though the strands.

He noticed her smile, and shook the mop on his head, watching as tiny particles fell out. Chad wasn't the kind of guy to primp about his looks, but she could tell it bugged him that she found his current disheveled state amusing. "Mind if I use your mirror?"

"Um, sure. The bathroom is down . . ." She stopped because he knew exactly where the bathroom was. He knew where everything was, probably better than she did.

Chad squeezed past her, his chest lightly grazing her shoulder. She tried to focus on the storage container in her arms and not the burn lingering on her skin where his touch had been. Setting down their old

DVDs, she ran a hand down her arm, hoping it would take away the sting. It didn't.

She heard water running in the distance while she moved the now-empty CD basket aside and replaced it with the plastic DVD storage. The faucet cut off, and she flinched, not quite ready to be in the same space with him again.

"Hey," Chad called from the hallway. "What's with the screwdriver on the floor?"

She followed the sound to their tiny half bath just past the kitchen. "I was trying to change the air filter, but Cooper tightened the grate so tight, all I managed to do was strip the screw."

He dropped to a knee and touched the metal, rubbing his finger along the grooves. "I'll take care of it." His voice was tight. "You shouldn't have to deal with this all by yourself."

They lapsed into silence, not daring to speak further, but he turned his head, and pain flashed across his face. "That's been the hardest thing about these last nine months. Not just the recovery, but recognizing how badly I hurt you. How much I lost, and how much I allowed my hurt inside to control my behavior."

Tears sprang to her eyes, and she looked down at the new filter propped against the wall. He'd never said those words before, not with so much personal responsibility.

Heaving a breath, she shifted away, the space between them widening like open jaws. He must have sensed her retreat, because he put his hand up.

"Don't worry. I'm not going to beg you again. You've made your position abundantly clear and then some. Making amends is part of the process, so I just needed to say that."

"Okay. Thank you." She swallowed. "I'll go start loading the boxes."

With surprising speed, he pulled himself back into that casual, let's-be-friends persona he'd shown up with. "Sounds good. Let me finish this, and I'll get my clothes next."

But the idea of Chad walking past the bed where'd they spent so many passion-filled nights, or entering the closet where they'd painstakingly hung rows and rows of shelving, or touching the suit he'd worn while promising to love and cherish her, was far too dangerous to consider.

"I'll get them. We can just pack everything in the living room."

He looked up, and his soft smile made her stomach flutter. For a second she caught a glimpse of the young man she'd married. The one with hopes and dreams and promises he still kept.

Worse, she found herself not wanting to let the image go.

CHAPTER 17

C had stared at the changes made to Katie's old home—the house he'd snuck into at least twice a week when he was younger. The exterior paint was new, the windows were now framed by blue shutters, and the owners were some couple who'd moved to Fairfield from Nebraska, or so Cooper had said.

But even weirder was the fact that Katie now lived next door, in the towering two-story Victorian that used to belong to Dr. Mills—a tyrant of a man who'd threatened them all with a 12-gauge shotgun. Of course, they'd been traipsing through his yard at the time, and had stolen some gnomes from his garden once before.

Back pressed against Betsy's hood, Chad continued to stare at the Victorian's front door, his feet no more willing to move than they had been five minutes ago. Katie was married now. She shared this monstrosity with a husband, living the kind of life Chad and Katie had made fun of as kids.

Chad's fingers strayed to the back of his neck, trying to massage the ache in his muscles. The motion brought no respite. His whole body was locked in a tension that would likely stay until he'd said what needed to be said.

With one last kick to the gravel, he shoved off the truck and took four strides to the front porch. A scrape of hinges had his stomach plummeting, especially when a heartbeat later, Katie pushed open the door.

At least she wasn't in that pretentious church dress. He could deal with this version. The cutoffs, loose T-shirt, flip-flops—even with that diamond ring on her finger and hair way too short.

Unblinking, she took him in, open-mouthed shock reverberating off her face.

"I bet you never thought you'd see me again." His words came out bitter and strangled, but only because something had shifted in her face. The surprise had worn away, and her eyes had filled with tears.

Katie walked down each step without a word, but her gaze blazed a trail across his face, over his chest, down to his feet, and back up again. "Chad?" She said it like he was an apparition, walking toward him without any hesitation.

He found himself wanting to back away from her, from the relief in her eyes, from the tremble in her lip. This wasn't how Katie was supposed to react. It was too soft.

She stopped within a foot of him and put her palms on his cheeks like a doting mother. "You look so good. Healthy." The first tear fell from her eyes, leaving him once again feeling paralyzed. "I thought . . ." Katie shook her head, but it only made more tears fall. "I worried you were dead. Or hurt." Her hands dropped away. "But look at you. Sober. I'm so . . . I don't know what I am right now." With a force that had him stumbling, she wrapped her arms around him, her head pressed against his chest, her arms tight enough that she seemed to fear letting go.

Tears pooled in his own eyes. He told himself he wouldn't cry, but he couldn't stop the moisture. His arms wrapped around her by instinct more than anything, and Katie's chest heaved faster. These sobs weren't like the last time he'd seen her—not erratic and labored by deep gulps and shaky hands. But her tears were just as unbearable to him. He'd expected a fight. Instead he felt a piece of himself return, and the relief wrecked every terrible thing he'd planned to say to her.

They stayed that way for hours it seemed, until they both found a way to control their emotions. Slowly, she eased away from him, her eyes red and puffy, but full of that same joy he'd seen in the church parking lot.

"When did you get home?" She took a step back and again examined every inch like she needed more proof he was real. Her right palm wiped away the wet trails on each side of her face.

"A few days ago."

She paused, and he knew her next question before it ever left her lips.

"Yes, Laila knows. She's the first one I saw." He used his shoulder to wipe away the evidence of his breakdown and felt some of the anger return now that they'd moved on to small talk. That wasn't what he'd come here for.

Katie glanced at her front door. "Do you want to come in? Asher's on a conference call, but he'd love to see you again when he's off."

"You think so?" He snorted, no more eager to make nice with her new husband than Asher probably was to meet him. "Cooper gave me the impression you're not too fond of your old friends."

"Cooper's not an old friend, so how would he know?" Her eyes turned hard, and though most sane people would recoil from the sharpness, the sight only made Chad grin. That was the Katie he knew.

"Let's just ease into this, okay? I barely recognize you as it is."

She fingered her much-lighter shoulder-length hair and bit her lip. "It's my natural color."

"I remember. I just haven't seen that color since the fifth grade, and even then, your hair was crazy long."

A smile crept across her face. "It had to be or I'd lose."

Katie and Laila used to make him measure their hair to see whose was longer. The winner got to pick movie preferences for a month.

Chad felt his own smile emerge. "You lost anyway."

"Not always."

They walked over to the front steps and sat. Katie fiddled with the frays on her shorts, while he laced his fingers together, still trying to sort through his jumble of conflicting emotions.

The bitterness was easier.

Silence descended and seemed to find the spot between them, bringing a tangible awkwardness that had never existed before.

Finally, he found the courage to speak. "It's funny how things turn out. Laila and I are divorced, I'm living with your ex-boyfriend, and you're married to the preacher's kid." He kicked a rock in front of his shoe. "I still can't wrap my head around that one."

"Yeah. Most people can't." She glanced over her shoulder to the front door, and her face visibly softened. "I never thought I'd love someone the way Laila loves you."

"Loved. Past tense." He'd worked so hard to act unaffected, to hide the sheer torment that came with having been in his house again. "I think I really lost her this time."

Katie rolled her eyes. "Please. Laila still loves you as much as she always did. Don't let her convince you otherwise."

"She's certainly trying." He thought of the ache that came with every CD, DVD, and piece of clothing that went into those boxes. It was as if someone had died and they were burying the memories. "We spent last night packing my stuff up. And despite my best efforts to reminisce and tear down her defenses, her only response was to ask me to give her *space*." He air quoted the word with disgust.

"Ouch."

"No kidding. Like two years isn't enough time to show both of us that we belong together."

She tilted her head, then shifted so she could face him head on. "Are you okay?"

He shrugged. "I'm dealing with it the best I can without a drink. I guess that's something."

"It's not just something, Chad. It's everything."

His chest tightened as that familiar bond came flooding back between them. As always, she understood his temptations. His pain. Time hadn't severed it after all.

She reached out and squeezed his hand. "Tell me what happened after I left. Laila's given me bits and pieces, but not enough to understand what you went through."

Part of him didn't want to, but a stronger part knew he needed Katie in his life. His talks with Mark were becoming less and less effective, and it was only a matter of time before he'd have to face Slim.

Chad looked up at the blue sky, bright with the sun popping in and out of the clouds. It should have been dreary or rainy or even dark, to match the things he was about to tell her. "Laila found the vial by the bed and brought it with her to the hospital. They analyzed it and found traces of fentanyl in the mix. That's why the high was so strong for you and why after only two lines, I went into respiratory failure. I'm lucky I didn't have a heart attack on top of it."

Katie dipped her head, the shame loud enough without words. He continued, recounting every ugly detail of the last five years. How Laila changed after that night, how their relationship disintegrated in front of him, how he got mixed up with Slim and the dealing. He told her about the many times he'd failed and the one time he succeeded. He told her about Mark and how Cooper's call broke his heart.

She listened to all of it without interruption, her only reaction being the shifting of her legs or the tightness in her mouth when she heard the blackest parts.

"I've blamed you for a long, long time," he admitted. "Probably more than was justified."

"I deserved to be blamed. It's my fault." She ran her hands down her face. "I've thought of that night so many times. At first, I just wanted to erase it from my memory, and when that didn't work, I tried to outrun it. Then I tried to fix all the heartbreak I caused by trying to reverse that one stupid decision." She turned and her eyes pleaded with his. "In the end, I finally had to forgive myself and hope that one day you could too."

Chad waited, unable to answer that hidden question. She wanted from him the same thing he expected from Laila. Forgiveness. Something so simple, yet so impossibly hard.

Instead of answering, he asked his own question. "What about you? Cooper pretty much gave me the summary of events after you came home, but what happened in Jacksonville?"

Embarrassment flushed her cheeks. "I took up with an ex."

"Which one?"

"Zander."

"You have got to be kidding me!" Rage seared through his stomach, forcing him to stand, walk two paces, then turn around. "That guy almost put you in the hospital." Zander had also tried to get Chad arrested when he'd tracked him down and showed the monster what it felt like to be battered.

"I was desperate."

"You were stupid."

She jumped up as well. "And what do you call making deals with Slim, huh? Because in my book, that's equivalent to signing your soul away."

The man's name was like a splash of cold water on his simmering anger. He put his hands on his hips and let his head fall back. "I almost have the money I need."

Katie stepped closer, that fiery temper of hers bursting between them. "'Almost' will buy you a casket or a shiny new pair of shackles. Either way, there is no way to face that man without every cent, especially after two years of hiding."

"I'll figure it out, okay?" His tone was scathing. "It's not like you care, anyway. You left me alone to die and then drove off to be with a man who considered you his personal punching bag."

Katie recoiled like he'd slapped her, but he didn't care. Knowing she'd run back to Zander made the betrayal worse. She didn't get to judge him. Not after all she'd done.

Tempers simmering, they each took a step away, knowing the other well enough to take a much-needed time out. The trees blew in the breeze, their leaves in full bloom as summer approached.

Arguing wasn't a new pastime for Chad and Katie. As much as they cared for one another, they often bickered more than siblings. Laila had been the buffer. The calm that would always bring their anger to a slow burn.

Finally, Katie's shoulders relaxed. "How much are you short?"

"Twenty-eight hundred dollars."

"Good night, Chad! How much did you owe him?" He went to answer, but she put up her hands and shook her head. "Forget it. I don't want to know. Just wait here."

With a quick lunge, Katie sprinted up her front steps.

Irritation washed over him. "I told you, I don't want to talk to your husband."

"Will you simmer down? I'm not getting Asher." She pulled on the door. "I'll be just a second."

It wasn't just a second, and the longer he waited, the more uncomfortable he felt just standing there. His eyes once again examined his surroundings. Katie's old Camry was parked under a tree, the shade protecting its faded paint. The familiarity calmed him. He knew that car. Knew the rip in the backseat that Laila had tried to fix twice, the carpet stain from him spilling Big Red, and the radio that only picked up five stations. He just didn't know the girl who owned it anymore.

Katie emerged. "Sorry. I had trouble finding my checkbook." She met him in the grass, her steps focused and determined. "Here."

Chad stared at the folded piece of paper she offered him. Not just a piece of paper, but a new beginning. A fresh start.

"Take it." She shook it at him again. "My parents gave me some money after their house sold. A thank-you, I guess, but I've never felt comfortable spending it. Not until now."

His hand shook as he gripped the check, unfolding it to see *$2,800* written in black ink. He lifted his head, watched her silver-blue eyes sparkle against the tears. "I can't take your money."

"Yes, you can." She closed his hand until the check disappeared from sight. "When I came home a year ago, no one wanted to believe that I'd changed. Except Asher." That same lovesick look returned to her face. "He gave me the second chance I desperately wanted. Let me give it to you."

Chad felt every muscle in his body tighten. "I'm an addict, Katie. I could be lying to you. I could be dead broke and the minute I leave here, cash this check, and blow the entire thing on a drunken binge."

"Yeah, you could. But I don't think you will. Like it or not, Chad. Forgive me or not. I believe in you. I believe God has amazing things for you to do. And I don't think for one second that your future lies in a bottle."

He embraced her like a lifeline. The same one she'd been since they were kids, only this time it wasn't in darkness. This time they clung to each other wrapped in light. In hope. In a new beginning.

"I'll pay you back. Every cent."

She squeezed him tighter. "You already have. You came home."

CHAPTER 18

Nervous adrenaline shot through Chad's limbs as he paced between his truck and the concession stand at Fairfield's popular drive-in theater. Five screens flashed around him, each angled so patrons could watch their chosen movie without interference or crossover.

He had ten grand in cash burning a hole in his pocket, and a small voice in his head screamed that he should never have come here without backup or his trusty 9mm.

Luckily, the old drive-in was full of people; Slim couldn't do too much damage in such a crowded place. Even with the starless sky looming black as death.

An engine rumbled in the distance, the boom of the sound system's bass competing for dominance as the vehicle bounced over the potholed gravel. Chad stopped pacing the minute he saw the make and model. He could pick out Slim's black Jag in a sea of cars. There was something about the paint. It gleamed as if never tarnished by Slim's insidious lifestyle.

A shiver ran down Chad's spine. He'd dreaded this moment for two years. Had stayed away from his hometown, his family, his future, all because he'd let this man seize control of his life. Never again.

The car pulled directly in front of him, and the tinted driver's window rolled down with agonizingly slow speed, revealing the thin, punishing face of Chad's greatest regret.

Only, the man he remembered wasn't scowling. In fact, he seemed almost happy to see him. "Chad Richardson. Welcome home." It was a voice he'd heard many times in his nightmares, that slow, southern drawl that was both deep and raspy. It made his skin turn cold as if a burst of winter had followed Slim to the drive-in.

The door handle clicked, and Chad stepped back when Slim emerged and rose to full height. The notorious drug dealer had been given his name in juvie when he was a tall, gangly fifteen-year-old. It no longer fit the man in front of him. His chest was broad, and his exposed bicep, lined with ink, could rival men ten years his junior. Not that Slim was old, but pushing forty, he'd definitely outlived most who took on his type of lifestyle.

Slim gripped Chad by the shoulders affectionately. "What's it been? Two, three years?"

Chad swallowed, having no idea how to even respond to Slim's odd behavior. "Two." The last time he'd seen his former dealer, he was on all fours, bleeding and begging for more time. He was sick and addicted and lost. "I have your money."

Slim waved him off as if the damage he'd done to Chad's life was as insignificant as the toss of his hand. "Eh, we'll get to that. First, we need to catch up. How have you been?" His slithery gaze traveled over Chad's face down to his dusty shoes. "You look good."

"Probably because I'm sober now."

"No kidding?" Slim turned back toward his open window. "Garcia, come meet your predecessor." His gaze returned to Chad, though he still seemed to be talking to his friend. "Chad would have easily been my best guy, if he'd stayed at it."

The passenger door opened, and a guy Chad didn't recognize emerged from the other side of the car. There was something nasty about his demeanor, about his obsidian eyes as they met Chad's over the top of the Jag. His skin was the color of mocha, and he appeared to be crafted in muscle and steel. Worse, he looked capable of crushing a man's skull in his bare hands.

Garcia approached them, and as Slim slapped him on the back, his winding snake tattoo moved across his arm like it was alive. "Chad, this is Garcia. He just joined our little operation."

"It's nice to finally meet you," Garcia said so dryly it made the hairs on Chad's neck prickle. This guy may have been new to Slim's world, but Chad could practically smell his ambition. Even his greeting felt laced with a threat. "Slim says your sales at the beach parties have never been matched. I plan to change that."

"Well, my dealing days are over, so the honor is all yours." Chad quickly cast his eyes to Slim. "I'm just here to pay the debt I owe you."

He had the audacity to grin. "And how much do you think you owe me?"

"Ten thousand."

"No. That's what you owed me two years ago. With the added interest . . ." He tapped a finger to his nose, his mind surely calculating a ridiculous figure. "Ten percent a year, plus my energy trying to track you down. I believe your debt is much closer to fourteen." Slim tilted his head. "But no worries. I'm sure we can come up with something that will benefit us both."

"I'm done selling. Just take the money. It's not that much to you anyway."

Garcia eased closer, ready to do whatever his boss needed, but Slim placed a palm on his chest. "Chad's family. A little bit of a black sheep right now, mind you, but still, we deal with family differently. Don't we, Chad?"

"Yes," Chad said, faking a calm he was nowhere near feeling. Slim hurt his enemies, but he disciplined family. Or at least that's what he'd called it the last time they'd spoken. "Which is why I didn't rat you out that night," he continued. "If I hadn't tossed the evidence, we'd both be in jail right now. I think that bit of loyalty has earned a pass on the interest."

Slim's casual smile returned. "I admit that little snafu motivated me to finally seek out some inside sources at the Brunswick PD. It's become much easier to move inventory."

Chad felt his pulse jump.

Slim slipped his arm around Chad's shoulder. "You and I were a good team, Chad. I liked you. I trusted you." Slim squeezed him tighter than necessary. "I still do. Even more, the ladies like you. They *enjoy* buying from you. Together we could make a killing. Together, ten grand would be pocket change."

Nausea rose up his esophagus. *Show no fear. Give him no power.* "I told you, I'm out." Chad pushed Slim's arm off and rolled his shoulders as if to remove the lingering stench. "The money. Do you want it or not?"

Before he could blink, Chad's spine was slammed against the slick black paint of the Jag.

Using his right forearm to cut Chad's air supply, Garcia pressed against him, nose to nose, his stale breath fanning over Chad's paling face. "You're being disrespectful."

"I'm not trying to be," he choked out, his chest now stinging from the lack of oxygen.

"Doesn't matter." Garcia's arm dropped, and Chad had only a brief second to breathe before Garcia pulled him forward and slammed a knee into his abdomen.

Chad knelt to the ground, gasping for air at the feet of Slim's new associate.

Two thick hands pulled him off the ground by his lapels. Garcia's eyes glimmered like he truly relished the thought of what he was about to do. The next two blows came to Chad's side with enough force to break a rib, and probably did. He went down with an agonizing crash. His vision blurred from the pain shooting through his chest.

"That's enough," Slim said with terrifying boredom. "I think he understands his tone was inappropriate. Chad?"

"I'm . . . sorry." Wheezing and coughing, Chad gripped the loose gravel, praying it would somehow offer relief. He lifted pleading eyes to the man he swore he'd never beg from again and did exactly that. "Will you please take this money and release my debt?"

"Of course. All you had to do was ask nicely." Slim knelt beside him and lifted Chad's chin, his eyes so sincere Chad wondered if he was an exceptional actor or a true sociopath. "We're family. Brothers bound together, and I take care of my own."

"So I'm clear? No more obligation?"

"As I said, you owe me no more money."

Chad reached into his pocket and pulled the fat white envelope into view. He set it in Slim's open hand. "Thank you."

The words stung. Thanking that man was like swallowing acid, but he had no choice.

Chad forced himself to accept Slim's offered hand and rose back to his feet, the pain still sharp and almost debilitating. Garcia watched from a distance, but Chad could have sworn he saw jealousy flicker in his eyes.

Slim chucked his chin toward the car, and Garcia marched to the passenger side without a word. Chad forced his eyes not to follow. He wasn't weak anymore, and if Garcia hadn't caught him by surprise, that fight wouldn't have been so one sided.

"Whatever you're thinking, just get it out of your head," Slim said. "Garcia is a little impulsive, but he's one of mine now. Just like you." Slim smacked his arm and passed by. Chad didn't turn. "I'm sure I'll see you around soon."

The door slammed and the engine rumbled to life. Chad closed his eyes and let the sound infiltrate his mind and body. Let it bring a blur of tears that had nothing to do with the lingering pain.

For the first time in years, he felt free.

CHAPTER 19

Laila efficiently worked her way through the seating areas, turning over chairs and wiping tables, all while trying to forget that Chad hadn't attempted to contact her since he'd hauled away all his stuff almost a week ago. She should be happy. Ben certainly had been when he'd asked for an update, although he hadn't rescheduled their beach trip. Nor had he mentioned her spending time with Caden again.

Done with the table arrangement, Laila clicked the remote to power on the two large TVs and set each channel to the upcoming playoff game, quickly muting the sound. At the chalkboard, she wrote out the night's drink specials, then grabbed extra bottles from the back.

But none of her meticulous routine would stop the anxiety welling in her gut. Had Chad left Fairfield? Was he still sober? Should she call Cooper, or would that send the wrong message? The questions only fueled her frustration. She shouldn't have agreed to keep his return a secret. She shouldn't have to carry his burden once again.

When she heard the front door push open, Laila glanced down at her watch to make sure she hadn't miscalculated. No. She still had twenty minutes before opening.

"We're closed," she called to what was only a silhouette, due to the unfiltered sunlight. The brightness faded as the door closed, and Katie stepped forward with two clear plastic cups in hand.

"I brought you some tea, freshly made by Lucy herself." Dressed in jeans and a fitted blue T-shirt, Katie seemed to get more beautiful with age. People thought it was the lighter, shoulder-length hairstyle she now wore, but Laila knew better. Katie glowed with happiness, even more so since marrying Asher.

Laila exhaled and reached for the blessed drink. "Thank you. I so needed this. I was running late and didn't have time to stop for my usual order."

"Lucy also said to make sure you eat." Katie passed a white bag full of mini muffins to Laila's eager fingers. "Something about recovering from a cold."

Laila turned away, unable to meet Katie's eyes. They'd been best friends since they could walk, and Katie could read her like her own diary. Especially when she lied. "Yeah. Just a little bug. I'm better now." Stalling, she set what was likely to be her dinner on the counter.

"That bug doesn't happen to be Chad Richardson, does it?"

Laila spun around. "You know?"

"Yeah. He came to see me on Monday."

"Oh, good. So . . . have you heard from him since?" Laila tried to act casual, but she hung on every expression, even the amused one that said Katie knew exactly why she'd asked.

"I have. We're meeting for lunch tomorrow." Katie eyed her suspiciously. "He's giving you space because you asked for it. Not because he messed up. You know that, right?"

"Of course. I'm just glad he's starting to tell people he's home," she lied.

"Me too." Katie eased onto a stool at the bar, and time seemed to drop into reverse. Back to when her best friend would spend almost every night at Joe's keeping her company or helping to serve, if needed. But those memories were long gone. Since Katie had been back in town, she'd only come into Joe's a handful of times, and never stayed once the crowd showed up. "I couldn't believe how great he looked. He's more fit than he was in high school."

"Yeah, he is." Laila absently picked up a towel and began wiping down tumblers. She didn't know what else to say. Chad didn't just look better. Everything about him was different.

"How are you feeling about all this?" Katie took a sip from her straw and watched her with piercing blue eyes. Why she bothered to ask at all, Laila didn't know. Katie had walked most of the journey with her. Heck, her actions had been at the root of Laila and Chad's biggest fights. The girl knew exactly how she felt.

"Angry, confused, surprised, grateful. You name it, and I've probably felt it at some point since he's been back."

"I bet." Katie paused and the break was almost as prickling as the subject matter. "So . . . what are you going to do?"

"About what?"

"About Chad. Are you going to give him another chance?" She shifted her drink, ice hitting the side of the cup the only sound around them. "I mean, he's done everything you asked him to. He's been clean for months. He's kept a job. He's even giving you space, which you know for Chad is like asking him not to breathe."

Irritation replaced her growing apprehension. They'd come a long way in the last year, but she and Katie were nowhere near close enough for this conversation. "It's not that simple anymore. Too much time has passed."

"Come on. You and I both know that's not true." The almost chuckle from Katie's lips had Laila's pulse spiking.

She slammed her hand on the counter. "When you came home, I didn't pressure you about Cooper. I didn't try and convince you to go back to him. I gave you what you needed. I let you hide away until you were ready to face your past." She glanced down and noticed her fingers were trembling. "I guess it's too much to ask the same from you."

A flash of Katie's notorious temper crossed her face. "Chad is not Cooper. And you are not me. Those situations cannot be compared."

"How would you know?" she practically yelled. "You weren't here for the worst of it. You didn't see what he became after you left." Her old resentment came bubbling to the surface. She'd tried to move past it, tried to forgive Katie, and maybe in some ways she had. But Chad coming home was like digging up a decaying body, and all the pain of what she'd lost, what all of them had lost, seemed far worse now than when she'd buried it the first time.

The silence that settled between them made her shift on her feet. Laila knew she wasn't being fair. Katie had already apologized for what happened years ago. There wasn't anything left for her to say. "Listen, I didn't mean to bring up old arguments."

"No, it's okay. And you're right. I wasn't here during the worst parts." She played with her straw, scratching the plastic as she pulled it in and out of her cup. "I guess I just don't understand. You've been pining all this time, waiting for him to get clean, and now, he's here." She glanced up, confusion and sadness swimming in her eyes.

"Actually, I haven't been pining. Not for a while now. I've been dating someone and it's . . ." She hadn't told Katie about Ben or her plans to move, but now seemed as good a time as any. "Well, it's serious, I guess. Serious enough that I'm moving to be closer to him."

The admission sucked the air from the room, and for a second, the hurt on Katie's face matched Chad's. Laila pressed her palms to the counter. She wasn't trying to hurt anyone, though that seemed to be all she was capable of doing lately. Ben, Chad, Joe. Now Katie.

"Chad mentioned another guy, but I thought he was exaggerating."

"His name is Ben. He's thirty, has a steady job, and doesn't drink." Laila stood to full height and resumed her glass wiping. Talking about Ben made her feel better. More centered. It reminded her that stability was possible. "I met him four months ago at that church I've been attending in Burchwood. We ended up at the same table during one of the fundraising events and hit it off."

"I have no idea what to say to that." The shell-shocked look on Katie's face said plenty.

"You don't have to say anything. But you of all people should understand where I'm coming from. Ben is just like Asher. He's kind and generous. He's stable and successful. But more than anything, he makes me believe I might be happy again one day."

But empathy was not the emotion on Katie's face. Instead, she seemed angry, almost insulted by the words. "I didn't settle for Asher." Katie's voice rose with indignation. "Nor was he in my life as a way to forget my feelings for someone else. Asher is my first love, my best friend."

Laila flinched at the sharp tone. "I didn't say he wasn't."

"You implied it. You compared him to Ben. And that's what you're saying, right? That Ben is a nice, easy consolation prize. A way to forget all your feelings for Chad."

She slid furious eyes to Katie, her throat so tight it hurt. "I'm not settling for Ben."

Katie met her with equal disdain. "Aren't you? Do you even realize what you said, Laila? I *might* be happy one day. Might. You've been with the guy four months. You should know if you're happy." Katie took a breath and seemed to calm whatever temper had been simmering. "I know you. I know Chad. I've seen your life together. The good, the bad, the really bad. Unfortunately, I've been a part of that really bad equation more times than I like to remember." Remorse leaked from Katie's words as if they hurt her as much as they were ripping at Laila's chest. "But one thing has never been in question. And that is that you and Chad love each other. A soul mates kind of love. The kind that happens once in a lifetime."

Laila couldn't look at her. It was as if she'd opened her heart and poured it right out on Joe's countertop.

"Are you truly ready to let him go? I know you think it's easy because you have a guy in the wings and you're moving. But have you thought about the other end, Laila? Are you ready for Chad to fall in love with someone else?"

That last statement went too far, its purpose solely to manipulate. Katie was doing what Katie did best—interfering. No matter how many times Laila had run to her old friend, how many times Katie had held her while she cried, the truth was right there in front of her.

Katie would always choose Chad. They were the same.

With a coolness she didn't know she had inside, Laila met Katie's eyes, and for once Katie was the one who pulled back from the stare down. "Chad can do whatever he wants. I don't care anymore. And in the meantime, you and the rest of this idiotic town can continue to placate and justify all his actions."

"You know that's not what I meant."

Laila crossed her arms. "I'm moving in a few weeks, and I'm starting over. You're not the only one allowed a second chance."

"There is no perfect life, Laila. And if you expect Ben to bring you that, he's going to disappoint you, just like Chad did."

An empty space unlocked inside her. "You should go. I still have a lot to do."

Katie opened her mouth to say more, but Laila didn't stop to hear it. She rushed to the swinging kitchen door and disappeared before the tears told the real story. That Katie's words hadn't just wounded.

They'd exposed Laila's greatest fear.

CHAPTER 20

C had sat with Katie in the corner of Weston's Café's outdoor patio, painfully aware that everyone was staring at him. The spot was intended to be less conspicuous, but Chad hadn't realized that the foot traffic through downtown had picked up so much. Weston's used to be the only business on this block. Now there were four other shops with painted windows and colorful signs announcing sales and specials.

Through the slats in the wooden arbor, the afternoon sun shined down as if to spotlight the duo for the entire town to see. They'd only managed to take two bites of their food before at least ten different people came up to offer him a hug or express their joy in seeing him back in town. Chad tried not to cringe if they squeezed too tight and fought to return their cheeriness.

The bruising had subsided a little, although the ache on his right side still caused his breath to catch if he twisted too fast. After Cooper had reamed him for an hour about meeting with Slim alone, he'd wrapped Chad's swollen torso. According to his friend, the bones were likely not broken. But even still, it'd be weeks before he'd be able to move freely without wincing.

"You know what this means," Chad said after another passing acquaintance stopped and chatted for five minutes longer than he wanted.

"That you now understand the immense burden your best friend has to endure under Fairfield's bright, shining limelight?" Katie grinned, and he threw a balled napkin in her direction. She'd been watching with amusement for the last thirty minutes, enjoying his misery.

"No. And don't act like you've always hated it either." They'd both been the type to bask in attention, but now all the niceties and fake smiles just felt daunting. "What I'd planned to say is that I better go see Barney. He's going to be ticked I didn't come to him first."

"Nah, your uncle loves you. In fact, when you go, you should ask him about a job. Between my dad, Cooper, and Barney, you're practically a legacy hire." She bit into her sandwich, able to discuss her ex with so little emotion that Chad felt a slight sting for his friend.

He picked at his own food. "I have a record, though."

"One arrest for possession five years ago, and you got probation. They can work around it."

"Maybe." Chad pushed the plate away. He hadn't had much of an appetite since he'd hauled all his belongings out of Laila's house.

He'd expected her to call. At least once.

He knew she missed him. He'd seen it in her eyes, the same wistful longing he felt every miserable day without her. And yet, despite having his number, and knowing where he was staying, Laila hadn't made one move to indicate she cared for him at all.

"I don't know what else to do to make her forgive me." Elbows on the table, Chad lowered his head to his hands.

"Well, we made it almost forty minutes before the conversation turned to Laila. I guess that's an improvement."

He glanced at her through his fingers, annoyed at her flippancy. "This isn't a joke."

"I know that." Her voice tightened, now on the defensive.

"Then give me some advice. I've tried begging. I've tried explaining and showing her how much I've changed. I've tried discussing the good times, apologizing for the bad times. I've tried putting myself in her way so she's forced to deal with me. Now, I'm backing off, but maybe that's wrong." Cooper certainly thought so, but Chad was out of options. "I don't know what's left to do."

Katie began to open her mouth, then paused. "You know what? It's not my business. I've been in the middle since we were kids, and I need to stay out of it this time."

"Seriously? *This* is when you decide to become Switzerland?" He dropped his hands. Katie was like the meddlesome little sister who always had an opinion, even when he didn't want one. And now, when he needed her interference and influence, she was bailing on him?

Katie shrugged. "Maybe I just understand the dynamics of a healthy relationship now. There has to be trust. You can't force that."

"I think I liked you better before." He scowled and quickly moved his leg when she tried to kick his shin. "I'm only sorta serious. This new you isn't totally terrible." Katie was the same fiery, sarcastic ball of energy he remembered, but without all the pressing darkness. She seemed content, happy, and he found himself feeling twinges of jealousy.

Katie polished off the last of her meal and sucked on her straw, her gaze bouncing from the gaggle of people by the door and then back to him. The patio was clearing out, with most of the lunch crowd heading back to work. "Speaking of the new me, when are you finally going to talk to my husband?"

"I've talked to your husband. We went to school together for twelve years."

"That's not the same, and you know it. I want to you be a part of my new life, and Asher is at the center of it. You two could be friends if you'd give him a chance." She was surprisingly loud, and a brief flash of hurt showed in her silvery eyes. Chad wasn't trying to be difficult, but he also wouldn't pretend that he was going to cast aside his past relationships the same way she had.

"Okay, fine. You want the down-and-dirty truth?" he asked.

"Yeah."

"Being friendly to Asher feels like a betrayal to Cooper."

"But that's ridic—"

He put up his hand, stopping her. "You may have moved on, and Lord knows that Cooper is trying to. But men are wired different. At least the two of us are. We're territorial, yes, but we're also loyal—sometimes to a fault. If Cooper chummed it up with *Ben*"—he said the name like a disease—"I'd be ticked."

"It's not fair." She crossed her arms, her diamond ring reflecting the sunlight. "You guys didn't even like Cooper at first."

"What can I say? The man grows on you."

"Yeah, like a fungus," she grumbled.

Their familiar bantering settled the storm in his stomach, and he was finally able to continue with his half-eaten sandwich. He had been right when he'd told Cooper that his friendship with Katie would eventually win out over their past offenses. And if Katie could fall back into her old patterns with him, he just had to be patient and wait for Laila to do the same.

"Ah crap." Katie stiffened, eyeing the patio entrance.

"What?" He twisted to find the source of her surprise, but his answer came when the empty chair at their table scraped against the ground.

Slim spun the wooden seat around and sat with his arms perched on the back. "Well, looky here. My two favorite people, together again." He grabbed a piece of bread from their basket and pinched off the corner, glancing between the two of them while chewing away at the mound in his mouth. "I feel a little hurt I wasn't invited to the party."

Slim wore dress pants and a button-down shirt with each cuff rolled once. The edge of his tattoo peeked out from under his sleeve, but to the untrained eye, Fairfield's most dangerous resident looked almost respectable. But that was what he excelled at. Blending in. Remaining unnoticed, untouched. Only those who darkened his doorstep or purchased his goodies understood the extent of his corruption.

Chad knew he should say something, but what? The man held the power to destroy all of Chad's progress, and had done just that many times before.

Katie, of course, appeared completely unfazed by their new lunch guest. "Oh, Slim, we both know you never wait on invitations." Her sarcasm practically rattled the glass as she added a packet of sweetener to her iced tea. An overt act of disrespect from a girl with no fear, and once again, Chad felt that ache of jealousy. "So what's with the drop-in visit?"

Slim swung all his attention to her. "Do I need an excuse to see my two best clients?"

"Former clients," she drew out, a masquerade of politeness dotting her voice.

"And yet, it feels like just yesterday that you were banging on my front door."

"Well, who says stupidity doesn't dissipate with age? I guess I've outgrown you."

"I guess you have." Slim's composed, imposing tone sent a new emotion down Chad's spine. Not just fear for his stubborn best friend, but rage. His wounds weren't even healed yet, and here she was poking a snake.

Slowly standing, Slim pulled on the cuffs of his sleeves. "Katie, it's been a pleasure, as always." He turned dark, irritated eyes to Chad. "How is your side feeling? Still tender?"

Chad absently pressed a hand against his throbbing rib. "It's fine."

"If you need to take the edge off, just let me know." Slim winked, and the atmosphere stilled until he strutted away, back out the way he came in.

The minute he was gone, Chad leaned across the table, hands fisted. "What is wrong with you?" he hissed, so angry she became a blur in front of him. "You baited him on purpose."

"Wrong with me?" she shot back. "You sat there trembling like a lost kitten. Why not just hand him your sobriety chip and say, 'Have at it'?" Chad flinched, but she wasn't finished. "And what was with the 'tender' comment?"

"It doesn't matter."

"Yes, it does!"

"No, Katie, it doesn't, because he took the money and my debt is paid. That was, until you shoved our sobriety in his face." Chad ran frustrated hands down his cheeks, filled with an overwhelming need to hit something. "I have to get out of here."

"Chad." He didn't want to hear it. Once again, Katie's stubbornness and arrogance was going to suck him back into the nightmare. "You have to stand up to him. It's the only way he'll ever leave you alone. Can't you understand that?"

"I understand that, as usual, I'm going to get hammered over your smart mouth." He tossed a few dollars onto the table and shoved his chair in. "See you around."

He made it only two strides when he heard her say, "It's not space Laila wants."

Pausing, he turned back. Her hard-armored shell was gone, replaced by the softness he still wasn't quite used to seeing. An empty table stood between them, and Chad pressed his palm to its wood, partially to keep him sane. Katie had sent his emotions into a free fall with only a few choice words. "How do you know?"

"Because she told me the same thing she told you. That I needed to give her time to forgive me. But time and space are her defense mechanism. What she really wanted from me was to *see* the difference. She wanted me to prove myself trustworthy again."

"I've been clean for almost ten months. What else can I do?"

Katie fingered her wedding band like it gave her the answer. "Be the husband you were never capable of being. Allow her to be your partner." She met his eyes, and once again she became his leader, his guidepost. "Tell her the truth. All of it."

Slowly, his anger surrendered. The man he used to be would never have told Laila about Slim. He'd conceal his wrongdoings or run away from the guilt. Katie was right. Trying to make Laila remember the boy she'd married wasn't going to win her back. She had to see a new person. A man she could fall in love with all over again.

CHAPTER 21

When Laila pulled up to her house Saturday evening, the yard looked as if a small tornado had passed through it. Long tree limbs lay across the grass. Old boards were stacked in a pile by the porch next to two black trash bags.

Laila parked the car and searched for any signs of life. "Uh, hello?" she called after slamming the car door.

"Back here," came a voice from the side of the house. She followed it around and practically stumbled when Chad appeared, shirtless with an ax in his hand. The dead bush he'd been hacking at lay on its side, a piece of root stubbornly fixed to the ground.

It had only been six days since she'd last engaged with him, but somehow the sight of him sober and strong made her world feel lighter.

"W-what are you doing?" she stammered, taking in the dark tan ripple of muscle across his abdomen. When in the world had he grown those?

"What I should have done years ago." He tossed the ax to the ground and stretched his hands over his head. On the far side of his torso was a wide strip of white medical tape, the skin around it slightly yellowed as if the injury had happened a while ago. He caught her looking and quickly dropped his arms.

She wanted to ask what happened, but the question felt too personal. "You don't have to do all this," she said instead.

"I know, but you're moving soon, and our jerk of a landlord is going to gouge you if he thinks you're vulnerable. You've been a steady stream of income for years. But if Mr. Novak realizes I'm back taking care of things, he'll behave.

She knew he was right, so even though she wanted to refuse his help and shield her eyes from his bare skin, she simply focused on the wood siding and said, "Okay. Thanks."

"I can get this all bagged up in about an hour. Mind if I stay and finish?"

"No, of course. Take as much time as you like. And thank you." Feeling a sudden spark of nerves, Laila backed away. "Well, I'm going to"—she pointed over her shoulder—"head back inside. I've been running around all day, and I need to get these shoes off."

Chad wiped his forehead with the back of his arm. "What kind of running?"

"Oh, this and that. I spent the day in Burchwood." She didn't need to say what she'd been doing or whom with. They both knew. "Anyway, I'll bring out some lemonade if you're thirsty."

"That'd be great. Thanks." He picked up the ax again, though she noticed now that he favored his right side when he did so.

She rushed away before she did the unthinkable and reached out to touch the tender-looking area. Her cheeks flushed as vivid images of caressing Chad's damp skin brought a fresh wave of guilt over her. She'd left Ben not even a half hour ago. They'd checked on the bathroom renovation progress in the cottage, caught a movie, and then ended the day with ice cream and a walk through the park. And yet, not once during their time together had she felt this all-consuming kind of spark.

As she walked through the entryway into the kitchen, she heard Katie's words again. Only she wouldn't accept them.

She wasn't settling for Ben. She wasn't.

Okay, fine, physically, she found Chad much more attractive. Big deal. A long, healthy marriage wasn't based on great sex alone. She knew that. The problem, though, was that the differences between Ben and Chad extended past the stomach flutters. She was more comfortable around Chad; they'd had a lot of good years together. And memories of those "good years" had been haunting her more and more during late, lonely nights. She found herself pulling out old pictures and dreaming of the future that had never come to pass.

But . . . she still trusted Ben more. He wouldn't hurt her. He wouldn't lie to her. And he wasn't an addict.

Frustrated by her double-mindedness, Laila grabbed the pitcher from the fridge, filled two glasses with ice, and poured the lemonade.

A sudden rush of memories made her stomach turn over. She gripped the edge of the counter and hung her head. She and Chad had met over lemonade. He'd come to her stand, handed her a wrinkled dollar bill, and when their fingers accidentally touched, she'd blushed.

No. She wouldn't let him do this to her again!

She swiped the glasses off the counter and stomped toward the front door. A person couldn't possibly meet their soul mate at five years old. Maybe she'd believed that once, but now she knew better. That kind of youthful romanticism didn't fit into the real world. She was an adult now; she had to make smart, mature choices. Betting her future on Chad's ability to remain sober was neither smart nor mature.

He was bagging up the abandoned branches by the time she returned outside. He'd also put a shirt on, to her relief. When he saw her approach, he dropped the bag and stared until her skin tingled.

"Here," she said, offering him the drink in her right hand.

He stepped closer and took the glass, but never pulled his eyes from hers. He must have felt it too, the surge of memory, the zinging way their bodies were programmed to be together.

She averted her gaze and took a calming sip from her own glass. "How long have you been out here?"

"Since about one. I met Katie for lunch, but we had an argument, so I needed to chop something."

"What were you two fighting about?" She peeked back and he was still staring at her. Her free hand found the end of her braid.

Chad turned up his glass and drank until it was empty. He seemed uncomfortable with her question, which made her want the information even more. Only she shouldn't want it. She shouldn't care anymore. One day he'd find someone else to confide in. Someone else to share his burdens with, and she would have to be okay with that.

"Actually, never mind. It's not my business." She turned to leave, but felt his hand on her arm. It was hot, and masculine, and just firm enough to stop her.

"It is your business." He let go once she quit her retreat. "Can we go sit on the porch? This conversation might take a while."

"We've already talked about everything." She didn't want another arduous conversation. She didn't want another apology or explanation. She just wanted her stupid new cottage done so she could stop feeling as if she were in a battle every time he came near her.

"I never told you why I left like I did. And before you say it doesn't matter and that you don't care, let me just stop you. You need to hear this. And trust me, telling you is the last thing I want to do."

She pressed her lips together, annoyed that he'd practically read her mind.

He started toward the front of the house, and she followed until they were seated side by side on the top step.

Chad set his empty glass aside and studied his interlaced fingers. "I spent a lot of our marriage lying to you. Not because I ever enjoyed it, but because I was so afraid of losing you that I thought it was justified for the sake of preserving our relationship."

She fiddled with the condensation on her glass as her buried emotion and anger came percolating through.

"I'm not going to lie to you anymore, Laila. And that may mean you hate the things I have to say, but at least you'll know they're the whole truth." He turned his head and paused until she finally set down her glass and met his eyes. "The reason I left so abruptly is because I got involved with Slim."

"With Slim?" She choked on the name until the magnitude of Chad's words slammed into her. Suddenly all the pieces began to unfold. "You were dealing?"

He cast his gaze to the ground. "Yes."

"How could you? After everything we'd been through?" She'd felt a lot of things over the years when it came to Chad, but never a level of disgust as severe and paralyzing as this. She thought of Sierra's mom, of her own mother, of the criminals who kept the addictions of people like them alive and active.

"It started after I finished rehab the second time. You'd already threatened to leave again. I tried looking for a job, but no one would hire me with my drug history. Meanwhile, you were working yourself to death, and the medical bills from my overdose had gone into default. I was supposed to provide for you, and here you were, stuck because of my addiction. I felt powerless and desperate."

She didn't want to hear more, but he kept talking, giving her details of the parties where he'd sold, the agreement he'd struck. Telling her how he was able to keep the creditors away and still feed his habit. And then came the details of the sting operation gone bad and how he'd just now had the money he needed to pay Slim off.

When Chad confessed the last terrifying truth, her hands felt numb. "He could have killed you."

"Not for ten grand. Slim can make that up in a weekend."

"You say that as if it's no big deal," she gritted out, disgusted.

"It *is* a big deal. I'm not dismissing what I did. I'm just assuring you that I'm not worth murder."

She wanted to argue, but here he sat, two years later, alive and well. "How long did you work for him?"

"Six months. But he started recruiting me long before I finally said yes." For the first time in years, he kept his focus on her. He didn't look away. He didn't try to change the subject. His expression looked expectant, as if ready to answer any question she had.

Truthfully.

Suddenly, she had a flood of words, a million demanding inquires, as if this new transparency would disappear at any moment.

"Why wasn't I enough?" She hadn't thought before speaking, but keeping that question inside seemed as likely as trapping a hurricane. Tears pricked at her eyes and spilled over without hope of stopping them.

Chad winced as if she'd struck him in the chest. He moved slowly and knelt before her, using the bottom step to balance on. His hand found hers, and he caressed the now-empty ring finger on her left hand. There wasn't even a white band of skin there anymore. She hadn't worn the ring since the day she signed the divorce papers.

"My addiction was never about you, Laila. I couldn't have loved you more." His eyes filled with tears, which made hers come that much more rapidly. "The problem was, I couldn't have hated myself more. I don't know how to explain it, because there is no perfect formula. Some days, I'm happy and good, and then suddenly, I'm not. It's always there, the temptation to escape and bury all the hurt, and somehow you convince yourself that it's better than the pain. Better than reality." He squeezed her hand tighter. "I thought I could hold on to both. You and my illusions. But then I lost you, and nothing made sense after that."

She pulled her hand away and wiped at her face. "How bad did it get after you left?" She had to know the extent of his addiction.

Chad eased away until he was back to the spot next to her. "The drug use stopped pretty quickly. I didn't have the money or the supply anymore. Plus, I was still nervous about Slim tracking me down. But the drinking got worse."

"Did you . . ." She could barely speak the words. But she had to know. "The women. Were there a lot of them?"

"Gosh, Laila, no." Chad's voice rose, half-angry, half-offended. "I've never touched anyone but you." He shoved his ring in front of her. "This meant something to me. It will *always* mean something to me." He turned away, his shoulders tense enough to break concrete. "Why? Have you and Ben?"

"No." She shook her head, bothered by her relief that Chad hadn't strayed. "We both feel sex is meant for marriage."

No one ever knew that she and Chad had waited until their wedding night to take that final step. Even Katie thought they'd been sleeping together for years. It was easier to pretend than to justify why abstinence mattered so much to her. She'd seen a flood of men come in and out of her mom's life. Had seen how they used her, claiming love, yet walked away the next day. Laila swore no man would ever treat her body with such disrespect.

Chad exhaled like a burden had been shoved off his shoulders. "I'll tell you anything you want to know."

She could barely process the information he'd already given her, let alone more. But this was her chance to have what she'd always craved, from her mom, from her marriage, from her best friend. And she wasn't going to waste this opportunity.

Shifting, Laila found a comfortable position with her back against the wooden post. "Let's start at the beginning."

CHAPTER 22

The first two hours of Wednesday's shift passed by in a blur of laughter, drinks, and clanking glasses. It was a game night, so Joe had brought in Charity to help with the seated customers while Eric stayed behind the bar, washing glasses and doing extra chores for all of them.

Laila had been working nonstop since Saturday's confession from Chad. They'd yelled, cried, and finally, after he'd promised there were no more secrets to tell, she'd stood, walked into the house, and slammed the door behind her. When she reemerged an hour later, his truck and all the yard debris were gone. She hadn't heard from him since.

Pushing thoughts of her ex out of her head, Laila focused on the night ahead of her. Ben would be stopping by, and she desperately needed him. She could feel herself getting restless and agitated with each passing day. He would calm her down, and remind her of why she had to move on.

"Hey, Eric, next time you go to the back, tell Joe we need to order more orange juice." She swished the last of the gallon jug around, then knelt down and placed it back in the mini fridge under the bar. "And find out if he plans to show his face tonight." She smirked, knowing Eric would never address Joe in such a casual way. The man may be fatherly to her, but to everyone else, he was a shrewd business owner.

Grabbing a new tray of dirty glasses, Eric leaned down. "Hey, your guy is here." Her heart froze, as did her hand, now gripping the handle of the fridge. "I'm not gonna judge or anything, but last time he came, Joe was a bear all night. You sure you want me to tell him to come out?"

She pressed her eyes closed. Ben. He was talking about Ben. Not Chad. "No. Just take the glasses."

When she'd found some measure of stability, Laila stood and turned to face the one person who could give her an escape from the madness in her head. Ben, who had already woven his way to the emptier side of the bar, leaned his elbows on the counter, and locked his warm hazel eyes on hers.

"It's not quite as crowded tonight," he said, reaching for her hand as if he needed to touch her. She needed it too. They hadn't seen each other since before Chad's confession, and their telephone conversations had been kept to short, light rundowns of their days.

"No, it's not. You can actually move and see people."

Ben looked good. Still too dressy for the bar in dark jeans and a polo, but she knew he was trying to fit in, and his effort spoke volumes. Maybe they would make it out of this rocky time in one piece.

"Come here." He motioned for her to come around the bar, and she did, though her heart fluttered with each step. Ben pulled her into a tight hug, brushing his hand down her back. "I missed seeing you."

She squeezed him around the waist, pushing aside the last of the doubt from her head. "Long day?"

His hand cupped her cheek. "Not too bad. Definitely better now." He leaned in, surprising her with a kiss that couldn't be labeled as a greeting. It was much more of the end-of-the-night kind, and definitely not one she wanted an audience for.

Stepping back, she tried to hide her discomfort. "Do you want a drink?"

"Sure." Ben's smile indicated that he didn't notice her unease, and he pulled out the bar stool next to him and sat. "So, I decided I was being insecure and rash. If you're still willing to go to the beach with me, we can leave Saturday morning around nine."

Saturday. The beach. Why did those words now bring panic?

She stumbled on her way back around the bar. "Yeah. I just need to make sure Joe didn't put me back on the schedule."

"Great." Her stomach dipped when his smile broadened. "And you were right about the sea turtle center. I showed Caden online, and he's beyond excited." Ben slid his hand across the counter and captured hers, lacing their fingers together. "We both are."

Glancing at their joined fingers, Laila found a way to return his smile. Everyone in the bar was looking—no, gawking was more like it.

Barney raised his hand from the center of the dining room, and for once she was relieved that Charity was too preoccupied to notice.

Laila pulled away. "I have to get some orders."

"Okay. I'll be here."

Confusion lined every step as she filled new glasses for Barney's guests. She'd been Ben's girlfriend for months, yet every eye in the place cast the same accusation she, herself, was starting to feel. Betrayal.

Ben's mere presence felt like cheating. How was that fair?

Exiting the bar on the opposite side from where Ben sat, Laila pushed through the crowd to Barney's table. He'd slid two square ones together, creating a rectangle that could easily seat eight, despite being only his standard group of four at the moment.

"Expecting more people?" she asked casually as she set the four drinks down in front of him. Joe wouldn't like Barney hogging the few seating areas, even with their long-standing friendship.

The grin that cut the man's face was so foreign, even the lines around his mouth seemed surprised. "Yep. We're celebrating tonight. My boy's come home."

"Your boy?" An icy, endless dread swept through her, wiping away everything but the man in front of her.

"You didn't know?" Barney seemed to enjoy every second of her panic, and that weird, joyous smile turned gloating. "Chad's home. He officially starts work at the factory tomorrow."

Her chest tightened. And this was how they celebrated? By getting smashed the night before? "How many do you expect, then?" she asked through gritted teeth. She'd thought Barney was different. He'd been one of the few who'd tried to get Chad to slow down on the drinking. He'd even come to the house a few times to remind him how bad his dad had become. Those were the worst confrontations, but they usually worked.

"'Bout ten. Chad says he's off the liquor, so make sure we have some soda in the mix."

"That's awfully considerate of you." She didn't even bother to hide her sarcasm. Like having a soda in front of him would automatically make the lure of alcohol go away. Barney was as delusional as his nephew.

Laila finished retrieving the empty tray when she felt a hush flow through the room, then a mass of loud voices that pushed past her to the front door. She didn't bother to look. Didn't need to.

Chad always knew how to make an entrance.

✕

The crowd was already by the door when Chad entered, a welcome he could likely thank his uncle for.

They shook his hand, welcomed him home. A few pulled him in for an embrace, some of which lingered too long for his comfort.

"Where have you been?"

"It's about time you came home."

"Have you seen Kevin yet? He's still owes you that hunting trip you never took."

Chad reacted to every person, his face alive with feigned excitement as he answered each one of their questions. They expected him to be boisterous and funny. Expected him to bring an energy he had no handle on anymore. The drinking had always helped, especially on the bad days. The days when his insecurity was louder than any sound around him—*failure, disgrace, coward.*

And now he'd face them all, sober.

Chad swallowed the lump in his throat. He'd done it before. Several times, in fact. But never without Laila by his side, squeezing his hand, encouraging him to be real, and never after two years of silence.

He'd also never gone this long without a drink either. And if he was truly going to fix things with Laila, he'd have to find a way to come to her workplace without falling apart. Besides, hadn't Mark told him that part of recovery was learning to live in a world where alcohol was always present? That saying "no" was a choice he would have to make every day, not just when the temptation was greatest? Well, now was his chance to prove he could do it.

It took several minutes before he saw Barney standing by a table, his arm waving erratically. Chad pushed through the crowd, his reasoning edging out the earlier doubt. His uncle hugged him tight, patting his back and shaking him proudly. The other guys did too. Guys who'd taken him fishing when he was ten and let him hang at the factory when he needed a break from his dad. They were as much his kin as Barney was, and a slow warmth began to build in his chest.

Home. He was really home.

"Gotcha a soda coming, boy," Barney hollered, his big hand still squeezing Chad's shoulder. "Sit down and tell us all what you've been up to." A beat later, he leaned in, spoke soft enough that only the two of them could hear. "Don't worry. Laila's working the bar, so she'll make sure nobody tempts you with anything stronger."

Chad's head snapped up, catching a glimpse of her for the first time since walking in. She moved with fluid efficiency, but her shoulders were tense, her lips drawn into a tight line. He didn't know what he'd say to her, but he had to say something, if only to head off the inevitable tension. They hadn't ended their last conversation on good terms, and he felt pretty certain she was still fuming.

"Excuse me for a sec." Chad eased around his uncle and made his way to the bar.

A large round torso suddenly blocked his path. "Chad Richardson! Where the devil have you been?" Beefy arms came around him and lifted him up off the ground.

Chad coughed and squirmed out of Orlando's tight grip, pain ripping up his side. He'd been healing quickly, but his ribs still hurt. "Here and there," he answered, carefully easing out of the giant's hold.

The guy had been an offensive lineman in high school—all-American with a full ride to Georgia. He came back a year later, got a job at the factory, and declared college a waste of time.

"Katie's back too. You seen her yet? She's all dignified now. Still hot as fire, though."

Chad couldn't help the smile. Orlando had been crushing on his friend for almost a decade now. "Yeah, I've seen her. What about you?"

"I'm officially a married man." He held up his fat left hand and belly laughed. Orlando had easily gained fifty pounds since Chad last saw him, all around the middle. "Two years running. She's a beauty, isn't she?" Fumbling with his phone, Orlando pulled up a picture of his wife, who was far better looking than her husband, to be sure.

"Yes, she is. Congratulations." He slapped his old friend's bicep and inched forward, a polite way of implying he was ready to move on. But the guy remained planted in front of him.

Orlando glanced over his shoulder to the bar. "Listen," he said, his voice barely audible. "You know I'd get your back any day of the week, but let's not start the night out with conflict."

"Conflict?" But even as the words came out, the world dropped out from beneath his feet. Laila stood on the far side of the bar, talking with a guy cut straight out of a Macy's catalogue. He leaned in, his hair so intensely gelled that it didn't move as it brushed up against her cheek. Chad's gaze dipped to their joined fingers on the counter.

"Yeah. Of course." His heart twisted with the words, but he turned until the two of them were no longer visible.

Orlando's shoulder bumped his. "Hey, don't look so freaked out. I saw her face when you walked in. That guy's a distraction. Nothing else. And if he becomes more, well then, you know where to find me." He lifted his chin and forked off to the right, leaving Chad alone and hollow.

Suddenly, all he could see, smell, and taste were the bottles on the table. He wanted to fill the void, block out the pain, and burn away the memory of another man's touch on Laila.

The walls began to move, pressing in, choking him. He eyed the bathroom, but escaping in that direction would put him directly in line with Laila's—his stomach cramped—date. And in this state, Chad couldn't be certain he wouldn't do something stupid.

The swinging kitchen door moved in his peripheral, and every muscle in his body began to unwind. Joe could calm him down. The room became a blur as Chad pushed toward his escape. More people came to speak to him, but he ignored them all with a curt nod. His skin tingled. Someone had spilled a drink on his boots, and the smell was working its way into his nostrils, beckoning him like a drug.

A figure knocked him to the left, just hard enough that he stumbled into a skinny little thing near the table by the back wall. "Sorry" echoed in the air as Chad regained his balance and kept the young girl from toppling over.

Her eyes flashed with shock, then slid into a grateful gleam when she realized he had a firm grasp.

"Sorry. I wasn't paying attention and got sideswiped." He let go of her arm and noticed the apron around her waist. "You work here?"

"Yeah. Joe hired me on a few months ago. And who might you be?" Though she couldn't have been much older than nineteen, her gaze swept over him in such an intimate way that he almost choked. Young or not, she'd long ago stopped being innocent.

He took a small step back. "Chad Richardson. I, um, recently came back into town."

"Yeah, I figured as much. I definitely would have noticed if you'd been here before." She glanced down at her bare legs. "Oh shoot. I got beer on my shorts." Lifting her apron to expose the shortest pair of cutoffs Chad had seen since high school, the girl slowly wiped a napkin across the smooth tan skin by her thigh. She glanced up through her eyelashes and caught him looking, but his awareness only brought a bigger smile.

"So you're a Richardson, huh?" She let the apron drop back into place and somehow managed to move closer to him in the process. Wow, this girl was . . . well, she undoubtedly made good tips. "You related to grumpy old Barney?"

Chad shrugged away his discomfort, happy to have something to focus on other than Laila. "Yeah. He's my uncle."

"So, does irritability run in the family?" Her lacquered fingernails invitingly grazed his forearm. "Or are you friendlier?"

"Charity, you need to serve tables seven and twelve." Laila's tight voice behind his ear made the hair on his neck rise. "They've been sitting there for ten minutes."

The harshness in Laila's tone seemed to have no effect on the girl. She turned slowly, pressing closer to his chest. "Nice to meet you, Chad. My shift ends at midnight." Her hand lightly brushed his thigh as she walked by.

Slightly amused and slightly horrified by Charity's brazen invitation, he spun around to find Laila, her arms crossed, her face cold and angry. She watched Charity like a cat, then turned accusing eyes to him. "What are you doing here?"

There were so many words trying to make their way out of him that he couldn't speak at all. She'd rejected him multiple times. She'd brought a boyfriend here, to Joe's, like their memories were that insignificant. And now she had the audacity to look ready to pounce simply because a girl flirted with him in her presence? No. She didn't get to have it both ways.

"Just because you don't want to see me doesn't mean I have to stay in hiding." Chad put his hands in his pockets, fought for some level of restraint. "Barney got me a job. The least I could do was come here and have a drink with him."

He couldn't help but glance at the guy she'd left by the bar. He was watching, and judging by his scowl, Chad was certain the guy knew exactly who he was.

He stepped closer to Laila. *Time to have a little fun.*

"What's with the mood? Does my being here bother you?" He lightly brushed the stray hair around her temple, a touch so familiar and intimate that Laila's careful composure seemed to slip. He dropped his fingers and smiled when her own ran over the same spot as if to wipe away the sensation.

"Yeah, it bothers me. You're in recovery. You don't need to be around a bunch of drunks." In her frustration, she moved closer to him, and all Chad could picture was pulling her to him and crushing his mouth to hers.

Laila's temper didn't flair often, but when it did, she was like a bright, furious flame of passion. He loved that about her, almost as much as he loved the fact that no one but him seemed to evoke such an extreme reaction.

He leaned in, and the heat from her flushed cheeks all but evaporated his earlier need to escape. Seeing her like this reminded him of exactly why he needed to fight. "You don't have to be jealous. Say the word, and I'm yours." Laila wanted him as much as he wanted her, and every person in that room could feel it. Including her soon-to-be-ex-rebound standing halfway across the bar.

Coming just a hairsbreadth from kissing her cheek, Chad straightened and winked at the guy watching with violence raging in his eyes. "By the way, you might want to check on your guest. Looks like he's ready to blow a gasket." He squeezed her fingers. They were cold and trembling. Exactly how he felt. "Hope you have a nice evening. I'm going to go catch up with Joe."

CHAPTER 23

Sometimes people didn't need to say when their feelings had changed; it was written in their facial expressions, the way they carried their shoulders, the sudden absence of affection.

And Laila knew, within the ten steps it took to return to the bar, that she was losing Ben.

"Can you take a break?" he asked, so calm and distant that she nodded without thought of the bar. She'd tell Charity on the way out and hope they still had cash in the register when she returned.

Ben allowed Laila to take his hand, but his fingers were slack in hers, even as he led her out the front door and into the parking lot. A gaggle of couples hung around two nearby trucks, so Ben continued walking until the lights from the bar were far enough away that half his face was veiled in shadow.

He took her other hand and just stared at her—face to face, breath to breath—without moving. "I can't do it," he finally said.

Tears swarmed her eyes, blurring his face in front of her. All her efforts, all her work to rebuild a future for herself, had been wiped away in one unexpected moment.

"I spent the last year of my marriage fighting off my gut feeling that something was terribly wrong. Courtney assured me everything was fine, and I wanted to believe her, so I pushed down that gnawing sensation time and time again." He paused and squeezed her hands, to comfort her or himself, she wasn't sure. "I was right back then, and, Laila, that feeling has been hounding me for weeks now, and tonight, I finally accepted that I'm right again."

She should have stayed next to Ben. Should have ignored the way Charity's eyes lingered on Chad, the way her mouth smiled wickedly and without imagination.

"But I want to be with *you*." Her voice cracked.

"I absolutely believe that, which is why I'm disappointed more than angry. I have no doubt in my mind that you are fighting every part of yourself to make this work between us. But, Laila, it shouldn't be such a battle."

Feeling her future slipping between her fingers, Laila detangled her hands from his and lifted them to his face. "A few more weeks. That's all we have to wait, then I'll be in Burchwood. We'll be minutes apart."

Fingers encircled her wrists, pulling, adding back the distance she'd tried so hard to close. "Our proximity won't make Chad go away, or the feelings you obviously still have for him." The words were spoken with such finality that a shiver coursed through her limbs.

He had to give her another chance. "Tonight wasn't normal. I was taken off guard. I didn't know he was coming."

"Maybe. But I can't take that risk. If it were just me, I don't know. But I have a son, and above anything else, protecting his little heart comes first." Ben's voice softened and he let go of her wrists. Her arms fell limply at her sides. "Every time we're together, I fall a little harder, but I'm not totally gone yet. If I walk away now, I can still recover."

"Ben." Her voice pleaded as much as her body did to fight through the wall he'd suddenly erected. "I just need a little more time. Can't you give me that?"

As if he were combating his own heart, Ben ran a hand down his face, frustration finally trumping the cool exterior. "Answer me this question, Laila."

She nodded, waiting for him to speak again. Whatever he needed to ask, she'd answer him honestly. He deserved that.

"Do you feel for me even half as much as you did for Chad the day you married him?"

Laila opened her mouth, hoping some fantastic explanation would fall out, but nothing came. She wanted to answer yes—wished she could answer yes. But she couldn't. Not truthfully. She hung her head, unable to admit what Ben already knew. She'd never love anyone the way she had her ex-husband.

Ben sighed, her hesitancy far louder than a no would have been. "The worst part of all of this is that I believe in marriage, in vows spoken and kept. If you were anyone else, I would encourage you to try and reconcile with him." She continued to gnaw on her lip, tears spilling down her cheeks. He lightly wiped one away. "Unfortunately, you're not just anyone, so you'll understand why I may need some distance from you for a while." She watched as his leather shoes moved toward her, then felt hot moisture on her forehead, his kiss light and nonnegotiable. "Good-bye, Laila."

Then he was gone, the echo of his retreating footsteps the only sound she could hear besides the chirping of crickets and the rolling fury that had begun to grow in her gut.

This was all Chad's fault. He'd come to the bar on purpose tonight. He'd known his presence would rattle her. And why not? Ruining her relationship had been his goal from the beginning. From the moment he'd received that stupid phone call from Cooper. It wasn't enough that he'd abandoned her and broken her heart. No, he intended to keep her captive until the day she died.

No!

She wanted to scream it so loud that it could be heard past the flower shop and all the way to city hall. The rage twisted and turned, vengeance spilling through her veins and into her fingertips. Chad's expression filled her mind. That half smile and amused gleam that could needle well below her skin. She whirled around, her steps carrying her across the gravel with a predator's determination. In two heartbeats, she'd be close enough to slap that grin right off his smug, cocky face.

CHAPTER 24

C had shifted in his seat, waiting for his old friend to respond. Joe tapped his steepled fingers together, his elbows resting on an array of paperwork spread across his wide oak desk. Chad had spent the last ten minutes telling him about Atlanta and why he'd been gone for so long.

"So Slim is definitely out of the picture now?" Joe's bushy silver brows lifted with concern.

"Yes."

"And you've told Laila why you left? Why you stayed away so long?"

For once, Chad felt a rush of pride. "Yes, everything. There are no secrets between us anymore."

"Good, I'm glad to hear it. And, Chad, I'm really happy you're clean. It's nice to see you home." Joe placed his palms on the desk and pushed until he stood. Despite his small stature, Joe's presence was formidable. "But, don't mistake my support for absolution. Your addiction hurt a lot of people. Your beautiful wife, especially."

And the pride vanished instantly. "I know."

"She's stronger than most, I'll give you that. But this is it. Your final chance. One screw up," Joe lifted a finger, "and I mean *one*, and I'll throw you out of this town myself. Do you understand?"

"Yes. Believe me. If I fail again, I'll let her go, for good."

The office door crashed open with a reverberating bang. Chad jumped to his feet, his heart a tumbling gallop until his eyes registered the tall blonde in the doorway. She put her hands on the frame, her forearms flexing as if she were holding on for balance. "Joe, I feel pretty certain you don't want me anywhere near your customers right now."

The man looked between Chad and Laila and held up his hands. "Fine. Just please, if you need to break something, take it out on your own glassware. Not mine."

Laila shifted out of the way when Joe slid by but never once took her furious gaze off Chad. Eyes wild, torso taut, Laila had never looked more beautiful.

The mask of civility was finally gone, and there before him stood the woman she used to be, the one who'd starred in every dream he'd had since childhood.

"Are you happy now?" she demanded, slamming the door once Joe was safely through. The black shirt she wore pulled tight against her chest. Her shorts were a decent length, but they still showed a pair of finely shaped tan legs. Ones he'd run his hands over too many times to count.

He forced his attention back to her face, but the glow of fury only made his fingers tingle. "Happy about what?" He squeezed the back edge of the chair, wanting to touch her so bad it hurt. She became a blazing inferno when her temper finally lit. Sometimes he'd push her on purpose, just to see her this way.

"Ben just broke up with me."

Mischief coiled and sprang within him. That had been much too easy. "Did he? I'm sorry."

"You're not sorry." She shook her head, and her wavy strands danced across her cheekbones. "You planned this from the very beginning."

Chad forced himself not to burst into a canary-eating grin. "I don't know why you're so mad at me. All I did was come in here and visit with some old friends. I didn't even talk to the guy." He shouldn't feel so smug, but if Ben wasn't willing to fight for Laila, he didn't deserve her anyway.

"You didn't have to talk to him." She took a step forward, eyeing his not so successful attempt at hiding his satisfaction. "Showing up was enough."

"And why is that, Laila? Maybe because everyone but you can see that we belong together? That we've *always* belonged together."

She backed away, her breath hitching as if he'd lanced her. "I had a chance to be free." Her lips trembled, reducing Chad's earlier glory to bone-chilling agony. "Do you really hate me that much?"

That look. He couldn't stand it. The broken, devastated look of a person who'd just lost her only chance at happiness. She truly believed he could never offer her more than pain.

"You know I don't hate you."

"Then help me understand. Because it feels like the moment I finally built a life outside of you and your addiction, the moment I finally let go of the memories and the dreams and moved on, you're back here again . . . telling me you've changed!" Accusation mixed with her growing volume, and he could feel his own temper sparking. "Forgive me if I don't buy it."

"Moved on?" he hissed. He wanted to grab her and shake all the stupid delusions from her head. "You really think that's what you've done? I've been gone two years, and you're exactly where you were when I left. Working at the bar every night of the week. Planting the same flowers you did every year. You didn't even bother to take my clothes out of your closet. You didn't move on; you simply pretended to." He met her icy stare with his own and welcomed all the fury he'd felt since those divorce papers showed up on his doorstep. "And don't you dare act like I'm the only one who did the hurting. You gave up. You signed your name to a document that ripped apart my soul."

"You left me!"

"And *you* kissed another man!"

The room fell silent, their chests heaving. Chad hadn't noticed how close they'd gotten until now. He swallowed, feeling that familiar sour taste in the back of his throat. "Every time I think of him touching you, I want to kill him."

She must have seen the storms in his eyes, because she inched back. "I will not feel guilty for my relationship with Ben. You and I are divorced."

"Like that matters. You still love me. And if for one second I thought you didn't, I could accept your choice. I could accept that you'd finally realized what I've always known about myself. But you were never with that guy because you cared about him. You did all of this to blot me out, to wipe away my touch, to try and erase me from your memory." He pressed in, his voice low and deliberate. "Sweetheart, if that's not betrayal, I don't know what is."

A sharp sting burst across his cheek, the handprint so scorching, he could practically feel the outline of her fingers.

Tears swam in her eyes while she gasped, "I hate you!"

"Yeah. Well, then I guess I have nothing to lose."

Before she could possibly resist, he had her back against the wall, his hands on either side of her face and his mouth over hers.

The kiss annihilated her. Forbidden, yet at the same time, she'd finally come home.

His lips were hot and demanding, as if daring her to stop the force they'd become. He released her only to whisper, "Can't you feel how right this is?" before trapping her again, one hand in her hair, the other splayed on her back. His touch was soft now, his mouth no longer a weapon but a promise of love that she shouldn't accept. Only . . . she couldn't say no.

He sighed against her lips, welcoming her weakness, pulling her tighter into his embrace. His mouth left hers, trailed kisses down her jaw, to her ear, to her neck.

She trembled with the need to touch him everywhere at once, to feel him touching her everywhere too. She slid a hand under his shirt, the sensations of his skin on her fingertips forbidden and intoxicating. She craved to bask in it, to drown in the luxury of feeling so incredibly alive after so many years of longing.

His lips found hers again, and two years of suppressed passion exploded between them. Her body ached, her heart pounded, and she pulled him closer, inviting him all the way into her soul.

He touched her face with his fingertips, so lightly it left a tingling sensation behind. Forehead pressed to hers, his body relaxed as if it had been locked tight for centuries. "I love you so much."

She gripped his shirt, pressed in, and demanded the earlier frenzy, the one with excitement and danger. She wanted the heat back, not this twisting soul-aching profession.

But he didn't respond, his lips going slack as he gripped her shoulders and pushed. She glanced at his face, confused. His cheeks were flushed, his eyes half-lidded with desire, yet he'd taken another step back.

Her hands felt empty without him, and she wanted to reach for him again, to hold him and remember that wonderful feeling of passion and carelessness. "What's wrong?"

"I said 'I love you.'" When she didn't respond with the same words, his body locked up, his jaw tightened. "I don't want just a moment, Laila."

She was still slightly stunned by his kiss, her head still spinning with how much she wanted to forget all her convictions and jump into his arms. But physically, they'd always connected. It was the tether that had held them steady for seven hard-fought years of marriage. But it was also a smokescreen that had covered all the real reasons why they eventually fell apart.

Unable to give him validation, she fingered the end of her braid. "That's all this is. I don't want things to go back to what they were between us."

He laced his fingers over his head and closed his eyes as if in pain. And it was likely he was, if his body felt anything like hers did in that moment.

She began to take a step forward but stopped herself.

A breath later, he lowered his hands. "Then I guess we have nothing left to talk about."

And for the first time since Chad had come home, he was the one to walk away.

CHAPTER 25

B en asked her not to come to Kids' Bible Club the next day. His text was brief, but not angry. He simply said it was too short of notice to find a teaching replacement for himself, and felt concerned that Caden would pick up on the tension between the two of them. She agreed, of course, and in turn texted Kim so Sierra would understand her absence.

Kim immediately countered with an invitation to the park, and despite the lingering sting of disappointment and rejection, Laila felt grateful she could do at least one unselfish thing.

So now she waited, the metal bench warm against the backs of her legs, and tried not to think of everything that happened the night before.

She missed Ben already. Missed his laughter and the way he made all her troubles seem to disappear. But her heart wasn't broken. She didn't sit and cry over the loss of him. And even more despicable than that? On the very night Ben broke up with her, she'd lain awake in bed while thoughts of her ex-husband crept in and out of her mind. Chad's wounded stare. His tender touch. The heart-wrenching way he'd left the bar without so much as a good-bye.

Ben had done the right thing by walking away from her. He'd saved them both a lot of pain.

Laila squared her shoulders, refusing to let her guilt dampen the time she'd been given with Sierra. Kim's trust in her sparked something inside. Something Laila hadn't felt since her miscarriage. She wanted to be a mother. She wanted a healthy family one day. The dream was no longer attainable for her, at least not any time soon, but she could still help give that to Sierra.

Laila checked the time and Kim's text, just to make sure she was at the right park, and then slid her phone back into her purse.

A car door closed in the distance, then another. Laila glanced across the parking lot and brushed away her sadness. Kim and Sierra walked toward her, each carrying baskets filled with paper and crayons. She met them halfway and offered to take the girl's smaller one. Sierra shyly handed it over.

"Sorry we're a little late. Sierra kept running back into the house for one more thing." Kim beamed with each word like they'd already seen a great victory.

Laila smiled at the little girl, who'd worn her hair down today, although the kinks and bends across the brown strands indicated that she'd just taken it down.

"Sierra wanted you to braid it," Kim offered. She must have noticed Laila staring. "She took them out herself and grabbed a bag of hair ties. You don't mind, do you?"

The little girl watched her with those careful brown eyes.

"No. Not at all." Laila offered Sierra her hand. "In fact, I've been watching some videos online and have some cool new tricks."

They walked side by side to a corner picnic table, arms swinging while Laila described the different shapes and tucks she'd learned. As she explained the third style, Sierra's eyes lit up and she nodded vigorously.

"Okay, then. The Dutch braid it is."

When they reached their destination, Laila set down the pink basket and took a step onto the bench.

A tug on her shirt stopped her ascent. She paused and glanced at Sierra over her shoulder. The kid began shaking her head.

"I'll need you to sit in front of me if you want me to braid your hair," she explained. "If we sit on top of the table, we'll have a lot more room."

Sierra still refused, her big eyes starting to fill.

"Hey, it's no problem." Laila quickly hopped back down, having no idea why Sierra was so against the picnic table. Her gaze swept the area. Most of the playground was either concrete or sand. There were two patches of trees about a hundred yards away by the corner of a soccer field. She pointed to the area. "Will that work? We can sit on the grass maybe?"

Sierra wiped her eyes and took off running for the trees.

Feeling completely unqualified, Laila turned to Kim. "What did I do wrong?"

"Nothing. Nothing at all. She has issues with climbing. Wants both feet firmly planted on the ground. We don't know why, and of course she won't tell us." Kim shrugged. "You pick your battles, and right now it feels like we're winning one, so I say let's just go with it."

Laila retrieved Sierra's abandoned basket, and she and Kim slowly walked toward the little girl. "I'm really not qualified to help her. You understand that, right? I haven't been around many children."

Kim only smiled. "Since Christmas, Sierra has seen a team of counselors with multiple degrees, and the greatest achievement we made was her sitting at the dinner table with us. After a few weeks with you in Kids' Bible Club, she's interacting, drawing pictures, and even gave me hug. All on her own." Kim fluttered her eyelashes, obviously trying to stop the tears. "Whatever it is you don't know . . . well, I say it's working for us."

Laila only sighed. She knew what was working. Her resemblance to Sierra's mother. "Have you considered taking Sierra to visit her mother?" Brianna was in a low-security prison only an hour away.

Color drained from Kim's normally cheery features. "No, and I won't. Not until she at least attempts to apologize for what she did to that little girl. Brianna knows where we are, and I've been told she can write and call. But it's been silence."

"I understand." More than Kim would ever know.

Kim halted their walk. "Listen, I know none of this makes sense, but I've prayed for a miracle every day since that little girl came to our house, and then . . . there you were. I'm not one to question whom God uses, and you shouldn't either."

Laila bit her lip, insecurity raging within her. She was a divorcée, the daughter of an addict, a fatherless bartender. "I just feel very inadequate sometimes."

"Well, honey, if you weren't, then God wouldn't get the glory, now would He?"

"No, I guess not." They continued walking again. "So what should we do today? After the braids, of course." They were close to where Sierra sat, patiently waiting for them to join her.

"Well, Sierra drew you a picture." The smile returned to Kim's face along with a gleam in her eye. "I'm sure she'd love to give it to you."

They stopped next to her.

"Sierra? Do you want to give Ms. Laila your picture now?" Kim offered the basket in her hand, and Sierra jumped to her feet. With careful fingers, she took the largest container, set it on the ground, and sorted through the stack until she pulled a thin, colorful page from its hiding place.

Suddenly bashful, Sierra handed it to Laila but wouldn't look at her.

Laila set down the other basket and held Sierra's gift with both hands. In the corner was a messy handwritten note. For Laila.

The picture was of the two of them in Kids' Bible Club. Sierra drew Laila with a big red smile but didn't put any mouth on her own figure. Just brown circles for her eyes and a nose. Laila tucked it to her heart. "It's beautiful, Sierra. Thank you."

The hour passed quickly between multiple attempts at the perfect braid and reading out loud from a book that Kim had brought. It was one the counselors recommended about a little girl who was adopted by a foreign family. Now they were lying on their stomachs, each drawing a picture in a sketchbook.

Kim sat on a bench several yards from them, having chosen to sneak away once Sierra appeared comfortable. Laila absently drew the playground with colored pencils and snuck a peek at Sierra's newest masterpiece. The little girl was talented. Her proportions were near perfect, and she even added shadowing to different areas.

She'd drawn another picture of the two of them. Only this time, Laila's face was gloomy and sad. She had a deep black frown and droopy eyes.

Laila reached out and lightly touched the braid she'd woven on Sierra's head. The girl remained vigilant in her work, barely reacting to the touch.

"Why did you draw me being sad?" she asked, even though she wouldn't get an answer.

Sierra shrugged and continued coloring.

"You know I'm not sad because of you, right? In fact, this last hour is the happiest I've been all day."

The little girl's fingers paused, and she cocked her head until she made eye contact with Laila. Though young, Sierra was immensely perceptive and didn't like being treated like a little kid. This was an opportunity to earn her trust, and Laila didn't want to waste it.

"I had someone very special in my life who left a long time ago. He made me sad a lot. And today, I was thinking of him again." She leaned up on her elbow, turning onto her side. "But when you came to the park, all my sadness went away." Laila gave her the widest, most genuine smile she had, and to her relief, Sierra grabbed her special colored-pencil eraser and scrubbed at the frown in the picture. A few seconds later, a bright-red smile replaced it.

"What about you, Sierra? Is there someone who makes you so sad?" Laila swallowed the lump in her throat and once again hoped she wasn't messing everything up.

Sierra hesitated, then scrambled to her knees and shuffled through one of the old sketchbooks in the basket. Finding the picture she wanted, Sierra shoved the book into Laila's hands.

The woman was drawn across a couch, her face covered in tears. There were messy scribbles all around, carefully drawn to mimic a horrendous living condition. In the corner was one simple word: MOM.

Laila felt her heart crumble inside her chest. "My mom was like that too," she whispered.

She didn't know if she was breaking a hundred rules, but she couldn't let that little girl sit there without being comforted. Laila spread her arms, an invitation she prayed would be accepted.

It was.

Sierra crawled onto her lap, small and broken, and let Laila hold her while she cried.

By the time Sierra was tucked safely into the back of Kim's car, Laila felt emotionally and physically exhausted.

"I'm going to set up an appointment with her counselor tomorrow. I think we may be on the cusp of a major breakthrough." As usual, Kim looked for the silver lining in every situation, but all Laila could see was the small, wounded girl lying in the backseat with her teddy bear clutched to her chest.

A feeling rose within her, an anger she'd never allowed herself to feel despite all the horror she'd experienced as a child. "I want to go see her mother," she blurted out, not even sure where the idea came from.

Kim's perpetual smile faded. "Why?"

Laila pulled her gaze from the car window and focused on Sierra's grandmother. "Because I need to say things—" She stopped herself, just as confused as Kim seemed to be. Everything was spiraling out of control. Her life, Chad, Ben. The stupid cottage that still wasn't finished. And now all she could feel was this insane, pressing need to scream at a woman she didn't even know.

"Laila, are you okay?" Kim's soft touch felt more electric than soothing. "You've gone extremely pale."

She tried counting, tried all the exercises she'd learned to keep her words hidden, to control the emotion when it got too great, but they all failed her. "I'm fine," she whispered, though she was anything but fine or calm or even rational.

Kim eyed her with concern and then dug around in her purse. "They do visitation on the weekends," she said, handing Laila a square information card. "I've never been, but they told us it would be good to call ahead and let them know you're coming."

"You're okay with me going?" The permission was all she needed to finally get her mind back in order.

The older woman squeezed her hand, crumpling the paper inside it. "If this is what *you* need, then you have my blessing. At first, I thought Sierra was drawn to you because you reminded her of her mom." She shook her head, tears forming in her eyes. "But I think it was more that you reminded Sierra of herself. Maybe somehow she sensed you would understand her. It's a pity our society underestimates children so much, isn't it?" Slowly, Kim let go of her hand and wrapped her in a comforting hug. "Go, Laila. Do what you need to finally release the pain."

CHAPTER 26

The sign for The Point stood like a battered white wall against the graying skyline. Clouds had rolled in overnight, and heavy storms were expected for most of the weekend. The weather seemed fitting for the day Chad had chosen to visit his father.

He pressed a hand to the sign's splintered wood, still remembering the day the city erected the brick-and-wood neighborhood badge. The city manager had put twenty of them up, marking all the subdivisions in his small town. The Point had been the last one to receive such a distinction. Possibly because, at the time, the new sign had been the nicest structure on the dilapidated street.

Fighting against the tug of memories, Chad slipped back into his running vehicle and slammed the door. He'd been in a wretched mood for days now, and coming here hadn't done a thing to ease his growing agitation.

He needed to get this confrontation over with. His father had somehow gotten ahold of his phone number and had been pestering him ever since. In his last text, he'd demanded that Chad come to see him, threatening to show up at the bar and visit with Laila if he didn't. Joe had banned his father from the bar eight years ago, after his unpredictable temper led to six thousand dollars in damages and a weekend in jail. His father knew mentioning Laila's name was all it would take to get Chad here.

He slid Betsy's gear shift into drive and pressed on the gas. He passed Katie's old house first, one of the few nonmanufactured homes on the street. She'd moved to the country the summer before second grade, but by then the bond they all shared surpassed any distance.

Laila's trailer came next, but Chad couldn't make himself look. He'd spent the last seventy-two hours trying to remove her from his mind. Touching her had been a mistake. It'd only made the pain deeper, the ache more pronounced. He had thought getting rid of Ben would bring her back. But now, he knew Ben was only an excuse.

She didn't want to come back.

Pressing his foot harder, Chad managed to lurch forward without the past ripping away at his memories. His dad only wanted to assert his authority, so Chad would play along. Let the man feel powerful for a few minutes and then go back to trying to rebuild his life.

There were two cars in the drive when Chad finally pulled up to the house, if it could still be called a house. The porch hung at an odd angle, and one corner of the home was yellowing, most likely from water damage. The roof had leaked when Chad was a kid, and he doubted his father had ever fixed it.

Lost in a sea of emotion, Chad closed his eyes and walked through the mantras he'd learned from his meetings.

If nothing changes, then nothing changes.

Chad hadn't been back to this house since the day they buried his mom six years ago. She hadn't been sick. Hadn't complained of any aches or pains. She just simply died in her sleep one night. Doctors gave some medical reason, but Chad always knew her death was because life had finally beaten her down.

The air caught in his lungs when he thought of his mother and the frail, wounded woman she'd become. He should have done more to ease her burden. He should have demanded that she leave the monster.

Chad forced himself out of the truck and up the sidewalk. The grass needed cutting, and there were four cracked plastic chairs in a circle by the fire pit. Inside the pit were remnants of burnt logs, and abandoned aluminum cans dotted the grass around it.

The front door was wide open, likely to air out the house that, on a good day, smelled like a brewery. Chad peeked his head inside and knocked.

He was greeted not by his dad, but by a pretty brunette in a pair of dark jeans and a thin, flowy-looking blouse. Two large hoop earrings hung from her ears, and matching hoops dangled from her wrists.

"You must be Chad," the woman said warmly. "It's wonderful to finally meet you."

She appeared to be in her midthirties, but it was hard to judge because she had what he would call "old eyes." Deep, soulful eyes that indicated a person had lived through several lifetimes already. Her poised posture and plastered smile hardly hinted at the hard times she'd likely seen, but the survivor in him immediately felt an odd kinship.

"It's nice to meet you . . ." Chad let the sentence hang on purpose.

"Megan."

"It's nice to meet you, Megan." He offered a hand, which she shook with very little strength. It was more like a touch than an actual handshake.

"Your father is in the living room. He'll be happy you came."

Chad did his best to swallow the sardonic snort that threatened to escape as he followed his father's new girlfriend to the living room.

When they walked in, his dad sat in a leather club chair, balancing a tumbler of brown liquid on his knee.

Cheap whiskey at two in the afternoon. Different year, but the image was exactly the same. Chad tried to ignore the way his skin crawled as he looked at the man who'd wrecked every moment of his childhood. Years had passed since Chad had seen him, but he knew what signs to look for. The deep, etched lines, the broken capillaries, the overly bright sparkle in the same green eyes he'd inherited. Andrew Richardson was exactly as he'd been most of his life. Drunk.

He hadn't aged much despite pushing fifty. Dark brown hair with only a hint of gray at his temples, the same quick smile—used to charm and manipulate. Chad knew his father was still considered a very handsome man. But then again, Lucifer was also known for his beauty.

"Thanks for coming."

"I thought it wasn't optional."

A smile appeared. "It wasn't, but I'd like to think a part of you is glad to see your old man."

He could almost feel the leash tighten around his throat. "I'm not."

Megan stepped forward, her voice calm and eager. "Chad, would you like something to eat or drink? I can make whatever you're in the mood for."

Chad took his eyes off his father to steal a glance at Megan and confirmed his earlier suspicion. His dad had already hurt her. Maybe not physically yet, as she didn't seem to be hiding her arms, but that would come soon enough.

The signs were easy to spot. The way she twitched with fear when his dad shifted in his chair, and rushed to interfere before Chad could set off the man's temper. His mom had been the same way. Always moving, always reacting, always flattering, whatever it took to keep his father calm.

"I'm fine. I don't plan to stay long." As Chad walked to the couch opposite his father and sat, he noticed that the man's knuckles were white. He could tell his father was barely maintaining his composure.

Concerned for Megan, Chad tossed her a look over his shoulder. "Would you mind giving us a minute?" If his dad was going to explode, the least Chad could do was take the brunt of the fury.

Her eyes flashed to his father's, a quick request for permission that made Chad's muscles turn to lead. His dad offered only a quick nod, and dutifully, Megan disappeared.

"She's kinda young for you, don't you think?" Disgust lined every syllable.

"Yeah. That's what I like about her. She's still firm and perky." He lifted his glass and swallowed the rest of its contents in one easy motion. "So, you're back in town, I hear."

"For now." Chad didn't know what his dad wanted, but there was no doubt that an ulterior motive was responsible for this little reunion. "Why did you want to see me?"

"What? A dad can't miss his boy?"

"Yeah, a dad can. You, however, have never been much of a father." He shouldn't poke him this way, but everything about being in this house without his mom made the atmosphere unbearable.

His dad stiffened. "You're trying to test me."

In the past, those blazing eyes and red cheeks would have made him flinch, but not anymore. Once he'd turned seventeen and gained an inch and twenty pounds on his father, Chad realized he no longer had to be afraid of him.

"No. I'm just trying to find out why you blackmailed me into coming here."

His dad lifted his glass, just to realize it was empty. He sprung out of the chair, walked to the drink buffet by the wall, and poured until the tumbler was half full.

"You always did have a problem with respect," he said after drinking it down and pouring more. "This town watches you. And you not coming to see me for so long makes me look bad." Steely eyes met his. "The Richardson name means a lot in this town, and I won't have you disrespecting it."

"Then you're delusional, Dad, because everyone knows you're a slobbering drunk."

He whipped his head to look at him. "Watch your mouth."

Chad felt his own temper start to break. "Fine, then let's get this circus act over with. What do you want from me?"

His dad let out an annoyed grunt. "Word on the street says Barney hired you at the factory."

"So?"

"So vouch for me. He'll listen to you and give me another shot."

The man was certifiably insane. Barney would never hire him again. "Why do you even want a job? Mom's insurance money should be . . ." And then the truth hit him like a fist. "You spent it all? That fast?"

"I told you to watch your mouth!"

"Or what?" Chad taunted, standing himself so his father didn't have the upper hand. "You gonna hit me? Maybe take a breather from hurting your new girlfriend?"

His dad's entire body went taut as he set down his glass on the chipping buffet.

"You don't think I recognize the behavior?" Chad continued to hiss out. "You don't think I see the same soul-piercing agony that Mom buckled under before you killed her?"

His dad stalked toward him, stopping only when they were a mere foot apart. For a second, Chad thought he might strike him, a jab to the jaw or, his favorite, a line drive to the stomach hard enough to knock the wind from him. Even worse, part of him wanted his dad to throw that punch, just so he could strike back. To smash his fist into the man's pathetic face, and show him what it was like to get hit by someone who was supposed to love you.

But his dad didn't lift his hand, and neither did he. The sour scent of booze pelted him with every breath his father took. Suddenly, the realization that he could face this confrontation sober, while his dad couldn't, changed the entire atmosphere.

Chad stepped away, still shaking. "You need help, and I really hope you get it before you hurt that woman any more than you already have."

His dad was the first to break eye contact, and the coward stumbled back to his lifeline, the bottle, and all the promises it never kept. "Get out of my house." But there was no power behind the statement, only the hoarse demand of a man who had nothing.

Chad gladly escaped to the front door, his adrenaline still pumping from his victory, even though basking in it felt all kinds of wrong.

Megan sat on one of the sagging chairs, arms crossed in a hug while her fingers ran a trail up and down her arms. He hesitated, then sat next to her trembling form.

"He's not a good man. He's sick and violent and will somehow convince you that it's all your fault. But it's not. You will never meet his expectations because they are impossible and constantly changing."

She didn't speak but began to rock in her chair.

"I don't know if he's hit you yet, but he will. And I hope you leave before that happens."

"He says he loves me," she finally squeaked out.

"Maybe he does. But not enough to do the right thing. Not enough to let you go until he gets sober and becomes a better man." Frustrated that she was desperate enough to stay with someone so vile, Chad left her sitting there, huddled in her shell.

Only, he *did* understand, more than he wanted to admit. He'd been a train wreck too. For a year for sure, maybe even longer. He may not have hurt Laila physically, but the emotional damage he'd inflicted was equally debilitating.

She'd practically begged him to let her go. To set her free. And all he'd ever done was connive and manipulate until she was trapped back inside his web.

I had a chance to be free of you . . . Do you really hate me that much?

His head fell forward, hitting the steering wheel with an agonizing thud.

He wouldn't be his father. He wouldn't destroy the people he loved.

CHAPTER 27

Laila had never been to a prison before so she didn't have much to compare it to besides TV shows and movies. Kim had told her the facility was one of the smaller ones and minimum security, but still, she had expected high fences with barbwire, clanging metal gates, and strict rules of engagement.

Instead, the atmosphere was fairly relaxed. There was only a small fence surrounding the barracks-like structure, and the guards were all efficient and friendly. They ushered her into a large cafeteria-style room and told her to find a table.

She found a secluded one in the corner and watched the other families. The facility women were in white jumpsuits, and most of them were smiling and interacting with their children. A few played games while others talked. Some kids sat lovingly in women's laps while others, mostly the older ones, looked put out to be there. Laila wondered how Sierra would feel. If she would rush to her mother or hang back and eye her with suspicion. Not that it mattered. Kim had no intention of letting Sierra anywhere near this place, and Laila didn't fault her for it one bit.

The door opened at the far end, and a woman who had to be Sierra's mom stepped through. Angular and bony in her shapeless prison uniform, Brianna walked—no, strutted—closer. Her hair was a light, dull brown and wasn't braided as Laila had anticipated. The strands had been coarsely chopped and now fell just to the collar of her white jumpsuit. Her chin had a large raised scar across it, but the rest of her skin looked surprisingly radiant and soft. Not her eyes, though. Two distrusting slits of brown raked Laila over as the woman sat across from her at the table. Kim had said they looked similar, but Laila didn't see it at all.

"So, they tell me you're a friend of my mother's." Brianna's tone matched her irritated stare, and Laila felt her spine stiffen.

"Actually, I'm a friend of your daughter's."

Brianna hunched closer, her words as sharp as needles. "My daughter, huh? Well, you go tell my mother I'm not signing over my rights. As soon as I'm out of this crap hole, I'm getting Sierra back."

Laila knew the state had already legally placed Sierra with Kim, so Brianna would thankfully have an uphill battle if she ever wanted her daughter back. However, her agitation and passionate delivery made Laila wonder if maybe there was some hope for her yet.

"So you do want to get better?" she asked, genuinely surprised.

"It was a misunderstanding. I didn't do anything they accused me of."

The words were Brianna's, but they could have been Laila's mom's. The denial, the complete lack of responsibility. "You pleaded guilty," she reminded her.

"Only to get the lighter sentence." Brianna shrugged. "What do you know about that anyway? You've only heard one side, and my mom likes to tell everyone I'm a junkie and an unfit mother. Well, I'm not. Sierra was happy with me."

Laila laced her trembling fingers together, not from fear but a vicious rage that grew with every lie from this woman's mouth. "She was? What did you two do together?"

That seemed to hit a nerve, either the question or the sarcastic tone in which Laila delivered it.

"I don't know. Stuff," Brianna said defensively. "What do you do?"

"Well, we draw pictures, braid each other's hair."

"There you go. We did the same things." Brianna flung her hand in the air, and lounged in her chair like she'd won some great battle.

"What changed the night you were arrested?" Laila hated confrontation, yet something inside her refused to let this woman sit smugly by as if she hadn't broken her daughter.

"I told you. I didn't do anything wrong. Sierra was supposed to stay with my friend. She never picked her up."

Laila knew that was a lie. The cops had found Sierra locked in her room. She'd been there three days with only a gallon jug of water and a box of crackers. She'd had to use the corner as a toilet. Laila closed her eyes, nausea rising in her throat, forgetting for a moment why she had even bothered to come here. Then Sierra's heartbroken face popped in her mind. The tears she'd shed all over Laila's shoulder.

"Brianna, you say you love your daughter. A part of me wants to believe that. So, I'm going to tell you what she's gone through since that weekend. Sierra doesn't engage with kids or many adults for that matter. She won't climb anything. She can't be alone in a room without the door open, and even then, she usually ends up on the floor by Kim's bed. But worse than anything, she doesn't speak, not a word."

Brianna's cool exterior slipped enough that Laila thought maybe this visit wouldn't be in vain. "Sierra's always been a quiet girl. She'd sneak in and out of a room like a church mouse."

"Kids tend to do that when they fear what state they may find their parents in."

Whatever softness Brianna had allowed disappeared before Laila finished her sentence. "Why are you here, again? 'Cause I'm getting real tired of this conversation."

Laila suddenly felt speechless. Why *was* she there? Why had she even come, knowing all she did about this woman?

Brianna suddenly laughed, bitter and cunning. "So, you're that type, I see. No wonder Mom took such a liking to you."

Laila swallowed. She didn't like the change in Brianna voice, from defensive to offensive. She began to speak, but Brianna kept going.

"Oh man, what a great replacement daughter you must be for my mom. You're nothing but a beautiful, empty shell who needs everything to be perfect." Her mouth quirked up. "What's the matter, sweetie? Will no one like you if you're not kind and happy all the time?" Brianna changed her voice to sound as pathetic as Laila suddenly felt. "I bet you surround yourself with failures or worse, make them feel like failures, just so your life doesn't seem so pitiful. That is why you came to see me, right? So you can go back home and feel all kinds of satisfaction that you're better than I am?" She pressed in, her voice getting low as if going in for a killing strike. "Well, I hate to shatter your delusions, but you're not Sierra's mother. I am. And no matter how hard you try, she'll never love you like she does me."

Something inside Laila snapped. Maybe it was the scars that had never fully healed from her miscarriage. Or maybe the years of silence she'd suffered through, first with her mom, and then with Katie and Chad. The excuses she made for them, the crippling pain she had let all of them inflict without ever truly demanding more. Or maybe it was just the agonizing truth in Brianna's accusation. She *did* fear their rejection. She *did* wonder whether, if they ever saw her deepest, truest self, they would walk away like her father had.

Brianna sank back in her chair, smug and all too aware that she'd delivered a right hook to Laila's heart. But she wasn't the only one who could read through the guarded stare and biting words. Laila had spent her entire life with a woman just like the one in front of her.

"You're right," Laila said with alarming self-awareness. "I do care what people think of me. I always have. And I do want those I love to be happy, often at my own expense. But my life is not pitiful. I'm not locked in a cell because I couldn't stop getting high long enough to take care of my own flesh and blood." Laila reached in her bag for the picture Sierra had drawn of her mom sprawled across the couch. The one that reflected every horrific moment of Laila's childhood. "And one day when my daughter draws my picture, it won't look like this." She slammed the colored page on the table and shoved it in Brianna direction.

The woman's stony face faltered when she saw the image Sierra had recreated with startling accuracy. The image of addiction and neglect and heartbreak.

"You're right, Sierra still loves you. She probably always will. And she will probably always hope and pray that you will one day be strong enough to love her more than yourself." Twenty-seven years old and Laila still waited for that day with her mom. "Brianna, I didn't come here to judge you or make myself feel better. I came because I held your little girl while she cried for the woman you once were to her. The woman I really hope you can one day be again." With more confidence than she'd ever felt in her life, Laila rose to her feet. "Don't let your time in here go to waste. You can change that image."

And with that last piece of truth, Laila walked away.

She was still shaking when she reached her car, the adrenaline crash leaving her stomach in a torrential whirlpool. She gripped the steering wheel and closed her eyes, the words she and Brianna had spoken to each other still replaying over and over in her mind.

Beautiful, empty shell.

Had she become that? Had she really lost any sense of who she was or what she wanted? Deep down, did she believe people would reject her if she ever dared to really verbalize her needs?

Heaven forbid that the world doesn't think you're perfect, her mom had said.

Katie had warned her, *There is no perfect life, Laila.*

Even Ben had seen what she refused to acknowledge. *I feel like I'm chasing a moving vehicle half the time.*

And then there was Chad. *The problem was I couldn't have hated myself more.*

All this time, she'd blamed him for his weakness. For not having the strength to walk away from the world they'd both grown up in. But was she any different? When they lost their child, when Katie walked away, when the bills and the hurt spiraled out of control, they both coped the only way they knew how.

He used substances. She used silence.

Was that what Kim meant when she said Laila was like Sierra?

Fumbling with the phone, Laila dismissed the two unheard voicemails and called the one person who would understand.

"Laila, hi!" Kim answered, surprise and affection in her voice. "How are you?"

"I'm okay." She swallowed, fighting back the tears she didn't want to shed. "I just left Brianna."

"How did it go?" Kim asked, slowly processing the information. She'd known Laila planned to visit, but had likely hoped she would change her mind.

"Exactly how you thought it would go, but I gave her Sierra's picture, and I saw a crack. I don't know. Maybe it will have an impact."

Kim's sigh was loud through the phone. "Maybe. Thanks for telling me."

"Kim?"

"Yeah."

"What did you mean when we were at the park? How Sierra connects to me because I remind her of herself?"

Kim paused as if searching for the right explanation. "Well, I suppose it's that guard you put up. You're personable and kind, but still very distant, and the minute that wall starts to falter, like at the park, you seem to panic. Sierra chooses to withhold her voice. I don't know, I guess it feels like you withhold part of yourself too." The line went silent, but Laila couldn't find the courage to fill the void. Kim's words had been too real, too insightful, and ones no one had ever cared enough to say to her.

"Honey, I didn't mean to upset you," Kim continued, her voice now ripe with concern.

Laila forced her heart to settle. "No. You're right. Everything you just said is true."

"You'll find a way to heal, Laila. I know you will. I've seen it already."

The strange thing was, she was starting to believe she might. Maybe part of her already had. "Kim, this may not mean much, but I want you to know, if Sierra is like me, then I think you're doing the right thing with her. You're loving her every day, and showing her every day that she can trust again." Laila couldn't stop the tears this time, especially when she heard Kim's own sobs. "And as soon as Sierra knows you won't reject her or abandon her like her mom did, and knows it's okay to be flawed and still be loved, then she'll open herself up to you. So don't give up. Even on the bad days."

Kim tried several times to speak, but her voice was broken up by her emotion. Finally, she calmed. "Thank you, Laila. I needed that today. I just prayed for strength right before you called, and God graciously answered."

They spoke for a few more minutes before saying their good-byes.

Laila stared down at the black screen, knowing she needed to listen to Chad's voicemail. Yet she couldn't seem to make her fingers move. She closed her eyes and found herself whispering her own prayer for strength and wisdom. Something she'd failed to do since Chad had come home.

She'd been fighting all this time to stay in control. But maybe that was the problem. Maybe it was time to give all of herself to a God who had never rejected or abandoned her.

"Lord, please show me what to do . . ."

CHAPTER 28

Chad stared down at the sand beneath him, his phone weighing in his hand like a knife. He'd tried to call her an hour ago, and when she didn't answer, he'd left a voicemail asking her to meet him at the beach. He didn't trust himself to say what needed to be said in their house, with their bed only steps away. He needed to do this, and he needed to do it right.

This spot on the beach had been the first place he'd told Laila he loved her, and today, he would tell her again for the last time.

Closing his eyes, Chad thought of the duffel in the back of the truck, the scribbled note on Cooper's counter letting him know he'd leave Betsy at the bus station.

Waves broke over the shore while misty drizzle pelted against his cheek. It would still be a couple of hours before the heavier rain pushed in, and he had no intention of staying that long.

He checked over his shoulder, scanning the bridge walkway. She could choose not to come, to ignore his offer to discuss what happened at Joe's, but he knew she wouldn't. That wasn't how Laila functioned. She didn't try to hurt people. Just the opposite, she spent her life trying to make peace with the most broken of broken souls. Her mom, Katie, him. It was as if she were a magnet for the undesirables of the world.

A shape appeared at the end of the bridge, coming toward him. He stood, not needing to see her face to know it was her. She had a distinct walk, a sexy sway to her hips that she didn't even recognize. He briefly closed his eyes, already regretting his decision.

When she hit the sand, she removed her flip-flops and navigated the soft, warm beach until they were within speaking distance. Her steps were tentative, her expression solemn, as if she too had lived through a hurricane of emotion today.

"You got my message," he said when she got close enough.

She'd worn her hair back in a clip, pieces falling around her face in unruly chunks. He ached to run his hand through the strands just one last time.

"I'm glad you called," she said, tossing her shoes near his. "Last time we talked, it was . . ."

"Bad. I know. I'm sorry I lost control like that." He shoved his hands into his pockets, not trusting them to stay away from her. "Will you walk with me?" Never did he imagine that he would be the one shoving Laila back into Ben's arms, but he would never, ever, let her end up like his mother. "I promise, I'll behave."

She silently nodded, as if she knew this moment was a turning point for both of them, and followed him down to the shore. White capped waves rippled together as cold, salty water slid over their toes.

"I've thought a lot about what you said at Joe's." He stopped walking. "It's what you've been trying to tell me since I came home, but I guess I thought I could change your mind."

"Honestly, Chad. My head is a little hazy right now. I don't even know what part you're referring to." She turned to face the ocean.

He could see the self-consciousness in the tense line of her shoulders and felt a similar tension in the back of his neck. She seemed lost. Stricken somehow, and it made his stomach clench with knots.

"Laila, are you okay?"

"I went to visit a woman in jail this afternoon," she said absently, still not looking at him. "She nailed me. In less than ten minutes, she ripped apart all my illusions."

He wanted to step forward, embrace her, promise to be the partner she'd never truly had. But instead, his feet stayed planted in the sand, waiting.

Finally, she turned, and everything she felt was evident in her face: urgent hope, desperate fear, and the struggle to contain both. "Chad, did I make you feel like a failure? Is that why you hated yourself so much? Because I made you feel like I couldn't love you if weren't perfect?"

"What? No." He shook his head, taken aback. "You did nothing wrong. It was me. Always me who screwed everything up between us."

"No. It wasn't just you." A shadow seemed to cross her face. "When we lost the baby, I thought it was a punishment."

His heart pounded in his chest, the pain of that time in their life coming back as if they were living it all over again.

"I was scared at first, when I saw those blue lines. I couldn't help but think I'd made a terrible mess of things, all because I'd forgotten to take a few pills. It just didn't feel possible." Tears pooled in her eyes. "We were so young and we had no money."

"Laila, everyone doubts at first. You can't really believe your fear caused the miscarriage to happen."

"Logically, no. But emotionally . . ." She wiped at her cheeks. "Instead of admitting how scared I was for our future, how uncertain I was of being a mother, of caring for a child . . . I just disconnected. And then your mom died, and I knew you were suffering; I knew you were struggling to cope, but still, I couldn't find my way back to you. After you overdosed, I was so angry, but I never told you. I wanted to hate you. When you needed me most, all I could think was that I wanted to hurt you too . . ." Her voice cracked. "I'm so sorry, Chad."

"Hey, it's okay." He pulled her into his arms, cradling her head against his shoulder. "There's nothing to apologize for." She sobbed like he'd heard her do in the bathroom when she thought he wasn't home, but never had she allowed him to comfort her this way. He whispered soft caresses in her ear and ran a hand down her back, until her shoulders stopped heaving and his shirt was drenched where her head had been.

"You don't have to be perfect," she whispered against his shirt. "We both walked into our marriage broken people. I should never have expected a fairy tale or blamed you when I didn't get one."

And with those words, he remembered why he'd called her here. Why, even though this moment felt like a breakthrough, he couldn't deny her the kind of future she could have without him. "You deserve a fairy tale, Laila. You deserve to be happy. You deserve to be with someone you can trust."

Chad released her, slowly. A small patch of light cut through the thick cloud cover, making her skin glow olive and her hair shine like a beacon for the sun. His eyes met hers steadily. "I told you I wouldn't lie to you, so here it goes." He spoke with more certainty than he had since stepping off that bus weeks ago. "I could never live in Fairfield and not be with you. I know this about myself. Just like I know I would do anything to get you to love me again, and that's not fair to you."

He needed her to know he wasn't leaving out of defeat. It was a choice. One made for her.

A larger wave crashed on to the shore, the water rising past their ankles, yet neither of them moved. He looked her in the eyes, saw those shining depths of blue that had loved him for so many years. "I don't want us to be my parents. My mom was trapped. She loved my father too much to leave him. That relationship eventually destroyed her, and I will not do the same to you."

"You're not your father." Her voice was thick with emotion, but her words only heightened his conviction.

"No, I'm not. And I'm not going be either." He studied every feature. The tilt of her nose, the pale eyelashes dotted with moisture from the misty air. The slightly parted lips that somehow stayed a perfect shade of pale pink. Ever so slowly, he reached up, pulled the clip holding her hair back, and tossed it on the beach. Blonde strands tumbled over her shoulders and down to her waist.

"I love you," he said, feeling his chest crush with the statement. "Enough to walk away. I didn't want to hear it before—you asking me to let you go. To let you have a life free from the scars I inflicted. But I hear you now. And I promise I won't mess up your life any more than I already have." He ran his fingers down the soft strands near her cheek. "I called my sponsor, and my room is still open. I'm going back to Atlanta tonight." Chad let his hand fall away and took two steps back. He could leave knowing that, for once, he'd sacrificed the way a husband should. "You should go to Ben. If he has half a brain, he'll take you back in a heartbeat. I won't interfere anymore."

"What?" Her jaw clenched, and her obvious exasperation confused him.

"Your great new life, Laila. I'm giving it back to you. I'm putting you first."

She paused for an agonizingly long time and then stepped forward, her body locked tight enough that he wondered if she might slap him again. "You're not going anywhere, Chad Richardson," she yelled. "This time I get to be the one who decides."

X

Laila could see the bewilderment all over Chad's expression, and honestly, she felt a little shell-shocked herself. She never spoke like this. Never raised her voice or demanded to be heard. But after years of bottling every emotion, she suddenly felt no capacity to pretend.

"I don't want you to leave," she admitted.

He flung his arms out in obvious exasperation. "I kissed you, and you said we can't go back to what we were."

"And I meant it."

"Then what do you want from me?" he pleaded.

Why was it so hard to speak her mind? To admit her needs? Did she even know what they were anymore? "I don't want you to leave, but I also want things to be different between us."

His arms dropped, his hands slapping against his thighs as if he had no more fight in him. "I can't be your friend, if that's what you're asking. I'll never be okay seeing you with someone else."

"I think the other night proved that would never work." She chuckled. "You know, I came very close to a catfight with Charity."

"You're smiling. Why are you smiling?" His brows rose, and he took a step closer. "What are you telling me here?"

She could see the recognition flash. She wasn't pushing him away. She wasn't fighting against the attraction neither of them could deny. And then it finally hit her what had always been missing with the two of them. What she was most sad about losing with Ben.

"I want to date," she said like an epiphany.

He stopped cold. "Date?"

"Yes. I want us to take it slow. Spend time together having fun without so much pressure and expectation." Confidence swelled in her chest. Why hadn't she seen it before? "We never did that stuff, Chad. It was intense, even from the very beginning. All-consuming."

"That's just how it is when you love someone." He took her hand and tugged, but she held strong, not moving until he truly heard what she was saying.

"It doesn't have to be. That's not how Katie is with Asher, and while I never loved Ben, I did see what it was like to be in a healthy relationship." He dropped her hand when she mentioned Ben, but she grabbed it again. "You and I brought so much baggage into our marriage that we've never functioned like a stable couple. I want to try again, but I don't want to go back to the roller coaster."

He continued to stare at her with careful consideration. "But you're willing to try? You're sure? I'd never want you to feel as though I pushed you into this or manipulated you. I have to know that being with me is what *you* want."

"It is." She slid her hands around his neck and played with the hair at the nape. "Even when the pain was beyond what I could stand, and all I wanted was to forget you and move on . . . I never really did."

Chad wrapped his arms tight around her, and tucked his head into the space between her neck and shoulder. She could feel his breath through her shirt, his heart erratically beating against her own. "I won't fail you this time."

His muffled promise came with a soft kiss to her neck. Then his mouth moved higher, behind her ear. She closed her eyes, and seconds later, they were lying on the sand, kissing furiously while thunder clouds rolled across the sky. She felt lost, consumed, as it grew dark around them.

It had been too long since she felt these sensations, too long since she'd been touched. His hand wove its way under her shirt, and her head fell back, her mind clawing to get out from under the fog of so much desire. But she had to be strong. She couldn't let them fall back into old patterns.

"Wait. We can't do this," she choked out.

"It's fine. No one is out here." Chad crawled farther on top of her, his body pressing over hers, so beautifully masculine, so familiar.

Her mind cleared even more. "No, I mean sex. We can't have sex."

He stilled as if she'd splashed cold salt water over him, and eased off of her. "Why not? We're married."

"No, technically, we're not." She had to swallow the amusement that came with the shock on his face as she sat up, attempting to brush the wet sand from her tangled hair. "But that isn't the only reason why I want to wait." She spied her clip a few yards away and hopped to her feet.

"Okay . . ." He continued to sit there like his brain was trying to clear, his gaze following her every move. "Can you give me an idea of how long we're talking here? Weeks? Months?" His eyes widened in horror. "Please don't tell me years."

She seized the clip from the sand and pulled her hair back into a manageable twist, holding in a laugh. "I doubt it will be years."

Chad stared down at his adorned ring finger and then glanced back at her, his eyes sad. "I want you to know that, in my head, you've never stopped being my wife."

She felt a twinge of guilt, not just because agreeing to wait seemed to cause him physical pain, but also because she was asking him to sacrifice for her. But if they stood a chance, he wasn't the only one who had to change. She had to start verbalizing exactly what she needed. And give him the opportunity to meet those needs.

She sat in front of him, legs crossed, and set a hand on his knee. "I understand that this is hard for you. Trust me, a part of me is ticked right now too. But I need this to go slower. I need to feel safe and secure before we add another layer of intimacy into the mix. I need . . ."

"To date," he finished for her.

"Yes. Can you understand that?"

His exhale ended with a resigned chuckle. "Okay, then. Let's date. When is your next night off?"

CHAPTER 29

Dating Laila was a lot easier in theory than it was in reality. Between his new evening shift at the factory and her work schedule, the best they'd been able to do were a few rushed lunches and some stilted conversation while he hung out at Joe's for the last two hours of her shift.

Cooper's mocking commentary didn't help his frustration either. The guy thought the idea of Chad "courting" Laila was absurd. But Chad wasn't interested in his opinion. He wanted his wife back, and besides, it wasn't like Cooper was the king of relationships. Chad had been in town for over a month now, and Cooper spent every weekend solo, either on the couch or at Joe's.

The phone dinged on his bed while Chad pulled his crisp, new shirt over his head. He'd asked Katie for a favor. A big one. And the text that had just come in would tell him if she'd been able to come through.

He lifted the device, half expecting disappointment.

Katie: I found it, but you owe me. Is Cooper there?
Chad: No.
Katie: Okay. I'll swing by and drop it off.

He tossed the phone on the bed and spun in an act of victory. Everything was in place and tonight would be magical. With an extra skip in his step, Chad practically pranced to the bathroom to brush his teeth and spritz Laila's favorite cologne onto his collar. It took three tries to get his tie on correctly, but finally, the knot fell into place, even if it was a little crooked.

A knock came from the front door, and Chad checked the mirror one more time. For once, the man before him didn't make his stomach turn.

He heard the door crack open. "Chad?"

"Coming," he called to Katie, still smiling at his reflection.

With a flick of the light, he strolled down the hallway to meet her, and spun when she whistled at his appearance.

"I'll have you know that I scraped my leg on Laila's decrepit wood siding, and if I get tetanus, I'm suing you," she said.

"I thought you loved the rush of climbing through windows."

"Yeah, my own, when I was thirteen. Not through Laila's with my rear nearly getting stuck because I'm no longer a size zero."

"Please, you were never a size zero."

"Shut up." Laughing, she offered him the white square jewelry box he'd bought when he was only seventeen.

The box was light, almost weightless, but the hope it brought made all these weeks of waiting worth it. It was time to move forward. Time for them to enjoy all the happiness they'd missed out on. He wanted the children they'd dreamed of and the future he'd been stupid enough to forfeit to the drugs.

Chad lifted the lid of the small box; inside lay the simple gold band with three diamond chips in a row. The tiny ring was all he'd been able to afford at the time, and now this delicate piece of history felt priceless. He popped the box closed.

"Thank you for doing this," he said through a choked whisper.

Katie's natural sarcasm faded, and she embraced him. "You're welcome. I hope tonight turns out like you want it to."

He hoped so too. Truthfully, he felt more nervous about tonight than he had the night he proposed.

Katie glanced around Cooper's house and ran a hand down her arm. "Well, I better go. Being in this house sorta makes me want to tear my flesh off."

"Cooper's not the same guy he was back then either." Chad's sudden indignation attested to his torn loyalty. "And if we all stay in this town, you're eventually going to have to speak to one other again."

"Maybe so, but not today." She moved toward the door "Besides, I need to go make dinner for a man I actually *do* like."

Chad followed, grabbing his keys off the counter. "Fine. You can avoid this conversation . . . for now. But not forever." He pushed open the screen for her to walk though.

She passed in front of him, pausing just long enough to tug on his tie. "You know, as much as I enjoyed breaking and entering today, I was a little surprised that Laila wasn't home. Shouldn't she be primping at least half as much as you did?" He could see her point. The last time he'd bothered to put on slacks was when he went to his drug possession arraignment.

"You know her crazy schedule. I was able to finagle a night off, but she still wanted to work happy hour and make sure the bar was covered."

"You're just going to hang out there until she's ready?"

"Sure. No reason to stick around here waiting." He felt a sudden need to justify his actions, although he didn't know why. This had been his and Laila's routine since they were eighteen.

"So you're back to hanging at Joe's?" Katie asked with a little too much judgment. "How often?"

"A few times this week. When Laila works, of course. Or with Cooper."

"Ah." Katie clamped her mouth like she wanted to say more, and despite the irritation it invoked, Chad wanted to know exactly what she meant by that "ah."

He locked the door harder than necessary. "Go ahead and say it."

"Say what?"

"Whatever has your brows pinching together like that." He turned and waited for her interference. Katie always had an opinion when it came to him and Laila.

"Just . . . be careful." She bit her lip, and the slightly insecure motion did more to rattle Chad than her words had. "A new beginning requires you to leave some things behind."

"Like?"

"I don't know." She shrugged. "I know you're different, and I know Laila is too, but everything else around you feels a little too familiar. You need to be aware, on your guard. Old patterns tend to form when you stop paying attention."

"You don't think I'll stay sober." The words came out harsh and bitter.

"I think it will be a lot harder to do in Fairfield than Atlanta." She folded her arms across her chest, her tone just as caustic. "Especially if your life goes back to hanging out with Cooper at Joe's on the weekends."

"If you don't support me, why are you even here? Why did you bother to bring me this?" Grinding his teeth, Chad held up the box clutched in his hand.

"I *do* support you. You know how much I love you and Laila. I want you both to make it. Together. Which is why I won't sit back and pretend I'm not . . . concerned."

"I'm fine."

"Have you even been attending meetings?"

Defensiveness rose up in him. "Yeah, once. But it doesn't matter. I haven't even really been tempted."

"Of course you haven't. Why would you need a drink when everything is going your way with Laila? She's your drug of choice right now. But what happens when the high of getting her back wears off?"

She tried to touch him, but he pushed past her, storming across the driveway toward Betsy. "I can't believe you're doing this when you know what tonight means to me."

"I care less about tonight than I do about tomorrow and the day after." Her voice rose when he opened his door, ready to tune her out. "You won't succeed if you try to do this all alone." He practically threw himself into the seat. "Chad."

Furious, he slammed the door, done with her opinions and her so-called help. Katie had come home a different person, wanted a different life.

But they weren't the same.

He wanted his old life still. His old friends, his old hangout; he wanted to live that same life . . . just better.

Laila wasn't behind the bar when Chad entered Joe's, so he grabbed a stool and tried once again to get his heartbeat under control. Katie was out of line. He'd been to a meeting in Brunswick and had every intention of going back when things slowed down a little. But between the new hours at the factory and spending time with Laila, he just hadn't had the time to get out there again.

But that didn't mean his commitment had slipped. If anything, he was more determined than ever to stay sober. He just had to figure out a way to work the program into his new schedule. And he would. Tomorrow. First thing.

But tonight was about him and Laila, and he wasn't going to let Katie's interference mess with his head any longer.

Finally noticing him, Danielle set down her current busywork and sauntered over. "Chad Richardson. I'm still not used to seeing you back in here." Her short brown hair was fastened into two low pigtails, the bands a mismatching blue and green. "Especially looking so fancy." Danielle had been hired six months before Chad left town. He didn't know her well, but Laila didn't seem to mind her too much.

"It's not every day a man gets to take his girl out." He ran a hand over his blue tie and tried not to pull at the collar. He felt a lot more confident in his jeans and T-shirts, but Laila had spent the last several months being pampered by her high-class boyfriend, and there was no way Chad was going to let any of those memories outshine tonight's. "Speaking of which, is she about ready?"

Danielle dispensed some Coke over ice and slid it in front of him. "I think so. Let me finish up here and I'll tell her you're waiting."

"Okay. Thanks." He lifted the nonalcoholic drink in silent appreciation and tried once again to get Katie out of his head. It *was* different this time. He understood what he had to lose. He understood the finality of this last chance.

The stool beside him wobbled. Chad glanced to his right in time to see a guy he didn't recognize slide the stool far too close for social acceptability and plant himself there. Chad shifted left and began to ease out of his seat when the man pushed his business card across the counter.

Chad didn't have to read for long. The words *special agent* and *Southeastern Regional Drug Enforcement Office* were in sharp black ink. He slowly sat back down, his entire body rigid. The cop worked for the state. He'd have jurisdiction anywhere.

"I believe we have a mutual acquaintance," Agent Edwards whispered, his focus on the drink in his hand. To the casual observer, the man looked like a drop-in traveler. He wore faded jeans and a cotton shirt that wasn't necessarily dressy, but wasn't too casual either. He was the kind of man you barely noticed, but if you did, you forgot all about him a few seconds later.

But the card in Chad's fist was not one he'd ever forget. "I don't know what you're talking about," he said, looking straight ahead and not at the man.

"Oh, come now. You know what I do, and I certainly know who you are and that, for a period of time, you were quite popular at beach parties."

Chad swallowed, fear creeping up his legs and into his midsection, but he didn't say anything. With guys like this, the less said, the better.

The agent took a sip of his drink. "I also know that you've stayed out of trouble since then, so whatever you think I'm here to do, you're mistaken."

"I'll tell you the same thing I told the Brunswick PD years ago when they searched my room. You have the wrong guy." Chad gripped his Coke, concentrating on not exposing his unease. He watched the kitchen door with acute focus, suddenly hoping Laila would take a very long time getting ready.

"Which is exactly why I'm here. We want the right guy. The one who's hurt you and many other people. And with your help, we might finally be able to nail Slim for more than a few insignificant misdemeanors."

Chad nearly choked on his drink. Now he did rise, needing to put as much space as he could between the eager cop and himself.

"You may not want to accept this, but Slim will eventually pull you back into his circle. We've watched him follow you." The cop paused, waiting on him to react. When he didn't, Edwards pressed in closer. "His fixation on you makes him vulnerable."

Chad dared to meet the man's eyes, and a fraction of understanding passed between them. The cops wanted him to become a narc. Wanted him to sacrifice everything he'd just finally gotten back, and for what? Slim wasn't going down. The man had at least two cops in Fairfield, and even more in the surrounding counties whom he paid off on a regular basis. Plus, he'd just told Chad the Brunswick PD were in his pocket as well.

"Like I said, you have the wrong guy." Chad set his drink down and pushed away from the bar. "Enjoy your drink."

CHAPTER 30

Laila finished unloading the boxes, the drink storage now ready for the weekend. She resented how much Joe relied on her, yet at the same time, here she was, coming in to check on everyone, even when she'd been given the night off. What that meant on a deeper level, she had no ability to process, at this point.

"I have the mixes ready and the bar is fully stocked," Laila told Eric when he came through the back door. "I called in Charity, but she won't be here for another hour, so you'll need to make sure Danielle has some backup behind the counter."

"You got it." Eric tossed his keys into one of the square cubbies by the sink and smiled at her. He was barely eighteen and a senior in high school, but Eric had been one of their most reliable hires this past year. "So, I heard you have hot date tonight."

"How did you . . ."

He laughed like she was delusional. "It's Fairfield. That's all Charity and Danielle gabbed about last night. I thought my ears would burn off."

Laila stared down at her smudged black T-shirt and suddenly felt the need for a shower. She'd brought a new T-shirt and a toiletry bag, but nothing that warranted a date the entire town seemed to know about.

Heading toward the door, Eric wrapped a half apron around his waist. "Oh, hey, did you happen to finish next week's schedule?"

"Yeah. I gave you the days you asked for."

The young man's eyes brightened. "Great. Wish me luck, then. I may have a hot date myself." And with that he bumped the kitchen door with his backside and disappeared.

Rushing into the back bathroom, Laila tried her best to make herself presentable. New shirt, a quick freshen up, some perfume, mascara, and lip gloss. But in the mirror was the same girl who'd stared into it for nearly ten years.

Why did she do this to herself? She didn't want Chad picking her up here. She wanted the night to feel special.

And yet, for the fiftieth time today, she thought of the call she'd received this morning. The cottage bathroom was almost finished, and Ms. Harrington had given her a firm date for move in. She'd also said that she understood if Laila had changed her mind after waiting so long, and that she could return the deposit if she no longer needed the cottage.

Laila hadn't called her back. She'd come here instead. To think or to hide, she wasn't sure.

A knock on the door made her jump.

"Chad's here. And, man oh man, are you a lucky girl." Danielle's laugh filtered under the door, and Laila did her best to calm the flood of butterflies in her stomach.

She'd told Chad not to leave Fairfield. Had practically begged him to stay and let them try again. And at the time, she'd meant it with every part of her soul. And yet, she hadn't considered one day beyond that desperate moment when she was full of self-awareness and her own hollowing regret. She hadn't allowed herself to picture what a new future with Chad would look like. Or if it would be new at all.

Zipping up her green makeup pouch, Laila took one last deep breath and pulled open the door. Tonight was just one evening together, a date. She'd been on several of them with Ben, so there was no reason to feel so incredibly nervous.

But her anxiety only increased as she trekked to the main room. What if the connection she'd felt was just wanting what she couldn't have? Or worse, what if everything remained exactly the same, as if the last two years apart hadn't changed either of them? She'd worked herself up into such a state that, by the time she pushed though the swinging doors, Laila could feel her entire body trembling.

Chad's back was thankfully to her when she emerged. He stood with his hands in his pockets, watching the game on the screen nearest to him. He'd worn dress pants and a long-sleeved, very stiff-looking shirt.

He turned when the door made a swooshing sound behind her, and all her nerves dissipated.

"You wore a tie?" she asked incredulously. For a second, she pictured Ben, with his starched shirts and leather loafers. She'd liked the look then, but Ben wore it with ease. Chad wasn't that guy.

"Hello to you too." His grin widened as he took two easy steps in her direction.

She stared as his clothes, ones she'd never seen him in, and then looked down at her faded blue jeans. "I guess I'm grossly underdressed."

"You're beautiful, as always." He slid his hand in hers, and she noticed his muscles were tense, his jaw tight enough that she was surprised he could even speak. Maybe he felt the same fear she did. The same pressure that tonight had to be monumental.

"Besides," he said, "if you'd dressed up, then you'd have killed my first surprise."

"Surprise?"

"Yes. Tonight will be full of them." He smiled and subtly tried to relax his shoulders, but all of his movements were forced.

A scraping sound came from the bar, and her eyes flickered to the man now rising from his seat. She recognized him. He'd been in here the last two weeks, every night she had worked. He caught her watching and dipped his chin right as Chad's torso blocked her view. He obviously wanted her full attention.

"Sorry. It's a habit to check on the customers."

"Then let's get out of here," he said, his voice even tighter than before. "It's time for your fairy tale to begin."

"My fairy tale?"

"Yes." He wrapped an arm around her and led her through the door, his body relaxing immediately when he took his first gulp of fresh air. "There is not much I do well, but knowing how to charm the people in this town is one of them." He stopped and pulled her to him, a hint of insecurity sneaking through his otherwise steady bravado. "I promise I won't always have so little to offer you."

Chad had always been a hopeless romantic. "The king of grand gestures," Katie used to call him, mostly with affection, but sometimes annoyance, when he'd disrupt their plans. Though they'd never gone to fancy restaurants or taken long, luxurious vacations, Laila never remembered missing any of it.

"You . . . like this." She didn't call out his sobriety, but they both knew what she meant. "It's all I've ever wanted or needed."

He leaned in then, kissed her boldly in front of Joe's, in the center of downtown, without apology. A few whistles came from those in the parking lot, but it only made her laugh.

"Come on," he said, returning her smile. "Our first stop is at Vintage Boutique."

"Chad, it's seven. Carol closes up at five." Vintage Boutique was one of the first major retailers in Fairfield and ran not only as a consignment store, but also as a nationally known vintage outlet for just about any decade.

"Not for us." Chad was half running with excitement as they crossed the street and passed Lucy's. Though the sign on the boutique's door clearly said CLOSED, Chad pushed it open, an obnoxious bell clanging against the glass.

"Carol, we're here," he called into the dim store.

Five years of heavy burden shed away as joy bubbled inside her chest. She'd missed this version of him. The spontaneity, the thrill of the unknown. "What are you up to?"

He winked. "You'll see."

Carol came around the corner with a huge grin on her face. She was a large woman and very proud of her Czechoslovakian heritage that attributed to her broad, six-foot frame. She wore a multicolored dress that draped to the floor, with hundreds of thin gold bands climbing up each arm. "My darling," she crooned with a voice that belonged in 1950s Hollywood. "You're ten minutes late."

Chad was quickly forgiven when he embraced Carol, kissing each of her pudgy cheeks. "My apologies, but I had to wait for the perfect girl."

Laila forced herself not to cringe and made a mental note to talk to him about the term later. She didn't want him to pretend everything was perfect this time. She wanted honesty. "Sorry," she called sweetly to the woman she'd know most of her life. "I had to work."

"Is Joe being obstinate again? That old cat. Don't you worry, I'll get on him about it. Now, come on." She waved Laila to the back. "I have your dress right here."

"My dress?"

Chad beamed, whatever tension he had earlier now completely absent. "You can't be Cinderella without a dress." He pushed her toward the dressing room, not bothering to entertain her protests.

When the door shut behind her, she just stared at the ice-blue silk masterpiece in front of her, the color an exact match to his tie. This evening had definitely been thoughtfully planned.

Laila fingered the delicate material. The dress was cut in a flapper style, but without all the fabric layering. It was simply two sheets of thin silk with a liner underneath. She changed quickly, the cool material dancing across her skin as it fell over her hips and down to her knees. On the bench sat a new pair of sandals, the straps matching the dress as if they'd been made at the same time.

Tugging at the bands in her hair, Laila released the braid and flipped her head over until a thick mane of waves encircled her face.

Her cheeks flared when she saw the final image, the dress shaping her body as if she'd been its designer's muse.

This certainly wasn't her grandmother's Cinderella. Not even close.

Shyly, she stepped from the dressing room, and Chad's silent stare was equally matched by Carol's booming approval. Laila twisted a stray piece of hair around her finger and waited for him to say something. "Well, what do you think?"

"Laila." He said her name like a caress, slipping a hand around her waist. He pressed his forehead to hers. *"You have been the last dream of my soul."*

The quote was from *A Tale of Two Cities,* and he'd said the same words at their wedding.

She closed her eyes, filled with the memories of falling in love with him so many years ago.

"Oh, you guys are going to make an old woman cry," Carol said, her voice notably choked up.

Chad slowly released his hold on her. "Are you ready for surprise number two?"

"Sure." Twenty-two years, she'd known this man, yet her knees suddenly felt boneless. After they'd each thanked Carol profusely, then been squeezed beyond comfort by her, Chad took Laila's hand, and they walked the sidewalk along Main Street once again.

They came to a stop in front of Lucy's, and he paused by the door. "I wanted us to have a little privacy tonight. I hope you don't mind."

"Not at all, but . . ." She glanced through the door at the crowded dining room. "I don't think we're going to find much alone time in there."

"I know." He kissed the tip of her nose, quick and sweet, and she couldn't help the schoolgirl giggle that followed. "Wait here. I'll be just two seconds."

He quickly pulled the door and disappeared behind it, leaving her to happily ponder what more the night could bring.

CHAPTER 31

The drive to The Point was a short one, but each mile felt more and more terrifying.

Chad thought he could push Agent Edwards's offer out of his mind, that he could go on with the date like nothing had happened to shake up his world. But every time Laila smiled or laughed or did anything that reminded him of old times, the burden of his secret came pressing down on him.

He'd give her the world if he could, but she'd only asked for one thing.

Honesty.

Sighing, Chad slid his hand into hers as he took the last curve into their old neighborhood.

"Are you taking me where I think you're taking me?" Laila asked, sitting erect in the passenger seat, clearly aware of the street he'd turn down. "I can't climb a tree in this dress, Chad."

"Don't worry, I brought you something to put over it." He eased his truck beside the culvert rail and parked, turning his lights off, but not the truck. He twisted in his seat to face her. "Before we go, though, I need to tell you something."

The tree house had been their sanctuary, a place of memories and new beginnings. He wouldn't tarnish it with Slim's name.

"Okay." She squeezed his hand tight as if preparing for the worst.

"That guy you saw at the bar. His name is Agent Edwards. He's a state drug enforcement officer." Chad ran his free hand through his hair, realizing too late that he'd messed up his sad attempt at styling it. "I hate that this conversation might spoil the mood, but I don't want anything but the truth between us."

"Are you in trouble?"

"No. I don't think so. Although he did seem to know a lot about my past." Chad rolled his shoulders, trying to force the tension to ease. "He wants me to help him nail Slim."

"Oh." Laila pulled her hand away, and he had to force himself not to grab it again. Touching her was the only thing keeping him sane right now. "What did you say?"

"I said no, of course." How could she even ask him that question? "I just got free of that guy."

"But maybe you should consider it. Slim's a bad person. He's ruined life after life. If you could help take him down, maybe everything we've gone through will mean something."

"It already means something. I'm here. You're here. We have a new beginning just waiting for us. I'm not going to jeopardize it to lock up a man who's spent the past twenty years mastering how to avoid getting caught."

"But if—"

"No. I'm not doing it. That isn't why I told you. You wanted me to be honest, to not keep any secrets from you. So, that's what I did. No more needs to come of this." He reached out and ran his hand over her beautiful blonde hair. "Now, let's go have our picnic."

She covered his hand with hers and pulled it from her hair and into her lap. "I was also contacted by someone today." When his entire body went rigid, Laila quickly added, "Oh, no. Not a cop or anything. Ms. Harrington called. My cottage is almost ready."

Though the clarification should have relaxed him, the idea of Laila moving felt just as terrifying. "What did you tell her?"

"Nothing yet. I need more time to think."

"Yeah, okay." He gripped the steering wheel and tried not to let the statement worry him.

She glanced at him. "Now I'm the one spoiling the mood."

He should say something, he knew he should, but he also didn't trust himself not to pressure her into staying in their old house. Then again, if tonight went as planned, it wouldn't matter where she lived, because he'd be right there with her.

"You know what? Let's just table this for now and go eat. I'm starving." Not exactly true—he'd lost his appetite back in the bar—but he also knew he needed to get out of the truck before he locked her in his arms and begged her not to leave him.

With a push to the squeaking door, Chad slid out of the vehicle. He'd tucked the food basket and a coat for Laila in the back, and after retrieving both, walked down to the path where she stood waiting for him.

"Since you left, I've only been inside the tree house once," she said absently, her gaze locked on the forest ahead of them.

The sun had begun its descent, and pink streaks danced along the tips of the branches.

"I'd never want to come here without you." He squeezed the basket handle and felt the same wave of nervousness he had as a kid when he brought her here for their first kiss.

"This place does have a way of dredging up the past."

"Not all of our past was bad, Laila."

She nodded. "I know. On those rare days when I didn't hate you or miss you so much it made me furious, I would park here and remember, but until six months ago, I never made it past the first tree line. Then Katie told me she was getting married."

Chad could hear the ache in her voice, and felt an identical one start in his chest. "That night," she continued. "I made it to the ladder, though I didn't climb. I simply sat on the ground, my back against the bark, and prayed. It was a strange feeling, talking to this force I couldn't see." She smiled then, sweet and content. "A lot like confessing to the wind."

"What did you pray for?" Chad remembered Mark's prayers for him. The way his sponsor dug deep into his soul and asked for peace and second chances. Chad had never tried himself. He just hadn't really seen much proof that a God existed beyond the wishes of messed-up people.

"I prayed for me." She turned, and there were teardrops on her eyelashes. "I wanted what Katie had found. I prayed that if He did nothing else in my life, if I were destined to live here, a divorcée with an addict of a mother, in a dead-end job with no real hope for more, then at least give me this one gift. Peace." She looked at the ground. "I met Ben two weeks later."

He winced, that name like a knife in his ribcage, and fought every instinct to pull her to him, kiss every inch of her body until Ben's name was a void in her memory. Instead, he squeezed his fist around the coat he held and continued to listen.

"I realize now that God's answer wasn't what I thought. Ben was never in my life to be my future. I truly think he was there to bring me to Sierra. The peace I needed was never about him, or even you. It was about allowing myself to have a voice when my entire childhood was spent stifling it."

She fiddled with her hair, tugging and twisting it so much he wanted to rip her hand away. "Whatever comes of this night, you need to know something. I'm not the same girl you married. I'm not the same girl you left. I won't swallow my voice anymore out of fear you won't love me if I do."

Chad set the basket down on the leaf-riddled grass and tossed her coat over the top of it. He felt explosive. His skin tingled, while he fought the overwhelming instinct to demand she give him more credit. He stood in front of her and cupped her face, not tightly, but firmly enough to ensure that she saw and felt his conviction. "I will always love you. Always."

Leaning down, he captured her mouth in his. He should have kept it light and sweet, but he couldn't fight the frustration he suddenly felt. He wasn't her mother. Hadn't he proven that to her? He pulled away, staring into her beautiful blue eyes. "There is nothing you can say or do that will change my feelings. Yell, scream, fight back. I want it all."

Her gaze blazed into his. "It means we're going to argue more."

"You're never more sexy than when you challenge me."

Her eyes narrowed. "You sure about that?"

"Yes."

"Fine, then. I hate you in a tie. You look like a stuffy accountant," she said.

"I'll burn it tonight."

"I don't want you to call me 'perfect' anymore." Her voice cracked. "It's too much pressure."

"Never again." He didn't budge, not his hands or his stare.

"I don't want you coming to Joe's when I work. It's not a healthy environment for you."

He paused on that one, but knew at the same time she was right. "Okay. But you have to cut your hours, because I won't go days without seeing you."

She startled, then slowly began to smile. "That feels fair."

As if the electricity found its way back into nature around them, Chad released his grip on her and felt his pulse settle. "At this rate, it's going to be midnight before we ever eat dinner. You must be ready to pass out."

"Oh, don't worry about me. I ate at Joe's a couple of hours ago." The minute the words came out, she pressed her lips together, her hand flying to her runaway mouth.

"Are you serious?" he asked, feeling genuinely insulted. "Did you really have that little faith in my dating ability?"

"I'm sorry. But the last time you promised me a 'fabulous' meal, you decided you were Bobby Flay and made the nastiest thing I've ever put in my stomach."

His jaw slacked. "You said you loved it. You bought me a new frying pan the next day."

"That's because our old one was so crusted with black gunk that I tossed it in the trash can."

He didn't know when it happened, but they were suddenly laughing. Hers, a raspy giggle; his, a deep howl so unfamiliar it seemed rusty. Chad hadn't realized how much he missed that sound. Not just of her laugh, but of his own.

She sauntered toward him, eyes determined, as her hands found the knot of his blue tie. In a quick tug, she unraveled the material and tossed it to the ground. Sure fingers unhooked the top two buttons of his shirt, and he swallowed, forcing his mind away from the images of the two of them on their wedding night, when everything had been new and achingly slow.

"That's better," she said, her own desire reflecting in her eyes. "Now we can go finish our date." Laila picked the long trench coat off the ground and wandered into the trees, leaving Chad, as usual, completely at her mercy.

CHAPTER 32

Laila stared up at the wood slats, the coat Chad had brought tightly wrapped around her and tied with a belt. It would protect the delicate material as she climbed, but there seemed to be no shield for her racing heart.

"Do you need some help?" he asked from behind her.

"No." Heaving a breath, she pulled with her arms and lifted her foot until it securely landed on the bottom rung. She continued, one foot after another until she was easily six feet off the ground, her dress and jacket swishing around her knees.

"No peeking," she called to the man below her.

He covered his eyes with his hand. "Of course not. I'm a gentleman tonight."

But when she looked down, she could see his fingers slowly separating. "Chad," she scolded, and he quickly closed them again.

"Sorry. Old habits."

Laila chuckled to herself as a rush of warmth spread through her. She had to give him credit; he really was trying so hard.

A few steps more, and she was at the opening of the tree house. Shadows lingered in the corners, but enough light was left in the sky for her to make out a blanket, several candles, and what looked like two champagne glasses.

She carefully crawled through, using the coat to safeguard not only her dress, but her legs as well, and found a comfortable seat on the quilt. While she waited for Chad to join her, she unbuttoned the long trench and shook it off her shoulders.

Grunting enough to be comical, Chad stuffed his body through the opening and crouch-walked to the spot opposite her. "That was much easier at thirteen."

"At least you're wearing pants," she reminded him with a hint of scolding in her voice as she motioned to her dress.

He winked. "I said it was easier. Not more fun." Chad pulled the basket toward himself and spent the next several minutes intently focused on creating a masterful display on the picnic blanket. Lucy had gone all out, placing all the containers in insulted carriers so the food stayed piping hot.

Laila inhaled the tart aroma of marinara and garlic. Cannelloni. Her favorite, along with a crispy loaf of French bread, a plate of brownies, and a large Caesar salad, though the dressing had been replaced with vinaigrette because she hated creamy sauces. It was a spread no one but Chad could have ordered. Because he knew her, and though many things had changed, some things were still beautifully the same. He'd been right. Not all of their past was bad.

He reached to the corner and tugged a small ice chest along the ground. Once open, he pulled out a bottle of sparkling grape juice and twisted off the top. They'd toasted with that drink before. Every time he was sober, actually.

Fear crept over her. Was she just setting herself up for a harder fall? Was this moment and all the ones to come just more memories that would torment her when Chad fell off the wagon again?

The liquid filled the glasses, and she watched with a mesmerized stare. Two years gone, and it had only taken Chad six weeks to get her right back to this place: the setting of their first kiss and the beginning of their tumultuous romance. Maybe she should have played harder to get. Maybe she should have *been* harder to get. Maybe, she shouldn't be here at all.

"You okay?" Chad wasn't pouring the drinks anymore. In fact, the bottle was back in the cooler, and he was holding his glass in the air, waiting for her to respond.

She swallowed the insecurity and reached for her own flute. "Yeah, I'm fine." So much for speaking her mind. Chad wasn't the only one who could fall off the wagon. She'd only lasted, what? A few moments?

"To starting over," he said, waiting for her to clink her glass against his.

"To starting over," she replied absently.

Their glasses chimed together, and Chad's face became a mask of happiness. She loved seeing him this way. Vibrant and content. But those feelings seemed to dissipate the minute life got hard and uncomfortable.

"So, how is the job going?" She cut her pasta and layered her fork with stringy mozzarella.

"Good, so far. It's been mostly training. Barney says when I'm done, I'll have to go on the swing shift for a while. Day shift is given for seniority. But with you working nights anyway, I figure an evening shift might work out nicely."

While she was glad Chad had found a job with people who seemed to support him, she wondered, again, how long it would take for the euphoria to wear off.

When they were younger, he'd wanted to be a fireman. Then he'd changed his mind and decided a career was more about making money, so he had taken business classes at the community college.

"What about school?" Her question was careful. She didn't want to open old wounds, but she also knew that staying in Fairfield, both of them working long, exhausting shifts, was not the future she wanted. They'd get tired and start lashing out at each other. Then, she'd retreat, and he'd start hanging with his friends more and more.

He set his fork down. "Well, right now, I think I just need to settle into a routine. Mark says slow and steady is the way to long-term recovery. Don't do anything extreme or rash. Just take one day, then the next."

Some of her tension uncoiled. That answer was not one the old Chad would have given. "Mark sounds like a great guy."

"Oh, he is. He saved my life." Seriousness leaked into his expression. "Probably saved this moment too." He twisted a napkin around his finger. "When I heard about Ben, I lost my mind. I was ready to storm the gates and reclaim my kingdom."

She smiled at the idea of their small two-bedroom house being a kingdom.

"But Mark calmed me down. He said you wouldn't want that person. He said I needed to show you how I'd changed, not just tell you. It's what I've been trying to do every moment since I got home."

Her stomach fluttered, a welcomed sensation after all the unease. Chad had been different, so it was fully possible her fear could be unfounded. "I've noticed."

"Good." He filled another heaping forkful and stuffed it in his mouth, his eyes closing in pure bliss.

The food was good. Amazing, really, yet she hadn't been able to eat much at all. "I'm still afraid," she finally admitted. "All this. You. It's wonderful. A dream come true. But in the back of my mind, I keep waiting for the guillotine to drop."

Chad's eyes flashed open and seemed to really look at her for the first time. His gaze lingered on her tight mouth, then fell over her fingers as she pushed the food around her plate. His chest seemed to deflate. "I see."

They ate in silence after that, the tension filling the small wooden cubby like a choking smoke. She hadn't meant to upset him, but then again, what else did she expect from those words? A thank you for having so little faith in him?

"I didn't mean to ruin our dinner," she said, quietly making tracks in her red sauce. She forced a smile. "By the way, if I'd known what a great *dater* you were, our teenage years would have been much more expensive for you."

A short laugh came, but it wasn't genuine at all. "Yeah, I guess so."

She leaned across the blanket and squeezed his hand. "What are you thinking about?"

"My third surprise. But I'm wondering if it's not such a good idea now." He ran his thumb over her skin. "I took your trust for granted. I'm sorry for that. Now that it's gone, I realize how much I want it back."

"I want it back too."

He rose to his feet, his body staying hunched over so he wouldn't hit his head. "Come here, I want to show you something." Picking up one of the lit candles, he walked to the corner near their wall where she, Katie, and Chad had etched their names the night Mr. Mortenson had hit her.

When she was next to him, he squatted down and brought the light near the old etching, but her eyes didn't fixate on the names they had whittled out with an old screwdriver. Instead, she ran a finger along the fresh grooves that formed an infinity symbol. In one circle was a *C*, and in the other, an *L*.

Chad set the candle down and sat on the floor, his legs crossed. "Come here." He patted the spot in front, and she matched his posture, their knees close enough to touch. "I was going to do something really stupid tonight." He smiled sheepishly. "I was going to ask you to marry me again."

Her breath caught.

"Don't worry. I'm not going to anymore."

She shouldn't feel so relieved, but she did. They were in no way ready for that step. She watched, her pulse spiking as he pulled her old wedding ring box from his pocket. "How did you . . ."

"Katie. She might have slithered through that testy back window. And she might have rummaged through a few of your drawers. But don't be mad at her. I asked her to do it."

"I'm not mad." And she wasn't. Just really, really confused.

Chad stared at the box in his hand and slowly opened it. The thin gold band caught the light, and a rush of emotion hit her the minute she saw that ring. She hadn't allowed herself to look at it in over a year. Not since the day she took it off.

"I understand you can't wear this on your finger yet. I haven't earned that privilege. But maybe"—he looked up, his eyes hopeful and somewhat terrified—"if I bought you a chain, would you consider wearing it around your neck? As a reminder of what we're fighting for? And maybe even a reminder to keep using that voice you've discovered."

The fact that he'd listened, that he'd chosen to do what she needed and hadn't pushed her for more, made her next words come all too easily. "Yes, Chad. I'll wear it around my neck. And when I'm ready, you'll see it on my finger."

He picked up her empty left hand and ran his thumb along the bare third finger. "That moment will be the happiest of my life."

Laila felt as if she really had spent the night in a fairy tale. After their picnic, they'd lain on a blanket together in the tree house. Chad had read aloud from his favorite Dickens novel, while she listened contently in his arms. Now, he walked her to her front door, his hand tight around hers. The night had grown dark, but it wasn't cold, nor was it windy or hazy or cloudy. It was enchanted, much like the entire evening had been, and somewhere between the truck and her first step onto the porch, she realized the answer she had to give Mrs. Harrington. Maybe she'd always known, but for the first time, she felt no fear in the decision.

Chad slid his hands around her waist when they reached the screen door, a devilish smirk forming on his lips. "They say a man who's interested in a woman will secure a second date before the first one is over. I propose we just keep this one going and worry about the second date tomorrow."

Laila touched his collar affectionately. "Nice try, but I'll be sleeping alone tonight."

"I figured you'd say that. But I still had to ask." He winked.

She let her fingers travel to his neck and leaned up to kiss him softly. His reaction was fierce and immediate, pulling her in tight and turning their good-night kiss into something far deeper.

Sensations rippled through her as the feel of his skin and the taste of his lips fought against all conviction.

"Chad," she mumbled, breaking away before she changed her mind and pulled him inside the house. "I'm going to take the cottage."

He jerked back, his cheeks slightly flushed, and his eyes layered with confusion. "You could have just said good night, if you wanted to stop. Dousing the moment with that declaration wasn't necessary."

"I'm sorry," she laughed, more out of anxiety than humor. She'd never been good at taking risks. Especially when Chad didn't support them. But she had to take this leap. Had to believe in herself enough to step out on her own. If she didn't, they'd be right back where they'd started. "I know the timing was bad. I just wanted you to be the first to know. Especially since you're the one most impacted by my decision."

A sparkle hit his eyes. "Because you're asking me to come with you?"

She had to look away from the hope in his gaze. "No. Not yet. This is something I have to do on my own."

"I know. You need time." He gave her a closed-lipped smile. "So, about that second date. Are you free tomorrow?"

She took his calloused hand and kissed the back of it. "I'd like to take you there, if you want to see it?"

He pulled her back into his arms, hugging her close. She rested her head on his chest while he kissed the top of her head. "I want to be anywhere you are, Laila. If that's Burchwood, then it's my new favorite town."

She grinned against his shirt. "Mine too."

CHAPTER 33

The brunch buffet at Jasper's Diner had become a much bigger deal than Chad remembered. What used to be a few donuts, muffins, and runny eggs was now Belgian waffles, eggs benedict, and hand-sliced ham. One of the many changes that Fairfield had undergone in the two years he'd been absent.

Laila appeared in the doorway, and Chad lifted his hand to wave her over. He could tell she'd woken up not too long ago. Her hair was piled in a mess on her head, and her makeup not much more than a sweep of lip gloss, yet he wondered if he'd ever seen her look more beautiful.

Watching her weave through the tables, he realized he missed mornings with her the most. How they'd lie in bed, cuddling to stay warm, both talking about the plans they had for that day. No matter what arguments had happened the night before, he and Laila always started each day fresh.

"Good morning, beautiful," he said, rising to embrace her. For two weeks now, he'd been free to touch her at will, kiss her in public, and practically shout across town that she was his once again. Well, almost his. The ring still hung from her neck, but he'd waited this long for her; he could wait a few more weeks.

She flung her arms around him and pressed her chest to his, her lips so soft and inviting, Chad felt a rush of warmth spread through his entire body. Despite the bliss of holding her, he eased away. Her growing affection was a positive step forward, but it never fully satisfied, and remaining patient had become another challenge for him, on a long list of many.

He pulled out her chair, and she plopped down with far too much energy for someone who'd been up until three in the morning.

"How was work last night?" he asked, settling back into his own seat. As promised, he'd stayed away from Joe's, even though doing so substantially reduced their time together.

"Exhausting," she sighed. "But, I made almost five hundred dollars in tips."

"Really?"

"Yes. A charter bus came through and stopped for drinks. They stayed two hours. Some rich kid's college graduation present." She rolled her eyes. "Can you even imagine having that much money to burn?"

"No, I can't." He picked up his glass of water and took a sip, his gaze never moving from her animated face. He loved the way her eyes lit up when she felt excited or frustrated. Loved how her cheeks would turn pink at just the slightest hint of embarrassment.

"So, what about you? You do anything after you got off work?"

The question was a simple one, but he still stiffened. Last night had been especially hard. "I drove around for a while," he admitted, leaving out where he'd driven. There was no need to alarm her when nothing had come of it. "It was kind of a rough night."

Her cheeriness fell, and she leaned closer, taking his hand in hers. "What happened?"

Chad rubbed her ring finger and pushed aside the ache that it was still bare. "Turns out, Barney and Cooper had to jump a few extra hoops to get me in."

"How so?"

"They created a position for me. One they didn't even need. My job was being done by a machine before." Chad snorted a laugh, the only reaction he could muster besides utter depression. "So not only is my job repetitive and mundane, but you don't even have to have a brain to do it."

When Barney said Chad would be working with wood versus metal, he had figured it was a gift. He'd loved working at the hardware store in Atlanta. But factory work was far different than he had expected. He stood in the same spot every day, doing the same thing over and over. There was no sense of accomplishment, no end to the continuous flow across the assembly line.

"I'm sure that's not true. Maybe they needed you there. Maybe that machine constantly broke and was Barney's greatest headache."

He smiled at her attempt to cheer him up. She always had more faith in him than anyone else. His biggest cheerleader, the one person who saw all his potential. "According to Mr. Slate"—his boss who was openly contemptuous toward him—"I was given the position so that *when* I screw up—which he says I will—the damage can be minimized. I guess my dad worked for this guy; that's why he hates me so much."

Laila's face flashed a bright red, not the kind he adored. No, it was the other kind that came with tears, rage, and often an outburst of truth. "Well, he's an idiot. Don't listen to a word he says." She bit her lip, gnawing away at the skin. "Maybe you should quit."

"And do what?"

"I don't know. What about fire school? That was your dream for years."

"There's no way the city would hire me." He appreciated how she wanted to protect him, but the truth was, he'd barely graduated from high school, had a misdemeanor on his record, and had a history of addiction. People in Fairfield were happy to see him back, but no one really wanted to deal with him long term.

He squeezed her hand. "Stop worrying. It was just a rough night. Cooper says if I stick things out, I'll eventually get a day shift and maybe even move into the metals side."

Her eyebrows pressed together. "And that will make you happy?"

"*You* make me happy. This other stuff . . ." He shrugged. "It's just stuff."

"Okay." But she still didn't seem convinced.

"Enough about last night. Tell me your plans today. It's our first Saturday off together in weeks."

Her face morphed into an apology. "I have to pack. There's still so much to do."

Despite his initial hesitation, he was happy she'd chosen to take the cottage. When she'd given him the tour, her face had glowed with happiness. The one thing he'd move mountains to give her.

"But I can try to hurry. Maybe we can still do something tonight." She offered a weak smile, the same one that had appeared when he'd hinted that he wanted to move in with her. She'd been kind with her refusal, but it still felt like a punch in the gut. Burchwood was only twenty minutes away, but twenty minutes, when they'd already been given so few, felt like a lot.

He pushed aside the insecurity, refusing to ruin their day with it. "Okay, fine. So we spend the day packing. At least we're doing it together."

"You'll help?"

"Of course. Consider me your indentured servant."

Her face beamed. "Yay! I was so hoping you would say that. Let's go grab our plates, and then we can sort through what all needs to be done. And tell Cooper to clear next weekend too. Mrs. Harrington is giving me the keys on Friday!"

She jumped from her seat, back to the excitable energy she had when she'd first arrived.

Chad pulled her to him, tucked a stray piece of hair behind her ear, and remembered how much he had to lose if he ever screwed up again. The darkness was creeping back in, getting worse every day.

"I'd like to hit a sobriety meeting before I come over, but it shouldn't take too long."

With a tender touch, she grazed his cheek with her fingertips, kissing him softly at the same time. He could see how proud of him that statement made her, but as he'd asked, she didn't linger on his struggle.

"That sounds great. It will give me time to get my honey-do list together."

She spun, and he smacked her rear when she passed, getting an open-mouthed gasp from her in response.

He put up his hands. "Hey, if you get to have some perks to this not-really-married-but-it-feels-like-we-are thing we have going, then so do I."

She shook her head, that gorgeous pink blossoming along her cheekbones, and continued to the buffet line. He followed, relief stretching through his tightened muscles.

They were going to make it through this season. They had to.

※

Chad stared across the group of men and women seated in the small room. Metal folding chairs were placed side by side in rows of seven, and surprisingly, the Saturday afternoon group was larger than at previous meetings he'd been to. He'd received his eleven-month chip only a few seconds ago, and now he'd been given the microphone to share his story.

"I had my first drink at thirteen with my best friend, Katie. We'd snuck up to a tree house in the back of my neighborhood, and Katie surprised me with a six-pack of beer she'd swiped from her dad. Like most of you out there, my old man was an alcoholic, although I'm sure he'd tell you I'm full of crap."

The crowd chuckled, and Chad felt a surge of confidence. "Katie was a wild one. She didn't like rules. And she wasn't the type of person you argued with, so when she offered, I accepted. And even though I hated my father for being such a lousy human being, I still took that drink, because I knew I'd never turn out like him."

Chad paused as he pushed through the first sting of regret. That night had been the first time he'd lied to Laila. With addiction in both their families, she'd made him promise never to try any of it. Luckily, by the time Laila realized what he and Katie were doing, she loved him enough to stay.

"Unfortunately, that night was the first of many, and soon I was drinking regularly and experimenting with drugs. Katie and I started with weed, then moved to Ecstasy when we had some extra money. Finally, our senior year, we switched to blow, and instantly, I knew I'd found my nirvana." He shuffled his feet and squeezed his hands on the sides of the podium.

"By the time I was twenty-one, I drank from the time I woke up 'til the time I went to bed. Despite being married, and my wife working fifty-plus hours a week, I'd still spend our money to buy coke on the weekends. Eventually, she left me, and I knew I had to get my life together. I quit the drinking and the drugs, and she came back. This pattern continued until finally, after my third failed attempt at rehab, she changed the locks on our house, and my fleeing to Atlanta felt like the only option. She divorced me a year later.

"Two months ago, I came back to town—nine months sober—and won my wife back again. Promising myself I'd never, ever fall."

The room was so silent, he could hear the seconds tick from the clock on the far wall. He took two big breaths until his racing heart matched the steady rhythm.

"Two nights ago, I drove by the liquor store for the first time. Last night, I pulled into the parking lot and stared at that brick building for half an hour, warring with myself the entire time. I finally found the strength to drive away, but I'm not so sure I will the next time it happens."

He clutched the chip that felt so undeserved. "I love my wife, but that ache is still there. A void I can't seem to satisfy. I want to find it, end it, control it. I want all the temptation to disappear." Chad eyed the faces in front of him. A few were crying, others nodding in solidarity. Most of them had fallen, like him, many, many times.

"I want to know how it is that I can have my dream but still want the nightmare. I want to know if it will ever be easy."

He stepped off the stage, relieved to have shared his failings, yet still numb from the truth that Katie had been right.

His fight was only just beginning.

CHAPTER 34

Another three days went by without relief from his struggle. Laila was moving this weekend, and despite his heart telling him all would be okay, Chad still had this irrational fear that the minute that house sat empty, his hope would die as well.

She would now live in the same town as her ex-boyfriend. She'd run into him at the grocery store, see him at the coffee shop. They'd sit together, catch up on old times, and then she'd realize she'd made a terrible mistake.

Chad pounded his forehead on the steering wheel, so physically and mentally exhausted that he didn't have the strength to pull out of the factory parking lot. Raindrops sporadically fell against his windshield, barely harder than teardrops, almost as if the sky felt his pain and was crying above him. He should have left town when he was strong, when conviction numbed the pain. Now all he could feel was the hollow ache of his impending failure.

He wasn't the only one to see it either. Cooper had started hovering, asking him every day if he needed a run or wanted to take a fishing trip to the docks. This morning Chad had practically taken Cooper's head off, threatening to move out if his friend continued to act like a pecking hen. Though which was worse, Chad didn't know: Cooper's overzealous mothering or Katie's deafening silence.

They hadn't spoken since she'd given him Laila's ring. It had been his choice at first, ignoring her voicemails, but then she'd stopped calling, and now even her texts had stopped. A sure indication that Katie had tossed him aside. And why not? Everyone else seemed about ready to as well.

A loud rap on his window had him jerking straight up, the face of his worst enemy only a thin piece of glass away.

Chad glanced in his rearview mirror, but that impervious black Jaguar blocked his retreat. Again, he eyed Slim through the water-streaked window, and the man motioned for him to get out with a quick chuck of his chin.

Feeling a rush of anxiety, Chad popped open his door. He didn't have the strength to fight Slim tonight. He was barely winning the battle against himself.

"What do you want?" he asked, holding the edge of the door so it acted as a barrier between them. The light rain had ceased, but a breeze blew across his face, wet with humidity and chilled with the last cold front they'd probably get before summer.

"I was wondering the same thing. Your shift ended thirty minutes ago."

Chad's fingers curled as he waited for him to continue.

Slim's eyes met his, probing and intent. "Don't you usually do your self-reflecting in Joe's parking lot?"

"Why are you following me?" he hissed, hating that Slim had seen him at his weakest. He normally drove to Joe's because it kept him out of the liquor store parking lot. But lately, even that escape hadn't eased the ache. Instead, it seemed to make the situation worse. He'd stare at the door, tormenting himself with the truth: that he was so messed up, his wife didn't trust him to step past the threshold.

"I told you, you're one of my own." Slim tilted his head as if he could read the torrent of emotions in Chad's heart. As if he could sense that tonight was the perfect time to go in for the kill. "And if my guys are in trouble, I want to be there to help them. To offer solutions."

Chad slammed the driver's door shut behind him, his heart all but galloping from his chest. Rage pulsed through his veins, crawling up his arms to his closed fists. "I paid my debt to you. I kept your secrets." A flash of the last few weeks tore through his mind: the frozen metal claws waiting to do his job; the ring locked in the V at Laila's throat; the front door at Joe's, closed to him alone; the flashing neon sign at the Liquor Barn that throbbed as much as his need to drown his pain in the bottle. "Why can't you just leave me alone?"

"Because, Chad . . . I know the depth of who you are." With two long fingers, Slim pulled a pouch from his pocket.

Chad fell immediately still, his eyes transfixed on what had to be at least a quarter ounce of cocaine in his old dealer's hand. "No. Not anymore."

"Do you know why I never bothered Katie after she floated into town all snooty and converted?"

Chad swallowed. If he was expected to answer, he couldn't. Everything from his throat to his stomach felt dry and cracked.

Slim smiled, and there seemed to be a small hint of respect for her in it. "I watched her. Like I watch you." He raised his hands to the sides. "But wouldn't you know, that girl didn't come home the same."

"Neither did I." The words fell out as if he was begging for them to be true.

"Oh yes, you did." Slim's voice was suddenly harmonious, purring with deep, soothing vibrations. "You're not Katie. You never have been, and that's why you clung to her for so many years. She's strong and you've always been weak. Like your father. You fail, because that is what's in your DNA." Slim wrapped a hand around Chad's neck affectionately. "But I care. I see this torture you're living in, trying to be something you are not. And I'm here to help you." Tears blurred Chad's vision, Slim's words sparking every insecurity he'd ever had. "Katie, she's gone. Laila, you know it's just a matter of time. She's always been way too good for you. But not me. And I'll never judge you or cast you aside." With his free hand, Slim tucked the bag of powder into the front pocket of Chad's uniform and snapped it shut. "I understand." His dark eyes blazed into Chad's. "And no one has to know."

Slim backed away, but Chad couldn't move, couldn't breathe. He heard the Jaguar's engine roar to life and the bump of bass as the car exited the parking lot, and still he remained frozen to the asphalt.

His fingers twitched and found their way to the snap at his left breast pocket. He just needed to get it out. Throw it away and then everything would be fine. But nothing ahead of him seemed better than the promise of escape.

Maybe he could just do a little and no one would find out.

But as the horrifying thought ran through his mind, his voice suddenly found its rebirth. Clutching his hair, Chad screamed into the night. Answered by nothing but the buzz and flicker of the halogen lights at the perimeter of the parking lot.

He couldn't fail. He wouldn't fail. There would be too much to lose, and this time he'd never, ever get it all back, including himself.

With staggered steps, Chad clutched the driver's side door handle and pulled it open. He crawled into the seat, feeling every last drop of energy draining as if being sucked away by the bag at his chest.

He couldn't touch it. Not even to toss it away. Slim was right.

He was weak.

But Katie wasn't.

Chad put the key in the ignition, Betsy needing two turns before grumbling to a start. Katie would fix this for him. Somehow, she'd make it all go away.

CHAPTER 35

Katie's house was dark when Chad pulled up to the drive. He should care, even a little, about bothering them, but he didn't. She owed him this. She blew up his world the night she brought the drugs into his house, and he'd do the same if he had to.

Slamming Betsy into park, he winced at the shriek of her transmission, a clear scolding for not fully stopping before engaging the gear. He felt a laughable need to apologize to the old truck. It bubbled in his throat, a mix of hysteria and shock.

The pouch inside his pocket burned, and looking down, he half expected to see an outline of red crackling embers, as if the powder had caught fire.

He had to get it out. Had to make the shaking stop, the twisting in his intestines disappear.

The wind had picked up, a hiss through the trees, and thunder bellowed overhead, a promise of more rain to come. Half stumbling across the yard like a drunk, Chad gripped at the air. His eyes blurred and need clawed at his chest. So close. He was so close.

The steps were his last hurdle, but he flew up them and pressed on the doorbell twice, his finger lingering enough to make a long stretch of sound. While he waited, he paced in front of her door, leaving a trail of wet boot prints across it.

The porch light flicked on and he stopped, swinging around to the door in anticipation of Katie's ticked-off stare.

But it wasn't her.

Asher Powell filled the doorway. His hair was sticking up around his head, and it seemed his shirt was on backwards and inside out.

He'd woken them up. The thought brought another round of hysterical laughter to his chest. Katie Stone, asleep before eleven. Would the world ever feel normal again?

"Can I help you?" Asher said, his voice thick with sleep.

Chad froze, breathing too fast, too hard. He was meeting Katie's husband—in his boxers—on their perfectly decorated porch. This wasn't how it was supposed go. He wasn't supposed to be a train wreck when this moment took place.

He needed to apologize for disturbing their pristine life, but he felt like he'd been punched hard in the stomach—no, punched everywhere. Achy and rattled, jacked up and wrong, and desperate for a target. Desperate to push against something, anything that would get this feeling out.

"Yeah, um, I'm sorry to wake you. Is Katie here?" His voice was strangled, and he knew he had to look wild and terrifying under the dim yellow light.

"I think it's a little late for—"

"Chad?" Katie appeared behind her husband, tying the sash of her robe around her middle.

Relief stretched through him. "I need to talk to you."

"Okay." She went to inch past Asher, and with a nearly imperceptible motion, he stopped her advance.

Chad turned away from the couple and shoved his hands into his pockets. He didn't need to get involved; no one told Katie what to do.

He could hear their hushed whispers as they argued, Katie reassuring her husband that Chad wasn't a serial killer. Asher arguing that he didn't care; he wasn't risking her safety.

So Katie needed protection . . . against him? The irony was uncanny.

With an exaggerated huff, Katie stormed across the porch until she stood in front of him, her eyes a brand into his.

"Have you used tonight?" she demanded.

"Not yet." He let the words linger in the air, let her see how incredibly close he was to failing.

Lips pressed together, Katie disappeared again, and more whispers occurred behind him. Finally, Asher conceded, but insisted the door stay open.

Chad heard a kiss, and then silence long enough to ensure that Asher had indeed walked away. He whirled around. "It's in my left breast pocket. You need to get rid of it. Right now."

Her eyes narrowed, shifting to blue steel. Unlike the Katie he'd grown up with, this version didn't hide her feelings behind a stone exterior. He could see everything she was feeling. Surprise and anger but mostly severe, gut-wrenching disappointment.

"No," she finally said. "Get rid of it yourself."

"I can't!" He took an aggressive step forward, but she didn't even flinch. Desperation enveloped him. It was visceral, physical. It lived inside him, and he didn't know where to put it anymore. "Do you think I would have driven here, banged on your door, and humiliated myself if I thought I could even touch it?"

"And what happens the next time, Chad? When I'm not home, or when you're too weak to get into a car? What happens then?"

"Just get rid of it!" he hollered.

"No!"

Chad felt himself break. "I did it for you. I took the drugs from your hands when you weren't strong enough," he whispered, loyalty the only thing left for him to cling to. "I sacrificed everything for you."

"And where did that get any of us, huh? We all died that night."

He dropped to his knees, his legs too weak to hold him, his head cradled in his hands. "I thought I was free. I thought I was past all of this. Katie, it's been almost a year. How am I still in captivity?"

"Oh, Chad." Her words floated like the wind past him, and she was there, kneeling too, her head pressed up against his. Her teardrops fell on his forearm and rolled down to his elbow. "You will never be free, not without help. You can try and fight, and maybe even sometimes succeed, but without faith, you cannot call it freedom. It's simply bondage on hold. Paused until it rears its ugly head when you least expect it. I know. I've been there, but I now know the difference between the truth and a lie."

"I'm losing *everything*. It's slipping away piece by piece."

"You're not." Her hand stroked his hair with a mother's tender touch.

She spoke like someone much older, much wiser, not the spontaneous risk-taker who'd shared his childhood. Chad raised his head, desperately wanting to believe her.

She didn't say a word as she opened the flap of his pocket and pulled out the drugs. Her eyes widened at the amount. "There's a lot of money in this bag. How did you afford—"

"I didn't buy it. Slim called it a gift." Chad barely had the energy to shrug. "He said he was helping me."

"Yeah, helping you straight to hell," Katie snarled. Tugging on his arm, she helped him to his feet, then pressed the pouch into his hand and held it with hers. "Go do what you should have done five years ago."

He gripped her fingers. "I can't do it alone."

"You don't have to."

Hand in hand, they walked to the back of her house, to the spot where the yard ended and a line of trees began. The drizzle was back, wetting their heads and exposed arms. Katie released him, leaving the pouch of powder closed in his fist, and stepped away.

He stared at the bag, yet no longer felt inferior to it. He pulled on its opening, creating a small circle to pour from.

A gust of wind surged through the trees, as if demanding Chad's compliance. Water beaded on the pouch, and Chad turned it over, watching the powder dissolve as it was whisked away. When the bag was empty, he let the plastic slip through his fingers.

Cold stretched through his body, and suddenly he began to shake, everywhere.

Katie wrapped her arms around him, but he couldn't embrace her back. In minutes, he'd nearly unraveled every positive step he'd taken in his life. If Katie hadn't been home, he truly didn't know what he would have done.

"How did you find your way back?" His words were weak, a whisper.

"I woke up one day and had lost everything. My life had no value. *I* had no value. And then this wonderful man showed me that I was priceless, a child of the King, and loved. So when I feel lost or afraid— which I still do, sometimes—I cling to my new identity now. I refuse to believe the lie."

Chad stared into the sky, his shirt damp, rain clinging to his cheeks. "I feel worthless. All the time."

"But you're not, Chad. You're worth so much more than you'll ever understand." She said nothing for a moment, and then: "Come inside. I'm cold and getting wetter every second."

"I don't think your husband would like it."

Katie glanced behind them, and he could almost picture Asher standing there with his arms folded across his chest.

"Asher has prayed for you, probably even more than I have." She smiled up at him, though he could barely see her features through the darkness. "Come on. I promise, if he doesn't win you over, I'll wash that stupid truck for a month."

Chad felt a flicker of warmth. "Whatever. You still owe me a month from the last bet you lost."

"Nuh-uh. You rigged that bet. The prize was void."

"Was not. You were just too stubborn to admit that I was right and you were wrong."

She smacked his arm. "Milky Way will never be better than Snickers."

"We took a poll. I won."

"You manipulated the answers. You only asked women, and you gave them that stupid I-think-I'm-so-irresistible smile of yours."

Chad laughed, head thrown back, and the ice through his body began to melt away.

"Please." She tugged at his arm. "Come inside."

He closed his eyes, realizing that his worst fear had happened, and he'd somehow found victory. "Okay. Maybe for just a little while."

CHAPTER 36

Even in the darkness, Laila spotted Chad before she parked the car. He sat on her porch steps, head hung, shoulders slumped. Dread punched her in the gut. She'd seen that posture before.

She shut her door and slowly approached him, but he didn't even look up.

Please. Please, don't let him be drunk. She didn't know what she'd do if he was.

"Chad?" she asked, placing a hand on his shoulder.

"Hey," he answered, still facing the ground. His hands were clutched together, his elbows on his knees.

She catalogued everything, shifting through the signs she'd memorized from past experience. There was no smell of lingering alcohol, and he was too docile to be high. If he'd smoked weed, she'd have recognized the scent long before getting this close. *Could he be coming down from something?*

Laila studied him again. He didn't shake or tremble, but he also didn't move. Even when she lowered herself to the space next to him.

"Honey, are you okay?"

"No. I'm not okay at all."

Her heart clenched. This was it, the final test to see if they really would survive this time around or not. "Will you tell me what happened?"

"Slim found me at work."

Forcing herself not to panic, she listened as he recounted the events of the night with sobering details. How close he'd come to taking a hit. How desperate he'd felt when Slim confirmed his worst fears.

And after he'd exhausted all the words he seemed to have stuffed inside, Chad leaned toward her, slowly, and went silently and thoroughly to pieces.

Laila held him to her chest, arms wrapped around his thick, shaking shoulders, and watched as her own tears disappeared among the black mop of hair he still needed to cut.

"I'm sorry I'm so weak, Laila. I'm sorry this is the life I've given you," he whispered.

She pressed her cheek against the top of his head and murmured small reassurances to him as though he were Sierra. She'd asked him for honesty. And though seeing him this way messed her up in ways she couldn't process yet, she also felt grateful that he'd allowed her to see him so broken.

He raised his face at last, wiping his nose and eyes with the edge of his T-shirt. "Can I stay? Just for tonight?"

She began to protest but he quickly added, "I just want to be near you. Nothing else."

"Okay." She didn't want to send him home any more than he wanted to go. They'd been through the fire tonight, him especially, and pushing him away just felt wrong.

Relief dominated the other emotions on his face. "Thank you."

He stood first and took her hand, pulling her to him the minute she was fully upright. "I love you," he whispered, lightly kissing her forehead, as if to prove he'd be on his best behavior.

Laila hugged him back without response. She hadn't told him she loved him yet. When they were younger, those three words had been automatic, meaningless sometimes. When she chose to say them again, she wanted to feel each one deep in her soul.

The house was quiet when they entered, lights off in every room. They didn't bother to turn them back on, both walking carefully around the stacks of boxes scattered around the house.

"I'll use the guest bathroom," he said quietly, his voice mildly insecure.

"Okay." They hadn't done this yet. Slept in the same bed. Heck, he hadn't even stepped foot into their old bedroom. At first, by her choice, but lately, it seemed he avoided the room like it was haunted. Maybe it was.

She went through her nighttime routine quickly—washing her face, brushing her teeth, pulling her hair up and out of her face. And with every movement, her nerves ratcheted higher. Why was she so nervous? Tonight wasn't about sex. It wasn't giving in to a rush of hormones or getting lost in their physical desires. Tonight was about so much more—the delicate balance between holding on and being held. They'd shared a bed many a times, but tonight they'd shared true intimacy, something she hadn't even known they'd been missing until now.

For the first time ever, Chad had completely and fully let her in.

Turning off the faucet, she felt her nerves calm.

She exited the master bathroom and quietly shut the door behind her.

Chad was already splayed across his side of the bed, shoes and socks off, his eyes closed. She drifted to the other side and slid under the covers.

He seemed to move instinctively, pulling her back to him and wrapping her in an embrace tight enough to suffocate. He pressed his nose to the back of her hair and inhaled. "Good night," he whispered.

She closed her eyes, feeling safe and warm and cherished for the first time in so, so long.

Seconds later, she drifted off to sleep.

Sometime before dawn Laila's eyes popped open, a pressing, chilling need growing inside her waking mind. Her pulse ticked hard in her throat as last night's events unfolded like a dream. But it wasn't a dream. This story . . . was her reality. Their reality.

Slowly, she pulled back the comforter, glancing at the sleeping man beside her. Resolute in her decision, she left the bedroom, knowing what she must do.

On the couch was her abandoned laptop. She picked it up, crossed her legs up on the upholstery, and opened her computer. Careful to check the bedroom door for movement, she opened her browser and ran a search for Agent Edwards.

A list of websites appeared, and she glanced at each before clicking on the Southeastern Regional Drug Enforcement Office link.

Ever so quietly, she dialed the listed office number and, as expected at four in the morning, got Edwards's voicemail. He rattled on about his agency location and whom to call if this was an emergency. When the message ended in a beep, Laila took a breath.

"Um, hi, I'm Laila Richardson. You spoke to my husband about working with you. I'd like to discuss it further. There was an incident last night." She quickly gave her phone number and hung up, her hand trembling when she finished.

Erasing her browsing history first, Laila closed her laptop and set it back on the couch. She robotically walked to the kitchen, drank a glass of water, and then quietly returned to her bedroom.

Chad hadn't moved, his hair dark against his cheek, his arm still spread out covering the spot she'd vacated. She watched as his chest rose and fell, his soft features absent of the torture that seemed to plague him when he was awake.

A ferocious truth slammed against her chest. She loved this man. Loved him with everything inside her, and would not stand by this time and let Slim take him from her.

Her fingers reached up behind her neck, undoing the clasp of the chain Chad had given her. The cool gold ring slid off easily, and Laila held it in her hand for only a brief second before sliding it onto her finger.

Feeling calm for the first time since waking, she crawled back under the covers, under the hold of the man she loved, and fell heavily into a blissful, dreamless sleep.

CHAPTER 37

C had woke up alone, sun streaming through the windows. He rolled over and inhaled, the scent of Laila still lingering on the pillow. He'd been too upset to notice the night before, but the sheets were new. So was the quilt over their queen-sized bed. He ran a hand over the blue material, the absence of her twisting a knot in his chest.

He'd never let her see him so weak before. He'd always hidden that part of himself, always found a way to escape or hide. He'd never wanted her to see him broken, even though they both knew he was.

Refusing to consider that last night had scared her off, Chad swung his legs over the bed and reached for his phone on the bedside table. Twelve fifteen. Barely time to talk before he had to get ready for his two o'clock shift.

He scratched his head, felt the filth from the factory, now mixed with sweat. His uniform was rumpled and dirty. His fingernails still dark from his work gloves.

No wonder Laila fled the bed. He was disgusting.

Feet on the floor, Chad stood and stretched, the exhaustion from the night before settling back over him. He'd almost failed. And if he were being truly honest with himself, last night wasn't the first time. All week, he'd felt tempted. It stirred in him, growing stronger with each passing day.

He couldn't continue on this hamster wheel. Not if he wanted to stay sober.

The bedroom door was shut, and he listened for any sign of life in their small house. He heard nothing but the hiss of the air conditioner through the vents.

Entering the adjacent master bathroom, he flipped on the light. It reflected off of the white counters and old laminate floor. Laila had added some new rugs, he noticed, the same blue as her bedspread.

The sink was riddled with her toiletries, and though Laila didn't wear much makeup, she still kept a bag full of cosmetics on the counter. He picked up her perfume, then the lotion she rubbed over her legs at night and in the morning. Every scent awakened a memory. Every trace of her reminded him of why he had to fight. Why what happened with Slim last night could never, ever happen again.

He set down the bottle and splashed water on his face and hair, using her soap to wash away the dirt. Water beaded on his skin while bubbles slid down to a puddle in the sink. He drew in the fresh, clean, soapy scent, the same one that lingered close to Laila's skin, the one he'd smelled all night long as he held her in his arms.

He couldn't let their future end here.

After brushing his teeth with his finger and some toothpaste, he shut off the water and used a nearby hand towel to dry his wet hair and face. His boots were still by the bed, his socks shoved deep inside. He grabbed one and yanked up his sock. The room was full of boxes, his and Laila's history stuffed away in four-by-four-foot containers. Even the pictures were gone. The last bit of proof that they'd truly been a couple.

When he finished tying his bootlaces, he walked to the living room. "Laila?" Surely she wouldn't have left without telling him good-bye, without at least discussing what happened last night.

A faint murmur of voices came from the kitchen. He followed the sound and froze the minute he reached the doorway, "What's going on?" His gaze bounced between Laila and Agent Edwards. "What are you doing here?"

As Laila's companion stood to greet him, Chad eyed the coffee cups on the table. This hadn't been a surprise visit.

"I called him." Laila chewed on her bottom lip, but met his shocked stare without apology.

"Chad, your wife told me what happened last night, and we want to help you. We know there's corruption within the departments. We know you fear for your safety, but I guarantee we have the resources and manpower to do this with or without local involvement." Agent Edwards had obviously practiced that speech more than once. His voice was smooth, unwavering, and, if Chad didn't know better, almost believable.

Bile crawled up his throat as his eyes flashed back to Laila. He'd told her the cost. He'd told her that he didn't want anything to do with Agent Edwards or his doomed plan. Yet still, she had trusted a stranger more than him.

"Get out of my house."

Laila took a step forward. "Chad, if you would just listen to—"

He stormed to the back door, cutting her off, and pulled it open. "Get out. Now."

Agent Edwards must have recognized Chad's indignation, because he pushed in the chair he had vacated and offered Laila another one of his stupid cards. "In case he changes his mind."

"Thank you," she said, her disappointment in Chad's response evident to everyone in the room.

The cop stopped halfway through the doorway. "I've yet to see one person walk away after working for him. He'll suck you back in, or he'll take you out. It's what he does. Paying him off makes no difference."

So the man knew about the money. Did Laila tell him? Did she really go that far?

As soon as Edwards cleared the threshold, Chad slammed the door hard enough to rattle the dishes in the sink. He pressed his palm to the wood, lowered his head, and tried his best to find control. When he finally stopped shaking, he met her eyes.

Laila didn't move, but from the way her blue eyes widened, he knew the shock was gone from his face and replaced by the ice he felt inside. The ice he'd never once felt around her.

"Why would you call him?" He could barely form the words. They ripped him apart. "Is this punishment?"

"What? No."

"Then why?" he yelled. "When you knew how I felt? When I told you, point blank, that I didn't want to work with the guy?"

"I spent too many years watching you dissolve in front of me without saying or doing anything. I won't be that girl anymore."

He watched her put up an invisible shield, watched her eyes go as empty as they'd been the night he stood on her front porch two months ago. So much for honesty being the solution.

"You should have talked to me first. You should have let us make this kind of decision together, not called him in dead of night while I ignorantly slept in your bed." He slammed his hand against his chest. "This is my life too!"

The guarded stare slid away, and her eyes filled with tears. He couldn't tell if they were angry or remorseful ones. Or even just instinctual, because that's what always seemed to happen when they fought. He'd thought he was learning to read her again, but he wasn't. All this time, he'd thought they were making progress, when really she was no closer to trusting him than she had been before.

She took a step forward, practically trapping him between the door and the table. "Chad, they have it all planned. The manpower, the technology, the take down. It's all ready. All they're missing is a guy on the inside who Slim trusts."

"Exactly! They're missing that guy because people are loyal to Slim, and when they aren't, bad things happen." His words rose into a strangled shout, a riot of rage and fear that rushed though him so fast he could hardly think. "They don't have that guy because we all know better!" He had to back up, had to get away from her and calm the hurricane in his chest. "You have no idea the position you just put us in. The risk you took."

"It's never going to stop, Chad. Never. Not until he's in jail." She took another step toward him, pleading. "And I can't live like this, wondering every day if he's going to stuff more poison into your pocket. Wondering if one day you won't have the strength to turn him down."

He grabbed her by the shoulders. "You don't turn on men like Slim!"

His guilt seemed to wrap around them both. Guilt for not getting help sooner, even when she'd begged him to. Guilt over what was happening now. Guilt over the fact that his innocent wife was getting sucked into this despicable world.

Caving under the weight of it, he pulled her to him, crushing her in his embrace. "I don't want you anywhere near this stuff. It's too dangerous."

Her arms tightened around him. "You heard Agent Edwards. Slim wouldn't find out until it was too late."

"So he says, but they don't really know that. Ask him how many drug raids have gone wrong. I guarantee it's more than they want to admit." Chad exhaled, releasing her. He cupped her face with his hands. "You can't make those kinds of decisions without me again. You asked me to be honest with you, to earn your trust. I have to be able to trust you too."

She nodded, her eyes full of anguish and remorse. "Okay. I'm sorry."

"Me too. I shouldn't have yelled." He tucked a piece of hair behind her ear. "Promise me you'll never talk to that man again."

"I promise." Her hand fell on his arm, soft yet firm. He glanced down at it, and everything inside of him went liquid.

His eyes flashed to her neck, the absence of her chain confirming what he'd thought he'd seen. "You put on your ring?"

"Yeah, well, I liked you a little more last night than I do this morning."

He didn't care that her tone dripped with sarcasm and annoyance. She'd put on his ring.

Without thinking, he cupped her face and kissed her so hard they almost fell over. "Thank you," he whispered, pressing his forehead to hers. "You won't regret it. I promise."

She huffed like she already did, but he saw a hint of a smile.

He dropped his hands and the world seemed brighter, full of possibility. "I'm going to check outside, just to make sure no one saw Edwards's car here."

"Does Slim really have someone following you?"

"Yes, Laila. That's why you can never talk to anyone involved in that world again."

She threw up her arms. "Sometimes I really hate this small town. I wish everyone would just mind their own business." She stomped to their bedroom, her hips swaying in a way that almost made him forget his bigger purpose.

Shaking the images from his mind, he circled the house first. No broken branches. No signs of footprints. He checked the tree line, the driveway, and the area by the mailbox. All looked undisturbed.

Maybe all his fear was unfounded. Katie had walked away from Slim, challenged him even, with no lasting repercussions. Maybe all this time, Chad had made the man out to be more threatening than he truly was.

Feeling his heart rate drop back to a normal level, he closed his eyes, truly grateful that everything he'd been through had led him here, with Laila, ready to start their life again.

Katie had talked a lot about her faith last night. How she had prayed that God would put someone in his path to help him stay clean. Someone like Mark, and even Cooper, though Chad kept him out of the conversation. They'd talked about her and Asher, how they fell in love and how dramatically she changed. By the time he left, Chad actually believed that maybe there was a divine power who'd generously given Katie her happy ending.

He looked toward the sky and thought of the ring on Laila's finger.

"Yeah, so I'm probably the last person you want to hear from right now. But if you did have something to do with all this—my wife's heart changing—then . . . thanks."

He stopped talking, partially because he felt stupid and partially because those words seemed truly insignificant, like he should be saying more or giving more.

Chad shook off the feeling and walked back to the house.

CHAPTER 38

Laila stood frozen, chewing down her pinkie nail as Chad and Cooper maneuvered her ridiculously heavy couch through the cottage's front door. They'd already had to readjust their hold on it twice, and both their faces were red and undeniably irritated.

"Where does it go?" Chad asked, his voice strained.

Laila jumped into action, walking to the space she'd reserved. "Right here. Facing the fireplace."

The men spoke in hushed tones as they walked the couch around to face the proper direction and lowered it to the floor. When they stood up, they both had deep grooves in their arms from its weight.

"It's perfect," she said, hoping her enthusiasm would wipe away their frustration.

"Good. 'Cause I ain't movin' it again," Cooper said.

"Well, no one asked you to," she snapped back, but with teasing in her voice. Laila and Cooper seemed to share equal parts friendship and annoyance, but their mutual love for Chad gave them the common ground to get past the hurt they'd caused each other in the past. Although Cooper had more than made up for his interference by the amount of work he'd done for them this weekend. Not just hauling her things out of the old house and into this new one, but also helping Chad repair any damage she could be charged for at the old house. And, really, if it weren't for Cooper's big mouth, she and Chad would never be in the place they were now.

And things were good. Better than good. Even with them arguing over Agent Edwards. He'd come by the bar again last night, but Laila had done as Chad asked and told him to leave. Thankfully, he'd finished his drink and walked out.

"I'm gonna grab a water and get another load." Cooper said, rubbing his forearms.

"Yeah. I'll be there in a minute." Chad dropped to the couch with a mischievous grin and pulled Laila onto his lap. She tried to struggle off, sure a tickling assault was coming, but her efforts only got her a long, lingering kiss that sent fire bolts to her toes.

"What was that for?" she asked, breathless.

"For putting my ring back on your finger."

"It's been there for days."

"I know, but it still makes me giddy every time I see it." He slid his hand up her thigh, his eyes bright green and happy. "When are we going to make it official?"

She smacked his chest, although keeping her distance was becoming more and more difficult. "Soon. I want to get all moved in first. And I want Joe and Katie to be there. And Asher too."

"Cooper's going to be my best man," he warned. "That's nonnegotiable."

"Well," she said coyly, slipping her hands around his neck, "the three of them will just have to put their drama aside for one day."

"When?" he asked again, with more force this time. "I'm done waiting. I want you to be my wife again, in every sense of the word."

She stroked the back of his head. He had been patient and loving and supportive. "Okay. Two weeks from today. On the beach. That'll give me enough time to plan it."

He slid his arm under her legs and stood, swinging her around while she clung to his neck. "Ah, baby. I'm going to make it the best day of your life."

"I know you will."

Chad let her slip out of his arms until her feet were firmly planted on the bare floor.

Her gaze did a 360 around the room. The joy of her decision came back every time she walked through the front door of the cottage. She loved how open the space was. No tight, separated rooms like their old house, just one big, open kitchen, living, and dining area, with two bedrooms in the back, the bigger one opening up to a patio surrounded by three gardens.

She walked toward the large bay window and took in the view she'd been longing for since the first time she'd seen it. Ben had been with her that day, and she had truly believed he was the beginning of her future.

How different life turns out sometimes.

Thick hands wove around her middle, pulling her back into a firm torso. "You're right. This place is perfect." Chad nibbled on her ear and she giggled, feeling more content than she had in . . . well, in forever.

"How much is left to bring in?" she asked, sliding her hands over his locked arms.

"Not much. Just a few more boxes, the mattresses, and our dresser." He kissed the back of her head. "You sure you want to stay here alone tonight?"

She unclamped his arms and spun around. He wanted to move in with her, had made that very, very well known, but something in her needed to see this one step of independence to the end. She wanted it to feel like her home before it became Chad's too. "Yes, I'm sure."

"When is the walk-through on our old place?"

She was glad he hadn't argued with her and let her body relax back in his arms. "Thursday. And don't think I'm cleaning it without your help." Their old landlord was a tyrant, but Laila wanted their deposit back, and he'd find every excuse to hold it.

Chad grinned. "I'll be there. And tell Mr. Novak to make the walk-through at noon. I don't want him trying to manipulate you."

"I can't. He already said five sharp."

"Fine. I'll talk to Barney about taking off a few hours during my shift."

She lifted on her toes and kissed the man she never thought she would kiss again. "Look at you, my big, strong protector."

"I'm trying to be." His tone turned serious. "I'm trying to be a lot of things I wasn't before. Like . . ." He paused. "How would you feel if I went to church with you sometime?"

"You want to go to church?" She'd considered bringing up the subject a few times, but in the end decided he needed to make the decision without her pressuring him. The last thing she wanted was him pretending just to make her happy.

"I don't know exactly how I feel about everything yet, but I think I want to learn more. And if you and Katie are so sure, then it's worth checking into."

Overwhelmed, she barreled into his chest and squeezed. Of all the changes, this one calmed the worst of her fears. Watching Katie's transformation had shown her the power that faith could bring to a recovering addict.

A throat clearing had her releasing him and wiping her wet eyes.

"Not to interrupt your honeymoon or anything, but I'd like to go home at some point tonight," Cooper said, holding a stack of two boxes.

"Yeah, yeah. I need to find that man a girlfriend." Chad winked at her, his voice scratchy as if he too felt the importance of his decision.

"Thank you," she said before he walked away. "Nothing would make me happier than you coming to church sometime."

"Then I'm there." He gave her his heart-stopping smile. "Without a tie."

CHAPTER 39

Laila walked down the hall of Burchwood Elementary feeling just as nervous as she had the first time she'd taken the same path months ago. Only she wasn't the same person anymore. Which was why, despite her trepidation, she found the courage to come for the final Kids' Bible Club of the school year.

Passing through the cafeteria doors, Laila found Ben right where she expected to, up by the stage, hooking the sound system to his speakers. She'd come earlier than necessary so the two of them could talk before all the other volunteers showed up.

"Hey," she said, carefully approaching him.

He didn't turn, but she could see his body go rigid. He knew it was her.

After a second, his shoulders seemed to relax. He set the wires down and faced her. "Hi. I didn't know you were coming."

"I hope it's okay. Kim asked me to be here today . . . for Sierra."

Ben shoved his hands into his pockets, his gaze zeroing in on the ring she now wore on her left hand. On instinct, she touched it with her fingers, then dropped her arms by her side.

"I'm sorry—"

"I'm sorry—"

They both said it at the same time.

Ben smiled and gestured for her to go first.

"You were right about my feelings," she said. "But I want you to know that when I was with you, I truly didn't think Chad and I would ever be together."

"I know." He glanced at his feet, then up at her. "Once again, my instincts were spot on. I just wish sometimes they would work in my favor."

"Oh, Ben. They will. You're such a great guy. Someday—"

He put up his hand. "Please don't say that. I know it's not meant to be patronizing, but it still feels that way."

"Sorry."

"It's fine." A heavy silence followed, and Laila wondered if she should go find something to do, but feared it would again be the wrong thing.

"I have something for you," he finally said.

"You do?"

He reached into his back pocket and pulled out his wallet. Opening it, he shuffled through some slits and then pulled out a business card. With one hand, he offered it to her. With the other, he slid his wallet back into its resting place.

"What is this?" She scanned the print.

HARRISON FAMILY DENTISTRY

"A friend of mine mentioned that he was looking for a new receptionist. One who was good with kids and smart enough to take on some office management duties as well." Ben watched as she read and reread the handwritten number on the back. "I still had your resume on my computer, and I thought you'd be perfect for the job. I hope you don't mind, but I sent it to him, and he was interested. If he hasn't called yet, it's probably because he knows we broke up and wasn't sure how I'd feel about it."

"How do you feel about it?"

Ben paused and seemed to scan her adorned finger again. "I guess I feel like if *I* hated you working at Joe's, I can't imagine how hard that must be for Chad, considering his history."

Laila bit her lip, knowing everything he'd just said was true. "It is hard. On both of us."

"I meant what I said that night. I believe in marriage, and if you two have a second chance at a happy ending, I really hope you do everything you can to get there." He smiled—it almost didn't seem forced—and pointed to the card. "You should call him. Jeff will be a great boss, and the office is located just north of downtown, near Burchwood Medical Center."

"Ben. I . . ." What could she possibly say to let him know how amazing he was? "Thank you."

"You're welcome." For a moment, he seemed to want to say more too, but then switched to the proficient businessman she'd seen him be with other people. "Okay, let's get to work. Can you start pushing the tables out of the way?"

She carefully slid the card into her pocket. "Sure."

They were going to be okay, she realized, and one day, whether Ben wanted to hear it or not, God would bring the perfect person into his life. A man so kind and caring deserved no less.

✖

Laila stood by Sierra, fighting the rush of tears that threatened to spill from her eyes. Not only had the little girl listened intently to the lesson, but she'd also smiled—twice—and now she clapped along to the final song of the day.

The room pulsed with energy, kids jumping and singing as loud as their little lungs would allow. Caden stood next to his dad, both of them clapping and laughing. Yeah. Ben would be just fine.

When the song ended, Ben stood on the stage, thanked all the volunteers and kids, then formed lines to bring the masses to the pickup area.

Sierra gripped Laila's hand and pulled her to Kim's chair at the back.

"What a day," Laila said, breathless with all the emotion.

"What a month," Kim said, her eyes filling. "Sierra, do you have anything you want to add?"

The little girl she had grown to love smiled sheepishly and waved Laila closer. She knelt down, and Sierra wrapped her arms around her neck. "I love you," the child whispered in her ear, barely loud enough to be heard.

Shocked, Laila wrapped her arms around Sierra's small torso and searched for Kim, as if needing confirmation that Sierra had actually spoken.

Kim nodded and wiped a stray tear with her tissue. The woman constantly carried one.

"I love you too," Laila whispered back. "Thank you for being my friend. I really needed one."

Sierra didn't speak again, but she did kiss Laila on the cheek before rushing to her grandmother.

"Will you be around this summer?" Kim asked.

"Yes. I just moved in, actually, on Rosemary Lane." She directed her attention to Sierra. "Would you like to hang out a little while you're out of school?"

Sierra bobbed her chin up and down quickly.

"Great. Me too."

"I'll call you and set something up." Kim pulled her in for a tight embrace. "Thank you, for everything."

Laila felt as if she walked on clouds all the way back to her car. She never expected so much in her life to go right, and it seemed like everything she'd ever dreamed of was now falling into place.

The feeling continued all the way into Fairfield. Now, if their land-lord agreed to release their deposit, Laila would know for sure that she'd entered an alternate dimension.

Still smiling, she dialed Chad to let him know she was at the house.

"Hey," he answered, and just hearing his voice made her pulse quicken. Ten more days and they'd be husband and wife again. "I'm changing right now and will be there in one sec."

She clicked the car door shut, her feet skipping more than walking. "You won't believe it. Sierra spoke. She actually told me she loved me. Out loud."

"Ah, babe, that's awesome." He seemed to take a gulp of air. "So, um, I guess you talked to Ben?"

Laila held the phone between her ear and shoulder while she unlocked the deadbolt. "Yes. He was really great, actually. Oh, that reminds me. He found me a job. A receptionist position at a local dentist office in Burchwood. I'm going to call the guy tomorrow." She pushed open the door and flipped on the light. It spilled through the empty house, reminding her once again how happy she was to let that sad chapter in her life end for good.

"Wow. I, um." He paused, and she heard his keys jingle in the background. "Okay, I admit. I totally hate it. Although I'm grateful. I just wish it wasn't him."

"Give it time, Chad. Maybe one day, you two will actually become friends." She heard the front door open behind her. "Oh, he's early."

But when she spun around, Mr. Novak wasn't the one slamming the front door shut.

Laila screamed.

And then there was nothing but pain.

CHAPTER 40

C had sprinted across the yard, stumbling once in his rush to get to the front door. He had to be dreaming. This had to be a nightmare.

Sirens blared from a distance, closing in on their house.

It can't be too late. God, please, please don't let it be too late.

The stairs passed in a blur; so did the screen door he ripped open.

Then the world slowed to the beat of a hollow, ageless drum. It rushed through his ears, echoed through the house.

He didn't feel a thing as he dropped to his knees next to her, his jeans sliding in the blood spreading along the floor.

Fingers trembling, he touched her face, then her neck, a faint pulse still detectible.

"Laila," he choked, his tears mixing with the panic.

He didn't know where to touch first. Her blonde hair was matted with thick red oozing from a gash along her temple. Her left arm hung lifeless next to her, while her right one lay in a position so contorted, it had to be broken in several places.

His gaze trailed down her bruised face, already swelling near her split lip.

The sirens grew louder, but Chad forced himself to continue his search for more severe injuries. There was too much blood to fall apart now. He had to stay strong, at least until he knew she was okay.

Finally, he spotted the rip in her shirt, just near the ribcage on her right side. He pulled up the soaked cloth, his eyes zeroing in on the jagged slice through her pale, white skin.

He tore off his shirt, pressed the balled material to the knife wound, and prayed for the blood to stop flowing so fast. Even through the streaks on her face, he could see the color leaving, the life draining slowly away.

"Don't you give up on me! Not now."

She gave no reply, not even a twitch as his shirt slowly began to saturate with blood.

Chad's head dropped, helpless, his tears becoming sobs. This wasn't a nightmare. This was real, and it was his fault. He was going to lose her, right here on this cold tile floor.

Shouts came from the yard, growing louder as they reached the room, but their words were somehow muffled, as though he were underwater, staring up at the surface.

Suddenly, his hands were pulled free, and blue uniforms surrounded Laila, like ants on a dropped piece of candy. He tried to get back to her, but warm hands pulled him backward, and somehow he had no energy to fight. He could only stare at his skin, still coated with her sticky blood, already starting to dry.

Shivers racked his body, his teeth chattering as he continued to watch his shaking palms.

Someone shined a light in his eyes, and he flinched, the nausea reacting in his stomach. Dry heaves pulled at his chest, arching him forward, a bolt of pain slicing through his abdomen.

The room suddenly began to move back and forth, up and down, and black coated the edges of his vision. He embraced it.

Without her, there was nothing but darkness anyway.

Chad sat in the ICU waiting room, still as a statue. They'd cleaned him up, washed Laila's blood from his body, and given him a pair of puke-green scrubs to wear until someone could bring him new clothes.

The police had asked him a million questions, or the same questions a million times, he couldn't remember. His recount never faltered. He'd heard her scream on the phone, called 911, and drove as fast as he could to their house.

Yes, he had been by himself when she called.

No, he didn't hurt his wife.

The men in blue had finally left twenty minutes ago with a promise to be in touch.

Now, he was numb. Completely, blissfully numb. Not even the whispered voices at the nurses' station or the woman knitting in the corner felt real.

"Chad?"

He lifted his head just enough to see Katie and Asher rush into the waiting room. He must have called them, but he didn't remember doing it.

Katie knelt before him, and he wanted to curse and push her away. His chest burned, his mouth swelled. The numbness was slipping away.

She touched his cheeks with her palms, her eyes lost in a sea of anguish.

"I'm going to kill him," he said, his jaw hard, his eyes burning almost as much as his throat.

"First, you need to tell me what happened." She glanced nervously at her husband, then around the room, as if a cop might jump out of the corner and arrest Chad. They probably should. He was responsible for all of this.

"Laila talked to a special agent out of the southeastern office. Slim must have found out, somehow. He attacked her." Every line felt disconnected, much like it had with the cops earlier. They were just words; they didn't equate to the broken body he'd seen on that floor.

Katie slowly stood and dropped into the seat next to him, shock and horror plastered across her open-mouthed stare. "Why would she do that?"

"To protect me. Because of what happened last week."

They met each other's eyes, and he knew she could see his promise to kill was not an idle threat. Chad knew exactly what he was doing. He'd make that deal with Agent Edwards. Only he wasn't just going to be their errand boy. When the time came, when Slim was close enough, he'd plant a bullet in his chest.

Asher stepped closer, then took the spot on the other side of him. Chad had almost forgotten he was there.

"What's your plan?" he asked.

Chad felt his body lock up. Asher's intrusion was unwelcome and unnecessary. "What do you mean?"

"For revenge. That's what you want, right? Vengeance?"

Chad met his eyes, challenging him. "Yes. Tell me you wouldn't want the same if Slim had smashed Katie's skull, broken her arm, and then stabbed her with a blunt knife."

Asher winced but didn't back down. "So, after you kill Slim, what then?"

The answer was simple. He'd die in the process or go to jail. Then Laila would be free. "She'll go back to Ben. They'll build a life in Burchwood, and she'll never get hurt again. That's what would have happened if I hadn't been so selfish. It's where she should have always been."

Katie grabbed his hand and squeezed, but it didn't bring comfort, only the blurring of his vision as he looked down at the blue carpet. "It's my fault. I should never have come home."

"It's not your fault. It's Slim's. Don't take on that man's guilt," Asher said, his voice unwavering.

Chad didn't respond. He didn't need Asher's reassurances. He needed this hole in his chest to go away. He needed the numbness back. He needed to erase every single minute of today.

The wretched tears came again, spilling down his cheeks and onto his neck. His wife was in surgery right now because he couldn't say no to that thin white line. Laila could die because, deep down, he was nothing but a weak coward.

Asher's hand fell onto his shoulder. He wanted to shake it off until he heard a soft prayer asking for healing and protection coming from the other man's mouth. A prayer for justice for those responsible.

Chad closed his eyes. He wouldn't stop a prayer. Not if it helped her somehow. God may have forsaken him, but he deserved no less. Laila, on the other hand, deserved everything.

"Mr. Richardson?"

Chad sprung from his chair and dried his face with the cuff of his borrowed scrubs. "Yes. Right here. How's Laila?"

Dr. Malone had on scrubs identical to Chad's, with a mask hanging from his neck. He was older, a chief of something, Chad had noted when they'd first spoken.

"Laila's in recovery. The surgery went well. The knife lacerated a small piece of her liver, but we were able to repair it without complications. The contusion to her temporal lobe is our bigger concern. The CT scan showed signs of swelling, so we've put her into a medical coma until the threat recedes."

"How long will she stay like that?"

"Hours, maybe days. Every patient is different." Professionalism emanated from his voice, steady and unfazed.

"Can I see her?"

"Not yet. I'll send a nurse up once your wife is settled in a permanent room. Probably another hour."

"Thank you."

Dr. Malone nodded once and left the waiting area with little compassion. This wasn't the end of his life. It was just another day on the job.

Chad watched the door until it clicked shut. *Liver, temporal lobe, coma.*

"We were going to be married in ten days. On the beach," Chad said to no one. "We were supposed to get a second chance."

Katie wrapped her arms around his bicep, put her chin on his shoulder. "You heard the doctor. Laila is going to recover. You are still going to get your second chance."

No, he wasn't. Not until Slim was dead.

"I have to go take care of something."

"Chad, stop," she pleaded. "Slim isn't worth your freedom or your life."

"My life is worth nothing!" Chad detangled from Katie's grip, his guilt, shame, and regret balling up in his chest, glowing hot and red. He was wrapped around it, growling at her; at the same time he wanted to beg her to rescue him from this pain. "All I've ever done is bring heartache to everyone who's loved me. My mom. You. Laila. Even Cooper. It has to stop."

"Yes, it does. But this isn't the way." Her eyes were soft with concern, unhurt by the sharpness of his tone.

He spun around and spread his arms. "So Slim just gets to walk away free? He has no consequences?"

"No." Asher had once again joined their conversation. "You work with the cops. You give them what they need to do their job. Trust me, revenge has no boundaries. There is no safe place once it takes over your heart."

He let his hands fall to his hips. Even though every part of him hummed with hatred for the man, Chad had no idea if he could pull the trigger on Slim. And if he did, what then? He was just trading one captivity for another. "I can't work with the cops. If I do, this will only happen again."

Katie stepped closer. "Okay, then let it go. Move to Burchwood. Change your life."

"What do you think I've been trying to do for the last year?"

"I'm not talking physically, Chad. If you want freedom, true freedom, surrender is the only way to find it. You have to give up control. You have to let go."

His voice cracked. "Let go of what? I am nothing."

"Exactly," Katie all but pleaded. She began to speak urgently, and since he had nowhere to go, he listened. But through the words and the promises, only one thought remained central in his mind.

This day would be avenged.

CHAPTER 41

The fade into consciousness happened slowly, like a thick fog lifting or turning into a soft drizzle. The haze was still there, just in a different form.

Laila felt soft sheets beneath her and a thick blanket against her skin. Her left hand was pressed into something warm and vaguely familiar. She tried to move her right one, but it felt trapped, locked away and immobile.

"Laila, this is Dr. Malone. Can you hear me?"

She tried to open her eyes, but they seemed glued together, her mind trying again and again with no response. The warmth spread from her hand, up her arm, and into her head, where a sudden rush of pain made her gasp. The throbbing grew, moving down her face, into her scorching throat, and across her torso. "It hurts," she whispered, barely able to form the words through her cracked throat.

She felt a straw at her mouth and sucked in the moisture, only that hurt too, a stinging across her lips like a paper cut.

Suddenly, the haze vaporized and her veins filled with icy awareness. She felt her body panic, the image of that face next to hers, the darkness in his eyes, the total lack of mercy.

A beeping sound filled her ears, growing faster and faster.

"Laila, honey, calm down. You're safe. I'm right here."

"He had a mask." The beeping jumped again as the memory of those eyes ripped at her mind—cold, evil, unwavering.

"Hey, it's okay. You don't have to think about it. Not right now."

Chad's voice wrapped around her, melting away the images.

"Chad?"

"I'm here." She felt a hand on her forehead, heard the ache in his voice as his lips pressed against her eyelids. A drip of moisture fell on her cheek, from her or him, she wasn't sure.

Her heart settled back down, and finally, her eyes seemed to cooperate, opening slowly, Chad's face a blur against the bright light above.

The other voice began to speak, the detached one that used medical terms she didn't want to hear.

She only wanted to look into Chad's eyes.

"Can you give us just a minute?" he asked, looking up.

"A brief one," the man answered and quietly left the room.

Chad watched him exit, then focused back on her with such grief and fear in his eyes that speech failed her. She couldn't imagine the horror he faced when he'd found her, battered and unconscious.

The inescapable scars etched in both of them would be deep and long lasting.

Soft fingers stroked her cheek—light, yet still she felt a sting of pain. "I'm so sorry," he said.

She knew that tone. It was the one he'd use before walking out. The one that meant he'd given up the fight.

"Me too." Her own defeat mirrored his.

He knew. They both knew. Things could never be what they had wanted.

Chad was going to have to deal with her attack his way, and she would have to let him, even if that meant the worst outcome for both of them.

He would die to protect her. Even from himself.

As if he could read her mind, Chad pressed his forehead to her chest and sobbed. Carefully, she moved her unbroken hand and ran her fingers through the dark strands of his hair, wishing like he did that they could go back to the beginning, before life became so burdensome, before one man's evil shattered all their dreams.

CHAPTER 42

Cooper slammed his front door with a fury that had Chad bristling in his seat.

"You skipped work again?" he demanded. "It's the third day this week, Chad. I can't keep covering for you."

"Then don't." Chad sat up on the couch, his chest bare, his eyes red rimmed and cracked from the lack of sleep. His head throbbed. His body ached. He checked his phone and winced. How was it already eight at night?

Cooper took a deep breath, ran his hands over his face, and sat down across from him, calm as a rodeo bull in a pen. "So Laila left you. This isn't the way to deal with it."

"She didn't leave me. We left each other," Chad corrected, rubbing his temples. It'd been two weeks since he'd last seen or spoken to her. Two horrible weeks of being a person he hated. But there was no other choice. No other option.

"Fine. You left each other. But that doesn't mean you have to fall back into the pit. Joe said—"

"I don't want to talk about Joe." With steely eyes, Chad challenged his friend. "He kicked me out. He called me my father."

"You ordered a drink in his bar, Chad, not a week after Laila was attacked. What did you think he was going to do? Tap the keg for you?"

He smirked. "It would have been more polite."

Cooper clenched and unclenched his fist. "There are rumors going around that you're using again. Heavier stuff this time. Is it true?"

Chad shrugged. "Does it matter? I'm not doing it here."

"Yes, it matters! I put my name on the line for you."

"Well, I never asked you to, okay? This is me. Take it or leave it." He slammed a hand against his chest, hating himself almost as much as Cooper seemed to at the moment. "Without Laila, I have nothing. So, yeah, I've gone out a few times. It's either that or lose my mind."

"I won't watch you self-destruct again," Cooper said, his face a mask of determination and unchecked anger.

"Oh, really, Mr. High and Mighty? Where have you been, by the way? Your shift ended five hours ago."

"I had some paperwork to finish up."

"Yeah, and happy hour at Joe's. I can smell it from here, so don't lecture me on drinking, you hypocrite."

"I'm not the alcoholic," Cooper growled.

"You sure about that? I saw your stash that first night. Don't tell me you didn't drown your sorrows after Katie booted you." Chad's stomach cramped with every cruel word. "You can't even say her name without grimacing."

Cooper stood, rage pulsing off of him. "You skip work again, and you're no longer welcome in my house. I won't enable you."

"Don't bother waiting. I'll be gone by morning." Chad grabbed his cell phone off the coffee table and stormed past his roommate.

Cooper gripped Chad's bicep, his hand tight and threatening enough to stop his retreat. "Don't be this person again."

He ripped his arm away without a word and slammed his bedroom door. A responding crash came from the living room. Chad ignored the rush of guilt and packed his duffel bag. What did it matter anyway if Cooper hated him? After tonight, it would be over, finished, his fate sealed tight.

He sat on his bed and gripped his phone. Slim's guy should have called by now. They had a deal: Chad would work another party if Slim gave him access to the monster who had attacked Laila. The meeting was supposed to go down tonight.

Finally, after another fifteen agonizing minutes, the call came.

"Richardson," he answered, trying to sound fearless.

"We're on. Two hours. Meeting spot is Ray's Storage off 95. Number seventy-eight."

"And Garcia will be there?" His heart pounded against his ribcage. Slim should have known the giant couldn't be controlled. Chad had seen that the first time he'd met him at the drive-in. It was in his eyes, that need for violence.

"Slim will give you the details. Just show up alone."

The man hung up before Chad could ask any more questions. He forced a calming breath through his lungs.

Katie had told him vengeance belonged to God. Well, tonight, he had every intention of helping things along.

Standing in front of the dark storage building, Chad's hands felt twitchy and cold. He'd been waiting for over thirty minutes now, and Slim was nowhere in sight. He checked the address he'd written down against the numbers on the steel building. They matched. This was where he was supposed to be.

Finally, headlights appeared, moving closer until they paused a few yards away. Chad cupped a hand over his eyes as fear wove its way through his bones, thick and pressing. Two weeks, he'd waited for this moment. To be face-to-face with the man who'd destroyed his life.

The lights went dark, leaving only spots in his vision to blink through.

Shadows exited the car, but neither of the men were Slim.

Chad squinted, scanning them both until recognition hit him square in the chest. "Dalton?" he asked as the gangly teen approached him.

Dressed in sagging jeans and a Fall Out Boy T-shirt, he looked ready for a night at the movies, not a sketchy drug exchange. "Hey, you remember me!" The kid grinned, goofy and unaffected by the atmosphere they were in.

Chad's stomach twisted. Dalton wasn't even twenty yet. What in the world was he doing here? He had his whole life ahead of him. "Of course I remember you. You followed me around our neighborhood like a lost puppy." He embraced the teen, ruffling his hair, then held him by the shoulders. "You shouldn't be involved in this stuff."

Dalton shrugged, and in it, Chad saw his resignation. "It is what it is."

Letting go of the boy, Chad's gaze swung to the other guy, the one who'd been driving. Older, average height, and bald under his black baseball cap. A sleeve of tattoos covered his right arm, while an inked eagle wrapped its wings around his left forearm.

"You, I don't know."

"Nor do you need to," the guy snorted. "Spread your legs. Slim says we have to frisk you."

"Ah, come on, Jack. It's Richardson. He's harmless."

The guy threw Dalton a lethal stare, and Chad spread his arms and legs out, mostly to avoid whatever argument might ensue.

Jack patted down his chest, thighs, and calves. He wasn't even Chad's height, but the way his shirt stretched across his chest implied the guy could do some damage if he wanted to.

"No wire. No weapons either," he mumbled, stuffing his hands in each of Chad's pockets.

Chad pushed him away. "Don't get so friendly."

"Just doing my job. Slim said no cell phones."

Dalton ran a hand over his head. "Sorry, man. He's all freaked out about Garcia going rogue, ya know. Especially with it being Lai—"

"Don't say her name," Chad shot back.

Dalton stepped back at the sheer violence in his tone. "Yeah, whatever." The kid put more distance between them and hung his head a little. "I'm just saying, Slim's on edge."

The town had retaliated after Laila's attack. They'd turned on Slim, closing doors that had once been open. His most loyal patrons now finding other sources to buy from. It was likely the only reason he'd offered Chad the deal. In his sick, twisted mind, he probably thought if he could secure Chad's forgiveness, maybe others would follow.

Jack put out his palm. "Your phone."

Still hot, Chad pulled out his phone and slammed it in Jack's hand hard enough to hurt. "Feel better?" he asked, his voice a calm fury.

Jack tucked it in his pocket and jerked his head toward the car. "Get in."

A bolt of trepidation passed through Chad. He'd been told the exchange would happen here.

Dalton must have noticed. He edged closer and whispered, "You sure you want to do this?"

"I'm sure." Chad took a hesitant step toward the vehicle, unsure what fate would bring once he entered it. But fear wasn't an option, not when Slim could sense it like blood on raw flesh.

He pulled open the door and tucked himself into the back seat.

The others slammed themselves inside too, the car jolting into drive a few seconds later. Chad silently wrung his hands, while Jack pulled out his own phone.

"We're good," he said into it, then paused. "No. Nothing suspicious at all. There was a blue Chevy and an old Toyota in the parking lot, but they both looked abandoned."

Chad pushed down a wave of nausea. Cooper couldn't have followed him. He would have noticed. Just to be sure, he twisted around, searching behind him for any sign of headlights. Nothing. Just black stillness over the car's trunk.

He turned back around and met Jack's eyes in the rearview mirror.

"You want to talk to him?" Another pause. "Okay." Jack passed the phone back to Chad.

Forcing his fingers to still, Chad gripped the phone and put the receiver to his ear. "This is a hell of a welcome party," he said as calmly as he could.

"Just a little test that you seemed to pass just fine." Slim paused. "Sorry about Laila."

Flashes of her injuries scoured his brain. The bruises on her cheek, her mangled wrist, the thirty staples required to close up her side. All Slim's doing. Chad never knew he could feel so much hatred. "Are you?"

"Of course I am!" he yelled, for once not hiding behind his polite shell. "She's practically Joe's daughter and beloved in this town. You think I like being in this position? Garcia saw the unmarked car and freaked out. I told him to stand down, but he acted without my knowledge or my consent."

Chad swallowed the bile in his throat. "If I didn't believe that, you would already have a bullet in your back."

"Be careful, Chad. I know you're upset, but be careful."

"This was your deal, Slim." Chad pulsed with fury, his voice a shout into the phone. "So, you tell me, are we doing it or not?"

The pause was long enough that Chad could sense Slim's irritation on the other line. That black-hearted arrogance that made him think he was beyond human. Invincible.

"Yeah, we're doing it," he finally said, and Chad felt his entire chest deflate.

"Good." Unable to keep his emotions restrained any longer, Chad shoved the phone back to Jack.

A crisp pop echoed through the car, and Dalton reached back with an ice-cold aluminum can. "One for the road. I figured you might need it."

"Thanks." Chad took the beer in his right hand and stared at the foam bubbling from the opening.

Jack slammed on his breaks and jerked the car to the right, cursing as Chad slid across the back seat and slammed into the door, the beer spilling over his fingers and onto the carpeted floorboard.

"Sorry. I can't see crap on these back roads."

Chad shook his hand, flinging droplets in all directions. "Then turn on your brights. I don't plan on dying before Garcia does."

The man eyed him through the mirror, and Chad lifted his can in a toast.

Vengeance was only a few miles away.

CHAPTER 43

C had's back straightened when Jack pulled off the road onto a tire-worn path behind the lake. The city owned this stretch of two hundred acres, and it basically sat untouched, except during the fall when hunters descended.

The small sedan bucked up and down over the rivets worn by rain and wind, skidding once, until the tires caught and surged them forward. Chad gripped his still-full can of beer, wishing his stomach would stop churning. It wasn't just the anticipation causing it, but also the foul smell of cheap alcohol that had permeated the car.

He scanned the woods through the darkened windows. Nothing for miles. No lights except the faint glow of the half moon. Chad slid his hand into his pocket, gripped the key fob he'd been so graciously allowed to keep, and hoped when all the dust settled, he was still left standing.

"We're here," Jack said, shoving the car into park.

"Good, 'cause I'm ready to hurl." Dalton practically fell out of the car and braced his knees. The kid had always had a weak stomach, and he'd drained at least two cans during the ten-minute drive.

Easing the door open, he took his time exiting the car, giving both Jack and Dalton a head start. Chad casually followed, allowing the liquid to subtly pour a trail out behind him as he walked.

Jack and Dalton continued to move at a quicker pace, not because they seemed nervous, just eager to have their part finished. He could tell they felt sheltered, protected. Chad scanned the trees again, and a shiver ran down his spine. If Slim wanted to, he could hide all their bodies out here, and no one would find them for years.

The trees gave way to a clearing where two more vehicles were parked: Slim's Jag with its trunk open, and a large pickup with two portable lights casting a circular glow.

He spotted Slim immediately, sitting on the edge of the Jag's hood, his arms crossed, talking to Bruno, the same guy who had originally contacted Chad about making a deal.

The aluminum crackled in his fist, and he forced his hand to relax.

Slim stood when Jack and Dalton approached, watching him lag behind.

Chad slowed, lifting his empty can to his mouth for a brief second before lowering it. "Where is he?"

"I'll tell you once the deal is done and I have my money." Slim stepped forward, and Chad had to fight every molecule inside him not to strike hard and fast and without mercy. Instead, he took his fury out on the can, smashing it in his fist before chucking it as far as he could.

"Why the secrecy, Slim? I thought we were family? Brothers?" He pounded his chest. "You said I was one of your own. And now you're protecting *him*?" Accusation rolled through his tone, heavy enough that even the guys around them tensed.

Slim eased back, his jaw twitching as if he were forcing his teeth to unclench. "I really hope you didn't come here planning to do something stupid."

Chad saw a glint of metal in Slim's jeans, his hand easing toward the pistol, ready to defend if needed. "I'm unarmed, Slim. I just want my day of reckoning."

Slim's hand relaxed, and he crossed his arms again, the snake tattoo bouncing as if deliberating on what to do next. He gestured his chin toward his Jag. "Well, come on, then."

Chad held his breath. This was it.

A tree branch snapped, and in a fraction of a second, all three men—Slim, Jack, and Bruno—had 9mms pointed at Chad's head. Dalton stood like a deer at the end of a barrel, his eyes wide with fear.

Heart pounding, Chad raised his hands. "Whatever you think this is, I had nothing to do with it." It wasn't supposed to go down this way. They were supposed to wait until the drugs exchanged hands.

"Don't shoot!"

Those two words sent Chad's world into slow motion.

Cooper.

I won't stand by and watch you self-destruct, he had promised. And Cooper kept his promises, even the ones that would get them both killed.

He emerged from the branches, arms up, his eyes fixed on the gun now pointed at his chest. "I'm just here to take Chad home before he does something he'll regret."

"Risky move. You know I don't like loose ends." Slim's finger pressed in on the trigger. He moved the gun between Chad and Cooper as if deciding which was the bigger threat.

"Coop, go home. This doesn't concern you." His own safety he could risk, but not Cooper's. Not the man who'd stood by him. Who treated him like a brother. Who now stood ready to take a bullet for him.

"The deal's off." Slim backed away, his gun a shield in front of him. "Bruno, Jack, shut it down!"

But before anyone could move, a black metal cylinder rolled into the circle, bouncing over the tufts of grass, and then halted.

A huge bomb-like blast rocked Chad backward, a flash of light and smoke clouding his vision, then another, and he felt the sting of shrapnel pound against his flesh. Two gunshots fired, one after the other, barely perceivable through the continued assault around them. Chad slammed to the ground so hard the air was knocked from his lungs, his head spun, and through the chaos, he'd lost sight of Cooper. Calling his name, Chad crawled, clawing the ground in search of his friend.

Feet pounded the grass, shouts echoed commands to seize and get down on the ground. Knowing the commands weren't for him, he stumbled to his feet, barely taking two steps before another gun fired. Chad dropped again. This time, he didn't fall on the ground, but on a still body, one too large to be anyone's but his roommate's.

Chad blinked, his vision still impaired from the blast of light. But even in the haze, his heart knew those big, lifeless hands could only belong to his friend.

"No," he whispered, but blood was already soaking Cooper's sleeve and rolling down to his elbow. "No . . ." His whole life, Chad had been told he was unworthy, worthless, a mistake. And yet Laila, Katie, and now Cooper had sacrificed themselves just to love him. Just to see him stay clean.

Chad dropped his head to his friend's chest, gripping the man's shirt in anguish. He still wasn't used to praying, but all he could think in that moment was that he hadn't told Cooper what he'd learned. He hadn't shown him the freedom he'd found.

Tears spilled down his cheeks. *Please, Lord, not yet.*

Why did Cooper follow him? Why did he have to be so stubborn and loyal?

"Get off me. You weigh more than a pregnant elephant."

The voice spilled through him, converting his desperation into shocked laughter. He was alive. Chad palmed Cooper's cheeks, kissed his friend's forehead, and continued to laugh hysterically.

"Have you lost your damn mind?" Cooper shoved him hard before frantically wiping his forehead. Then he locked up in visible agony, gripping his right shoulder.

Chad lunged to help him.

"Kiss me again and I'll deck you," Cooper threatened, rolling to his knees.

The air around them had stilled. No more blasts or gunfire. Even the smoke had cleared. He stood, his body shaking from the flood of emotions and adrenaline. It took several seconds before he could process the scene in front of him.

SWAT teams swarmed in all directions, shouting commands and securing the narcotics. Through his hazing vision, Chad could see Agent Edwards, the lead on their sting operation, talking to one of his men. A joint venture, an agreement forged in the aftermath of tragedy, and a risk he'd had to take in order to protect his family and his future.

Slim lay face down in the grass next to his men, their hands cuffed behind their backs, while at least seven cops pulled bags of cocaine, marijuana, and meth from Slim's vehicles.

He never saw it coming. Never even considered that a spineless alcoholic could outsmart him. Chad had once told Laila that a man with nothing to lose was the most dangerous person on earth. He was wrong. A man with everything to lose was a far greater enemy.

Agent Edwards tipped his head and smiled. He whispered something to the guy on his left and strolled over. "Nice acting job, Chad. I thought we were done when they sent the car for you."

Chad pulled his keys from his pocket and detached the fob they'd given him. A drone. A silent, tracking twelve-inch drone had saved his life. "I guess it's good we had a back-up plan. Although, I don't recall it including flash grenades."

"He pulled a gun. We had to react."

"Those things hurt like hell," he said, rubbing a palm over his sore chest.

"That was the stinger grenade. It's supposed to debilitate the suspect."

"It works," Chad deadpanned. His eyes fixed on the terrified face of young Dalton. "So, what happens now?"

"We let the law do what it does best."

"Dalton's just a kid. He didn't even have a weapon."

"Don't worry. Slim is our target, and I imagine with the plea bargains we'll offer these other guys, Slim is going to be locked away for a long, long time."

"What about Garcia?"

"My guys picked him up an hour ago. Idiot used his credit card."

Relief pulsed through every vein. "So you definitely got what you needed?"

"And then some," Edwards said, smiling. "Thank you."

"Thank my wife. I did it for her."

Cooper moaned from the ground, still clutching his arm. "What do you mean, your wife?" His arm was a sickening red, blood still streaming from the bullet wound in his shoulder.

Eyeing him with concern, Edwards pulled a radio from his belt. "We need an ambulance. Gunshot wound. White male, two hundred pounds."

Cooper attempted to stand and almost toppled over.

Chad immediately reached for him. "Whoa. Just sit, okay? You're hurt." He couldn't hide the rumble in his voice, the buried temper. "And you're lucky you are, 'cause if not, I'd hit you myself for being so stupid!" Emotion choked him when he looked at his friend. Dark smudges lay under Cooper's eyes and coated his jaw. Utter exhaustion lined every inch of his body.

Barely conscious, yet still attempting to get to his feet, Cooper clasped Chad with his good arm. "I just took a bullet for you. A little gratitude would be nice," he grumbled, but his voice sounded weak and was beginning to slow. "Or at least the truth. Since you're not on the ground in handcuffs, I assume you were a part of this masquerade."

Resigned that Cooper would do more damage if he fought to keep him seated, Chad helped him to his feet. "Laila came up with the plan herself. The separation, the drinking, the drugs. We had to make Slim believe I could be bought again."

More strangled curses came, mostly Cooper's fury at Chad for keeping secrets and letting him worry for two weeks.

Chad stifled another round of laughter. It wasn't funny, but seeing his friend turn back into his cantankerous, bull-headed self brought a wave of relief. "Sorry. I didn't exactly anticipate you stalking me like a jealous ex-girlfriend."

Despite Cooper's protest, Chad wrapped an arm around his waist, steadying him. His face had gone pale, and Chad could feel him swaying.

"By the way, you owe me a Dr Pepper," Cooper said right before he collapsed.

EPILOGUE

Laila stared at the shimmering water, the wind off the ocean barely moving her sprayed hair. She wore it down, like Chad had insisted, the weight heavy across her bare shoulders. The ivory dress clung to her hips, light and airy as the wind around her. She traced a finger along its beading, watching it sparkle in the afternoon light.

"It's show time," Katie said, her own dress spilling out behind her, ice blue and empire cut to match Laila's. She handed her a bouquet of wildflowers—bright, cheerful, and so unassuming it made Laila smile.

She gripped the stems with her good hand, the other still trapped in the cast she had to wear for a few more weeks. Katie had wrapped it with lace, a sad attempt to make it work with her wedding dress.

Laila stepped off the wooden bridge, her eyes fixed on the small white arch Chad stood under. His white linen shirt blew around him, his tan legs exposed beyond the hem of his khaki shorts. His feet were bare, like hers.

A true beach wedding, the one she'd always wanted.

Katie took her place in front, and Laila watched as she walked slowly down the makeshift aisle they'd created with folding chairs.

She followed when Katie passed the first row, and soon their forty guests rose to their feet, each smiling at her, some with teary eyes that matched her own. She turned, and just a few feet ahead stood her future. Dark hair, bright-green eyes, and a sheen of tears.

Cooper looked almost as choked up as her husband-to-be, his arm still in a sling. White, to match his shirt. Laila had thought he and Katie would kill each other when she asked them to help plan the event. But after multiple passive-aggressive comments and averted glares, they'd found a way to call a truce, working together to give Laila and Chad the wedding they never had the first time.

Through all the hurt, they'd grown, moved forward. The ugly past, now only a memory to remind them how far they'd come.

She finished her last step, passed her flowers to Katie, and stood face to face with the man she'd love for the rest of her life. They'd been baptized together just last Sunday, a profession of faith they'd both been eager to make. This time would be different, and not just because they were different, but because they had a new foundation, one so much stronger than anything on earth.

He took her fingers in his. Sturdy, strong.

"*I would not wish any companion in the world but you,*" he said, lifting her left hand to his lips.

"You've quoted that one already," she teased. "You'd think I'd get something new at our second wedding."

He smiled, a gleam in his eye that said he accepted her challenge. He slid a hand around her waist and pulled her tight against his chest. Their guests snickered at his boldness.

> "*I loved her against reason, against promise, against peace, against hope, against happiness, against all discouragement that could be . . . I loved her none the less because I knew it, and it had no more influence in restraining me, than if I had devoutly believed her to be human perfection.*"

Laila felt the heat rise in her cheeks, not just from his beautiful rendition of Charles Dickens, but from the vow laced through each word.

"I suppose that will do," she whispered, her own heart ready to promise forever one last time, and to embrace the unexpected hope of a new beginning no longer a dream too far to grasp.

ACKNOWLEDGMENTS

Before I ever wrote the last word in *My Hope Next Door*, I knew I wanted to give Laila and Chad their happy ending. I hope their journey was as fun to read as it was to write. And to all those who helped me along the way, I am truly grateful.

To the Waterfall Press editors and staff, working with all of you has been a wonderful ride. Thank you for respecting my voice, for giving me plenty of say in every aspect of publication, and for your steadfast professionalism. I have learned so much from all of you.

To my fabulous agent, Jessica Kirkland, for bearing with me as I wrote and rewrote the concept for this book. Thank you for always striving for greatness. You inspire me to do the same.

To Sgt. Alan Eddins, for giving me insight into drug law enforcement and helping me tackle a very difficult scene. Your help was immeasurable.

To Nicole Deese, for being the best writing partner a girl could have. Thank you for your honesty, encouragement, forever-long phone calls, and laughter. You make writing fun.

To my sister, Angel, for being my very first beta reader and never caring that you get the "worst" version. You are my champion and I love you so much.

To my amazing writing critique partners—Connilyn Cossette, Dana Red, and Lori Wright—your love for writing makes me love my job. Thank you for pushing me, for your constructive criticism, given so carefully and with genuine kindness, and for helping me make this book one that I will always feel proud of.

To my magnificent readers—you have allowed me to share my life with you, and in turn have shared yours with me. I call some of you friends now, and appreciate all the ways you lift me up and push me forward. Thank you for your e-mails, notes of praise, and consistent reviews. You are the reason I write.

And last, but absolutely not least, to my incredibly patient family—you give me lots of material for my books. Your sense of humor, crazy stories, and never-ending affection make writing about unconditional love very easy. You are my greatest joy in life and my heart. Love you.

ABOUT THE AUTHOR

Photo © 2015 Karen Graham

Tammy L. Gray writes modern Christian romances with true-to-life characters and culturally relevant plotlines. She believes that hope and healing can be found through high-quality fiction that inspires and provokes change. Writing has given her a platform to combine her passion with her ministry. She lives in the Dallas area with her family. They love all things Texas, including the erratic weather patterns. Visit her online at www.tammylgray.com.